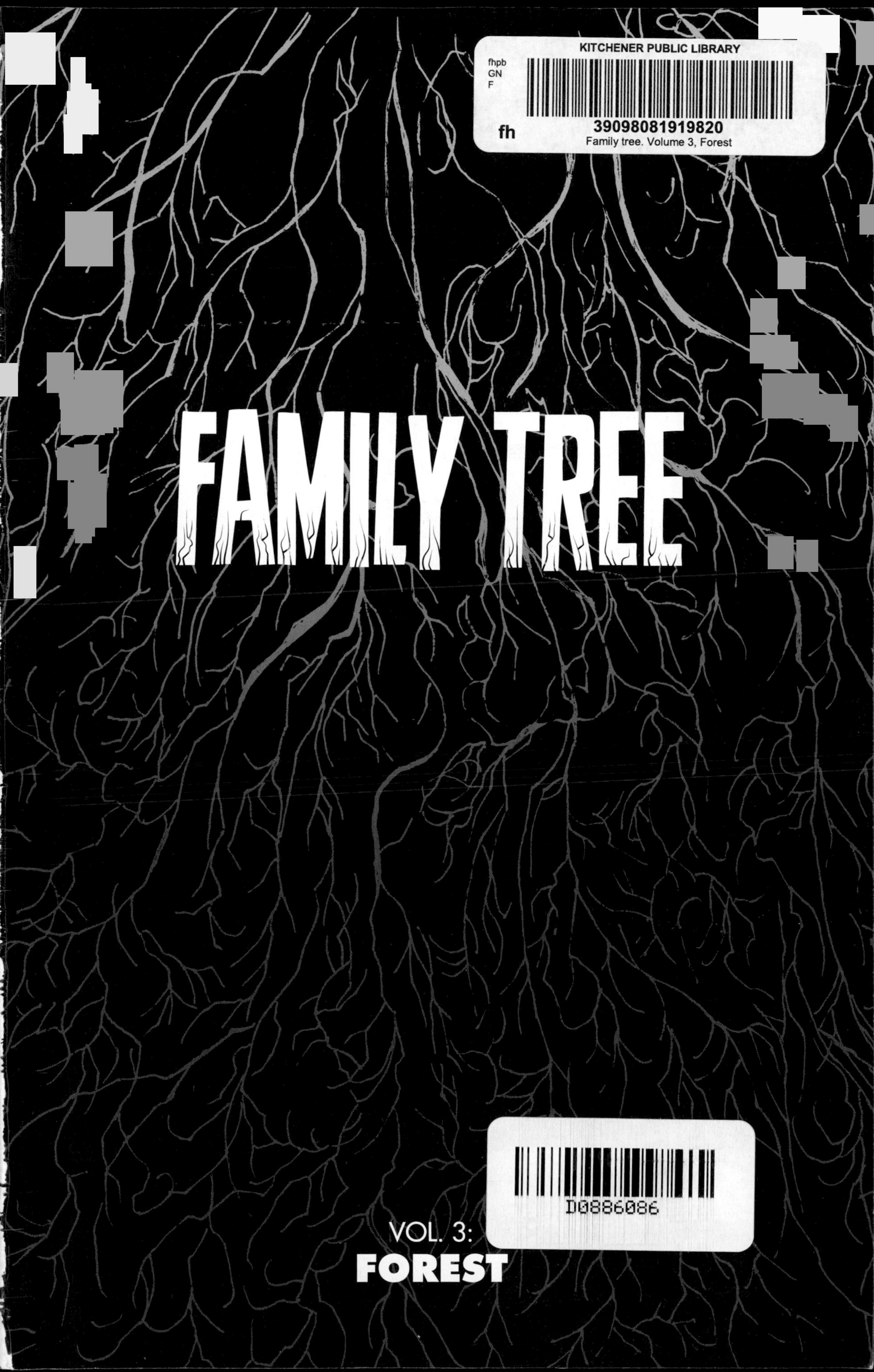
FAMILY TREE
VOL. 3:
FOREST

IMAGE COMICS, INC. • **Todd McFarlane:** President • **Jim Valentino:** Vice President • **Marc Silvestri:** Chief Executive Officer • **Erik Larsen:** Chief Financial Officer • **Robert Kirkman:** Chief Operating Officer • **Eric Stephenson:** Publisher / Chief Creative Officer • **Nicole Lapalme:** Controller • **Leanna Caunter:** Accounting Analyst • **Sue Korpela:** Accounting & HR Manager • **Marla Eizik:** Talent Liaison • **Jeff Boison:** Director of Sales & Publishing Planning • **Dirk Wood:** Director of International Sales & Licensing • **Alex Cox:** Director of Direct Market Sales • **Chloe Ramos:** Book Market & Library Sales Manager • **Emilio Bautista:** Digital Sales Coordinator • **Jon Schlaffman:** Specialty Sales Coordinator • **Kat Salazar:** Director of PR & Marketing • **Drew Fitzgerald:** Marketing Content Associate • **Heather Doornink:** Production Director • **Drew Gill:** Art Director • **Hilary DiLoreto:** Print Manager • **Tricia Ramos:** Traffic Manager • **Melissa Gifford:** Content Manager • **Erika Schnatz:** Senior Production Artist • **Ryan Brewer:** Production Artist • **Deanna Phelps:** Production Artist • **IMAGECOMICS.COM**

WRITTEN BY JEFF **LEMIRE**

ART BY PHIL **HESTER**
ERIC **GAPSTUR**
RYAN **CODY**

LETTERING BY STEVE **WANDS**

EDITED BY WILL **DENNIS**
TYLER **JENNES**

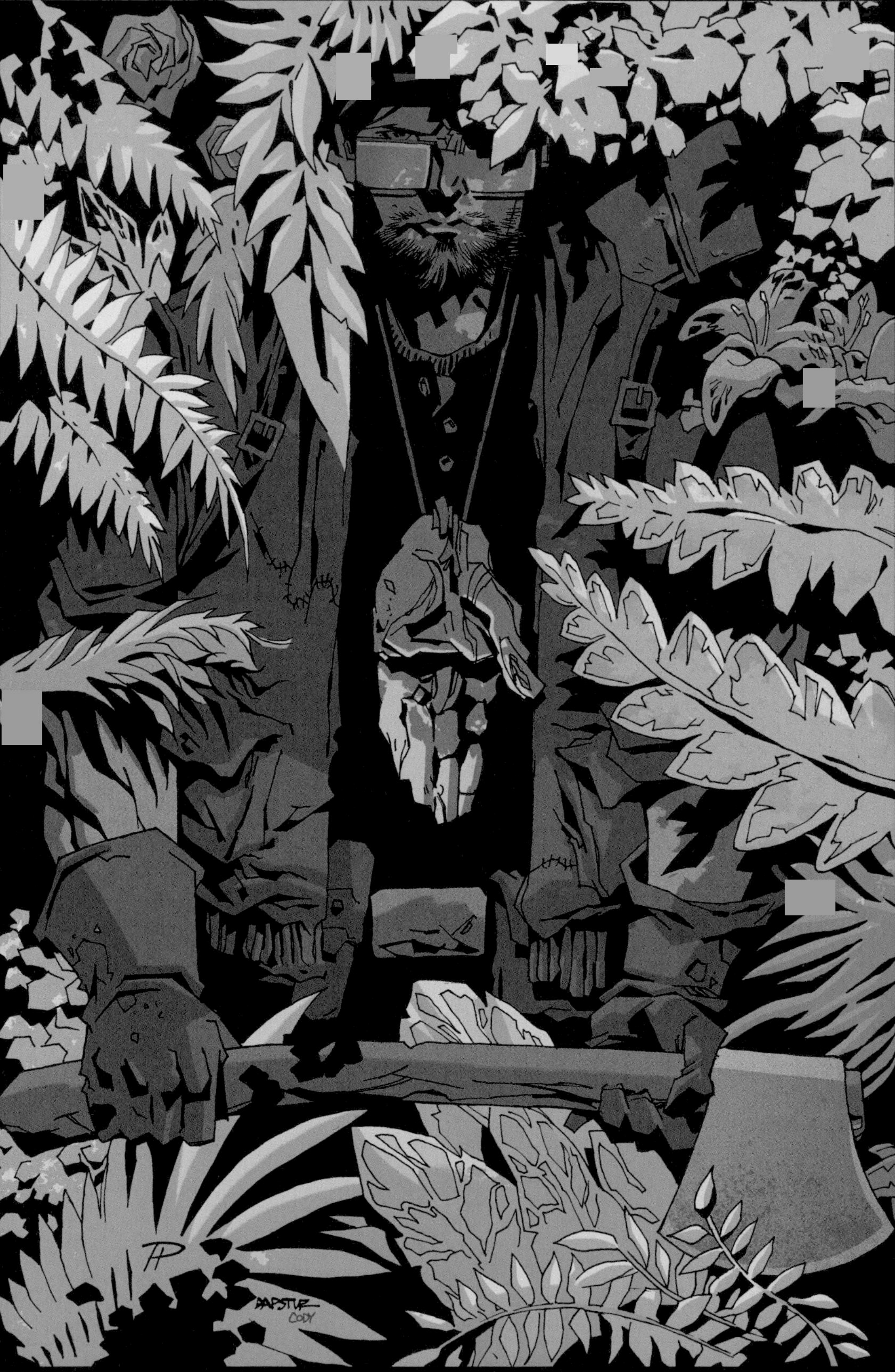

CHAPTER
NINE

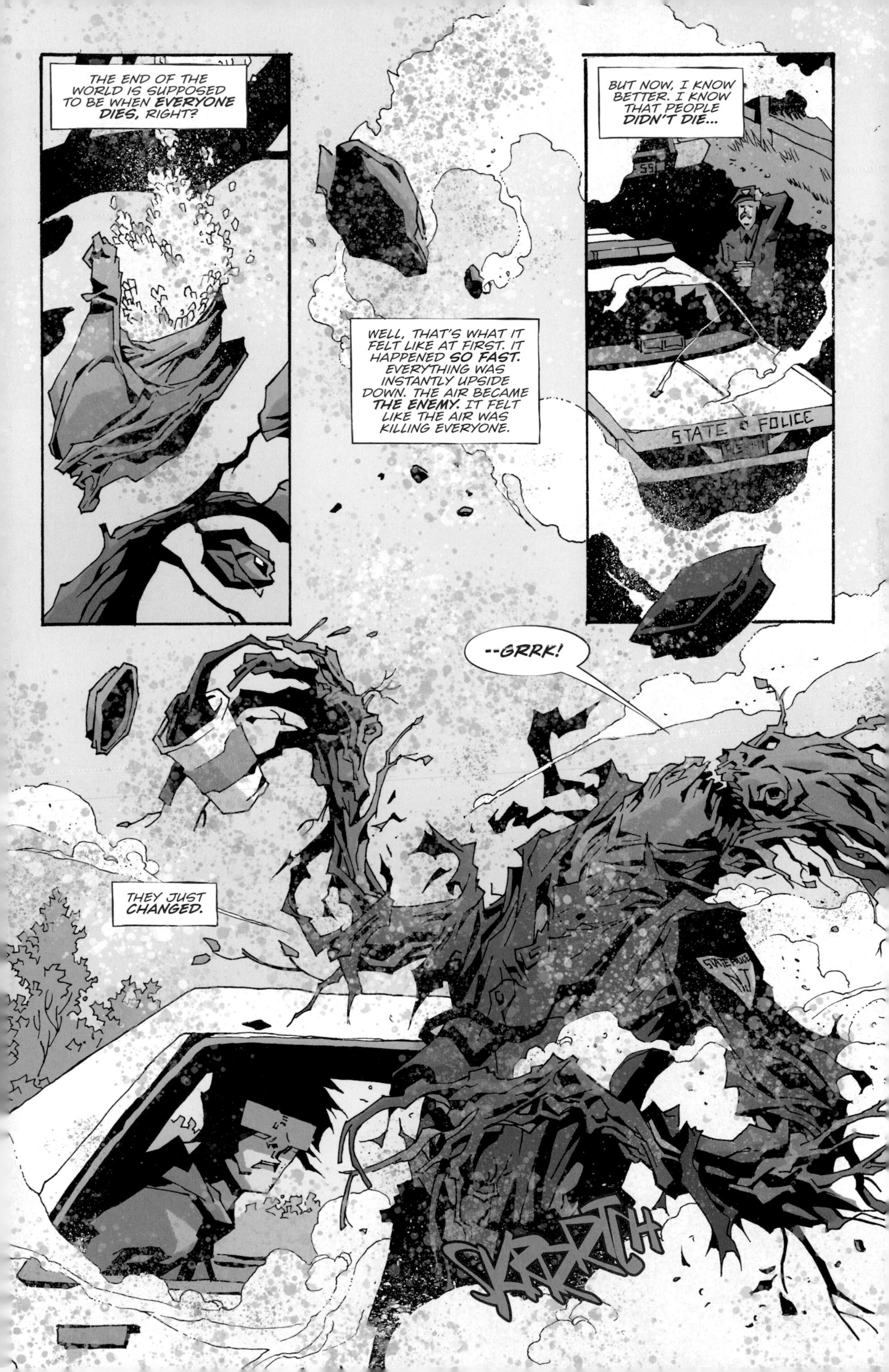
THE END OF THE WORLD IS SUPPOSED TO BE WHEN EVERYONE DIES, RIGHT?
WELL, THAT'S WHAT IT FELT LIKE AT FIRST. IT HAPPENED SO FAST. EVERYTHING WAS INSTANTLY UPSIDE DOWN. THE AIR BECAME THE ENEMY. IT FELT LIKE THE AIR WAS KILLING EVERYONE.
BUT NOW, I KNOW BETTER. I KNOW THAT PEOPLE DIDN'T DIE...
STATE POLICE
--GRRK!
THEY JUST CHANGED.
SKRRTCH

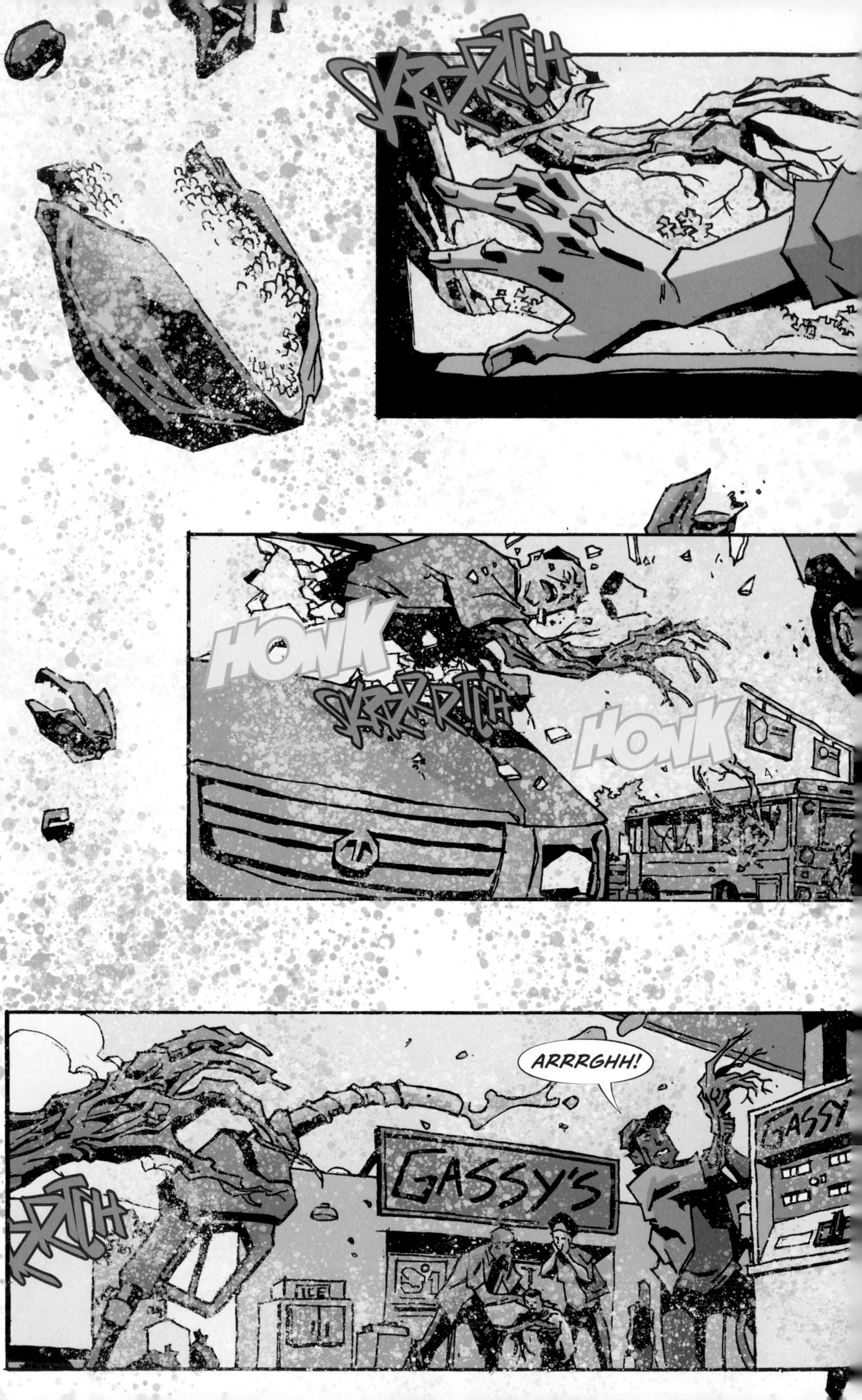
SKRRRTCH
HONK
SKRRRTCH
HONK
ARRRGHH!
GASSY'S
RTCH

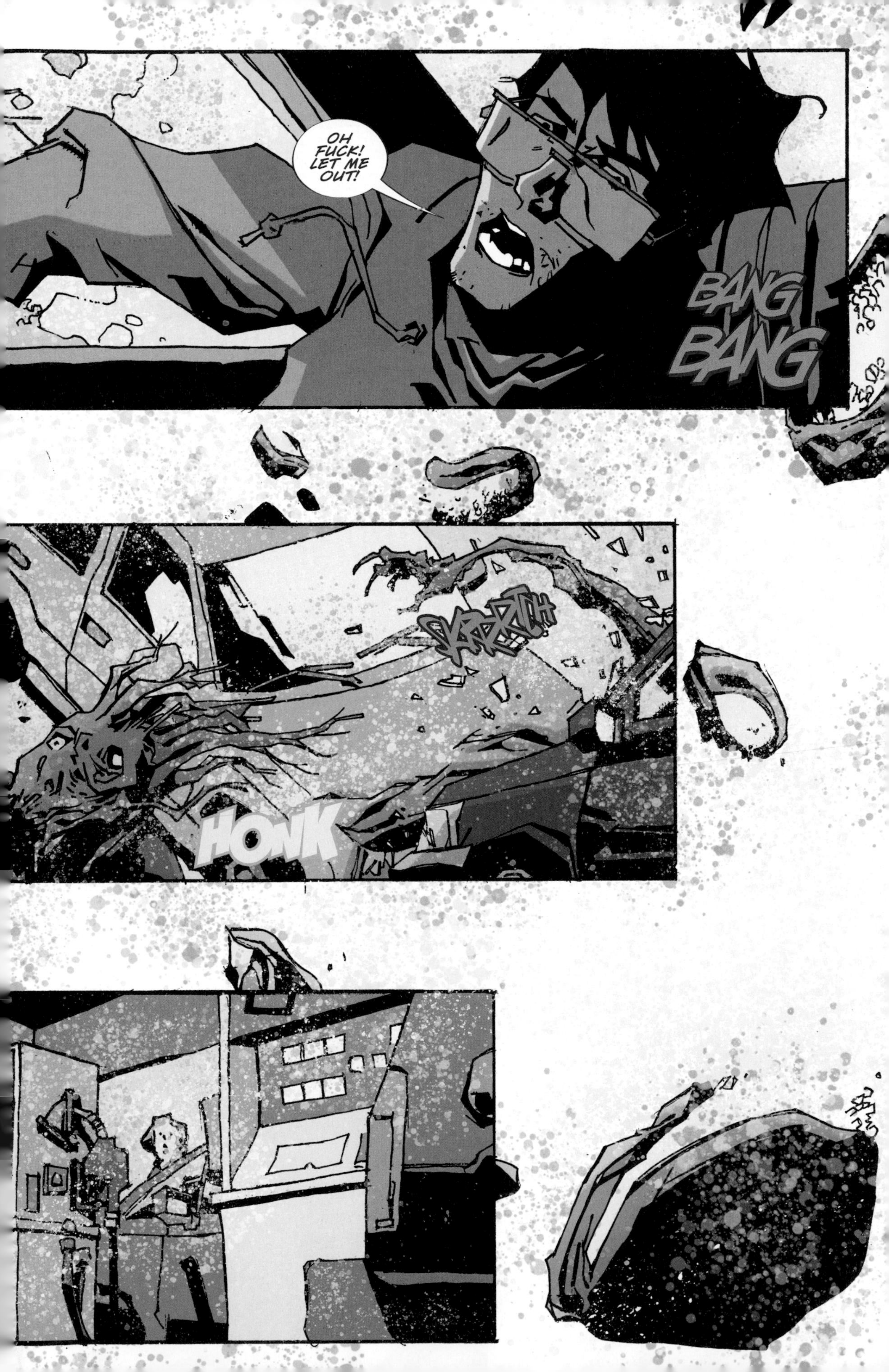
OH FUCK! LET ME OUT!
BANG BANG
SKRRRTCH
HONK

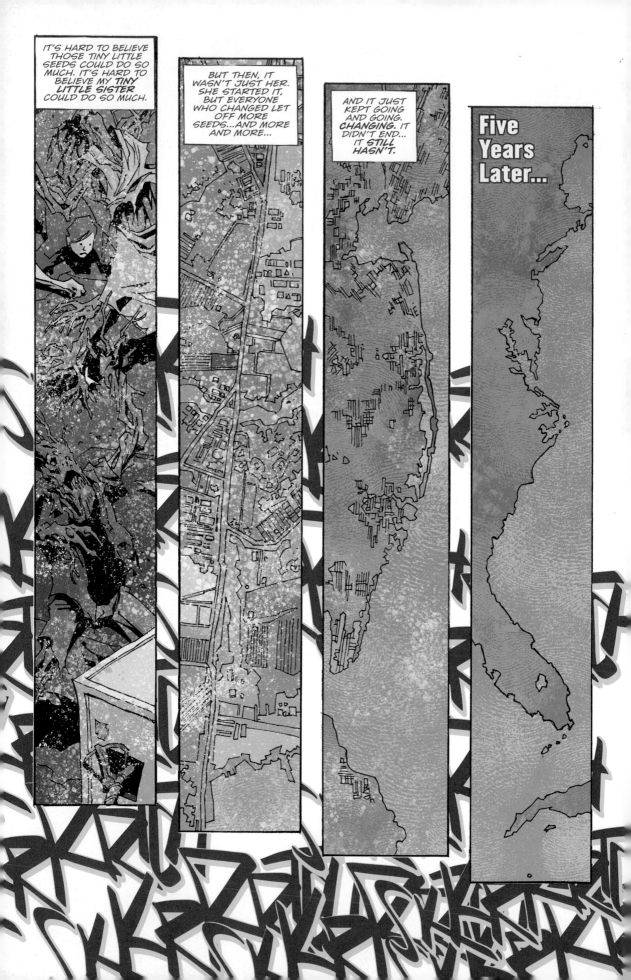

IT'S HARD TO BELIEVE THOSE TINY LITTLE SEEDS COULD DO SO MUCH. IT'S HARD TO BELIEVE MY *TINY LITTLE SISTER* COULD DO SO MUCH.

BUT THEN, IT WASN'T JUST HER. SHE STARTED IT, BUT EVERYONE WHO CHANGED LET OFF MORE SEEDS...AND MORE AND MORE...

AND IT JUST KEPT GOING AND GOING. CHANGING. IT DIDN'T END... IT *STILL HASN'T.*

Five Years Later...

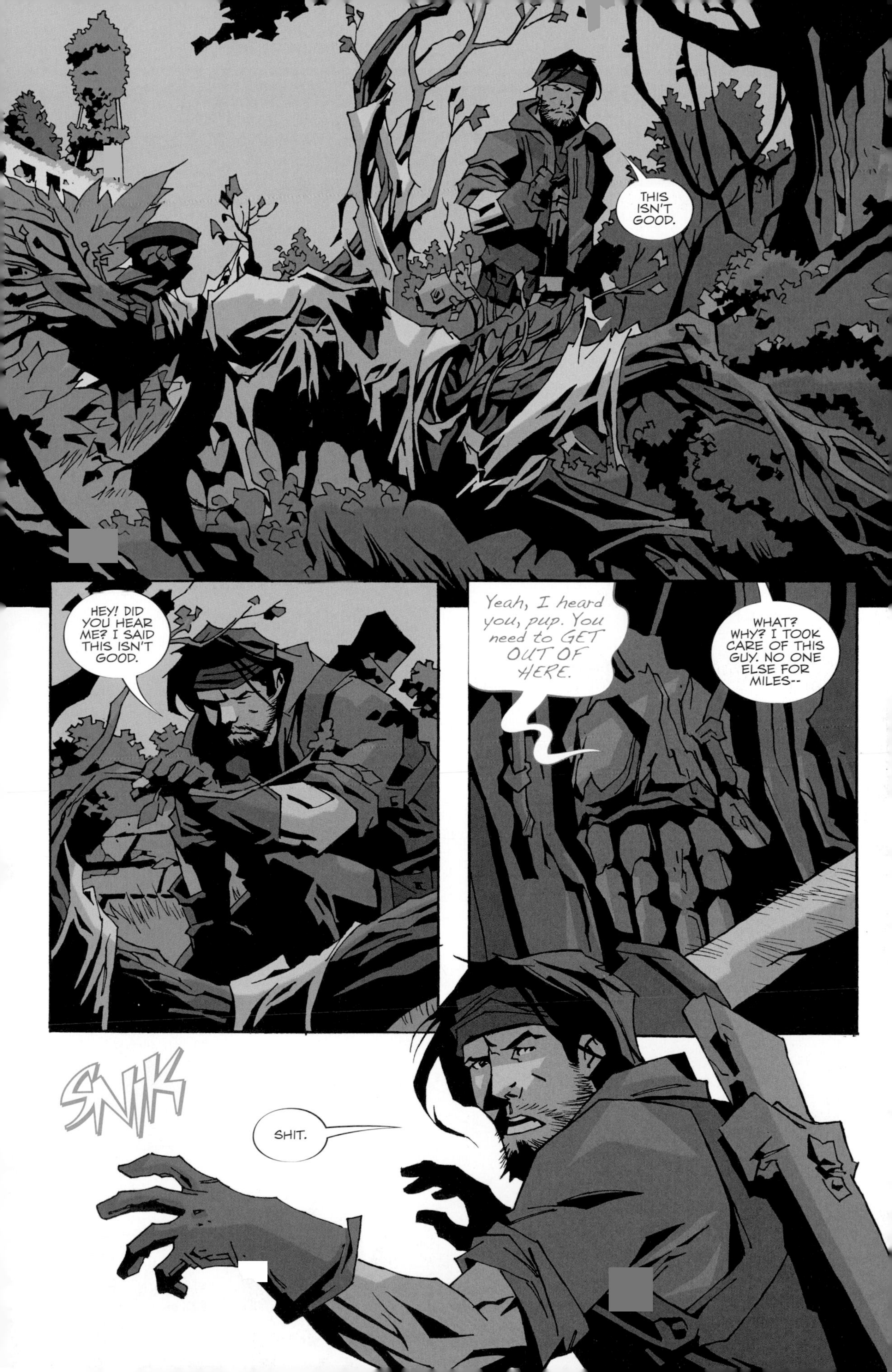
THIS ISN'T GOOD.
HEY! DID YOU HEAR ME? I SAID THIS ISN'T GOOD.
Yeah, I heard you, pup. You need to GET OUT OF HERE.
WHAT? WHY? I TOOK CARE OF THIS GUY. NO ONE ELSE FOR MILES--
SNIK
SHIT.

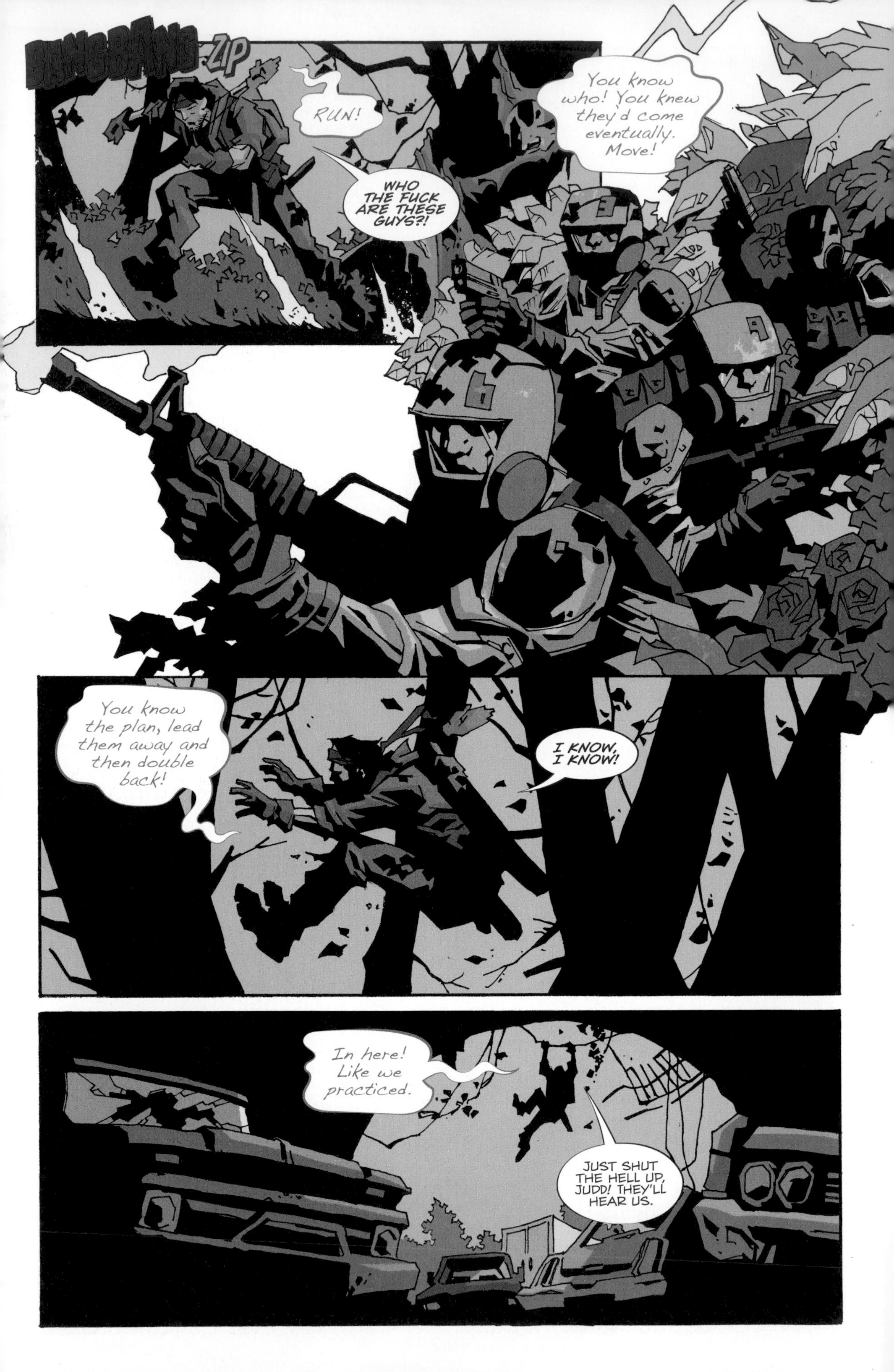

ZIP
RUN!
WHO THE FUCK ARE THESE GUYS?!
You know who! You knew they'd come eventually. Move!
You know the plan, lead them away and then double back!
I KNOW, I KNOW!
In here! Like we practiced.
JUST SHUT THE HELL UP, JUDD! THEY'LL HEAR US.

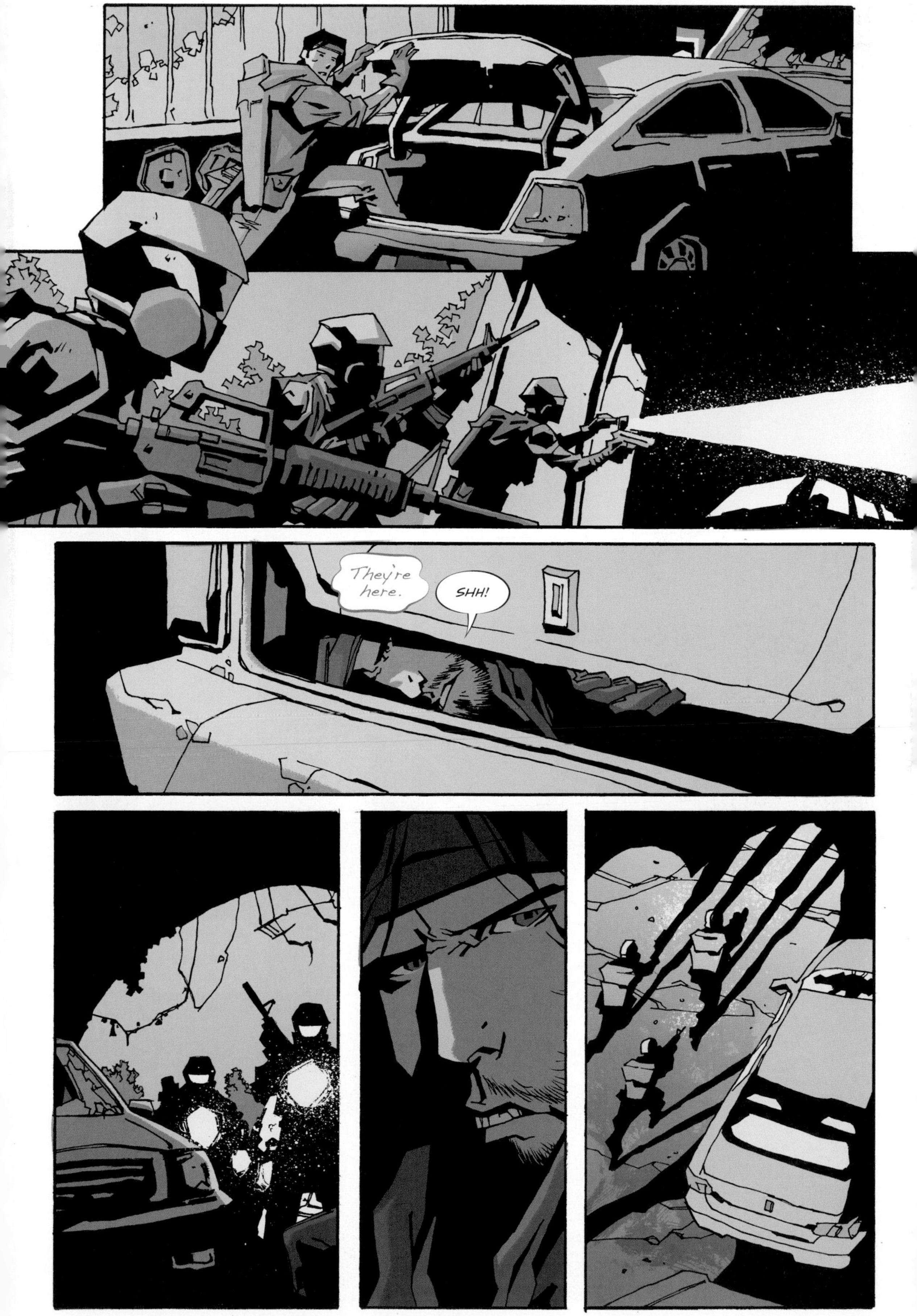
They're here.
SHH!

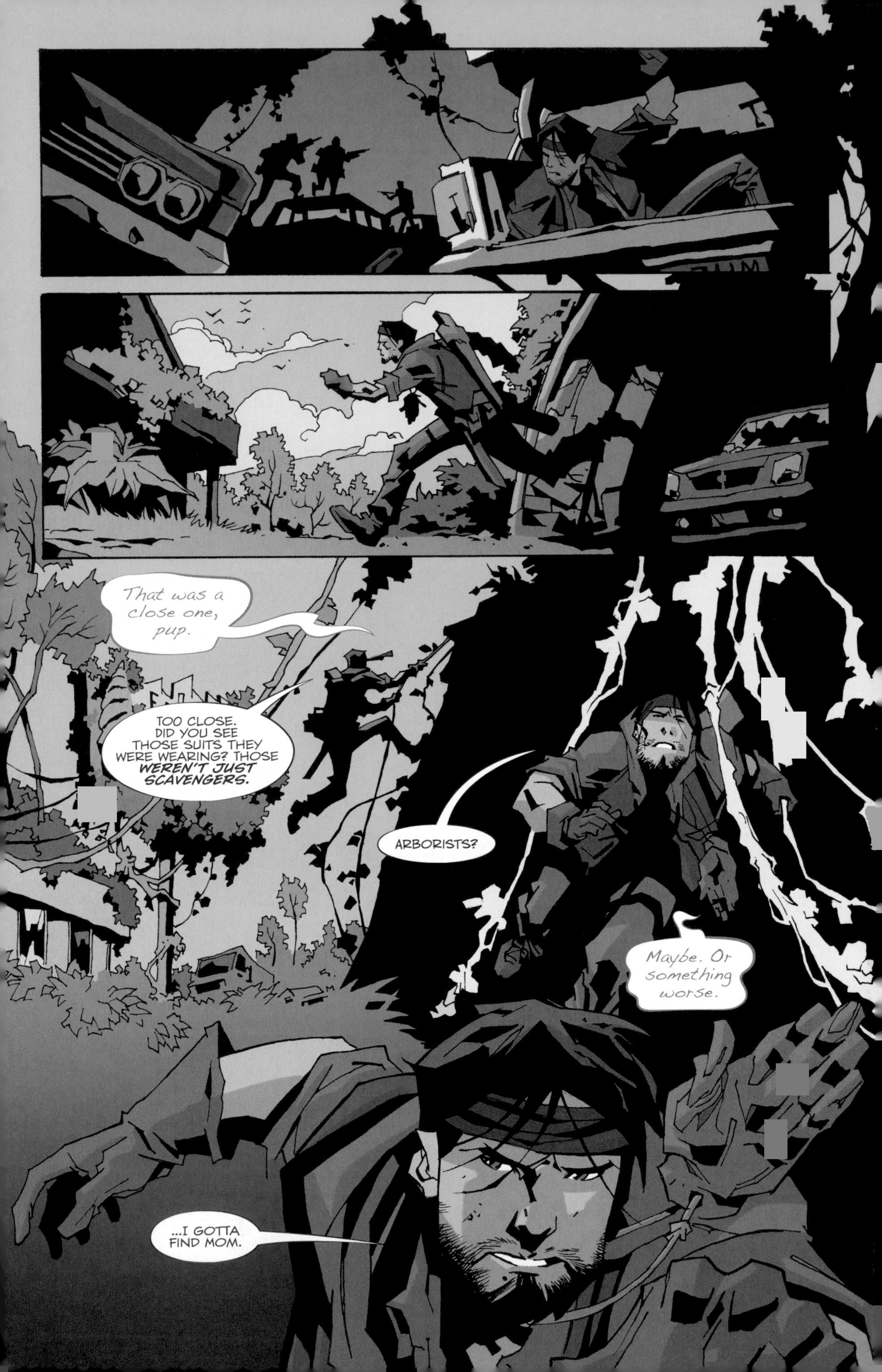
That was a close one, pup.
TOO CLOSE. DID YOU SEE THOSE SUITS THEY WERE WEARING? THOSE ***WEREN'T JUST SCAVENGERS.***
ARBORISTS?
Maybe. Or something worse.
...I GOTTA FIND MOM.

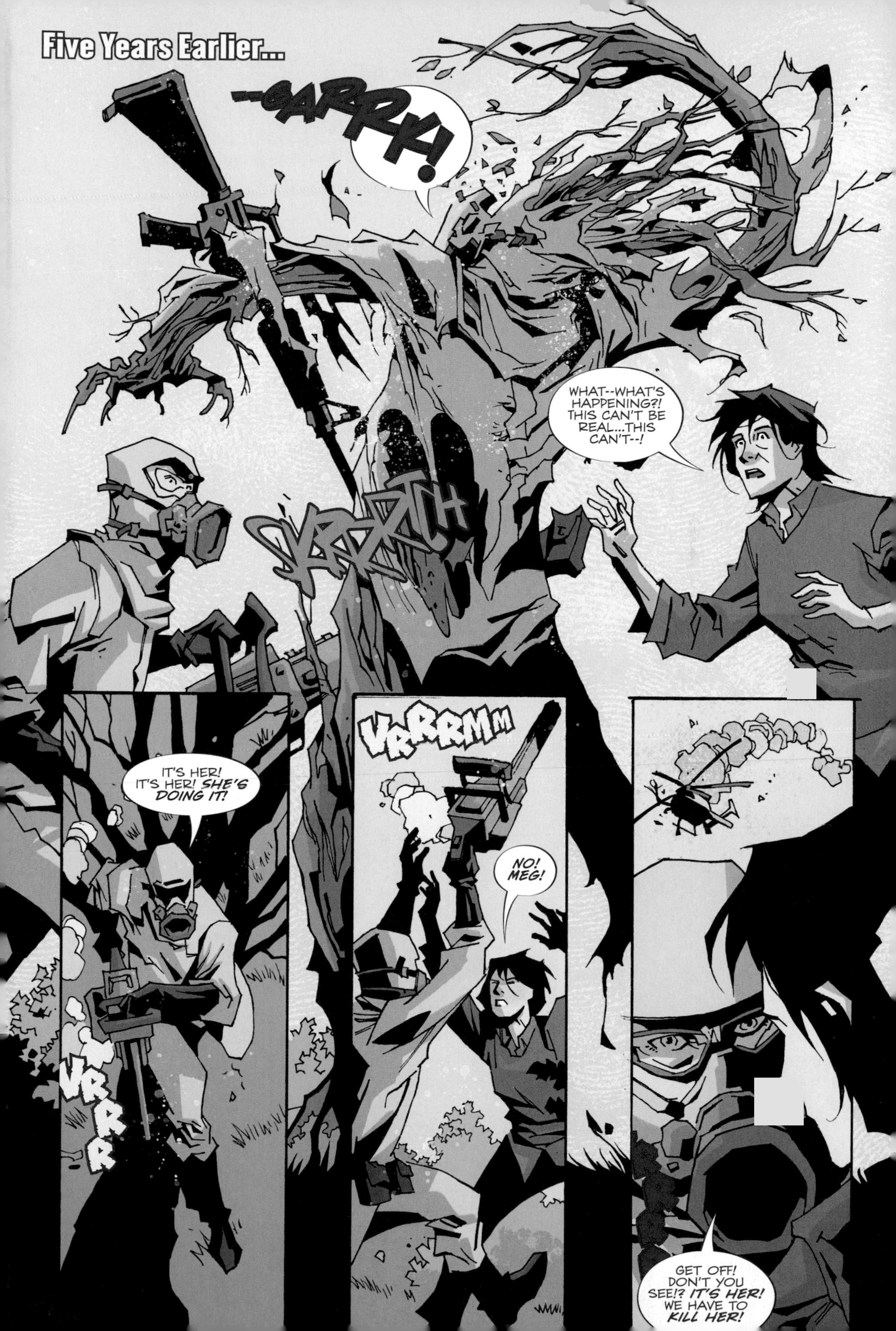
Five Years Earlier...
--GARRK!
WHAT--WHAT'S HAPPENING?! THIS CAN'T BE REAL...THIS CAN'T--!
SKRRRTCH
IT'S HER! IT'S HER! SHE'S DOING IT!
VRRRR
VRRRMMM
NO! MEG!
GET OFF! DON'T YOU SEE!? IT'S HER! WE HAVE TO KILL HER!

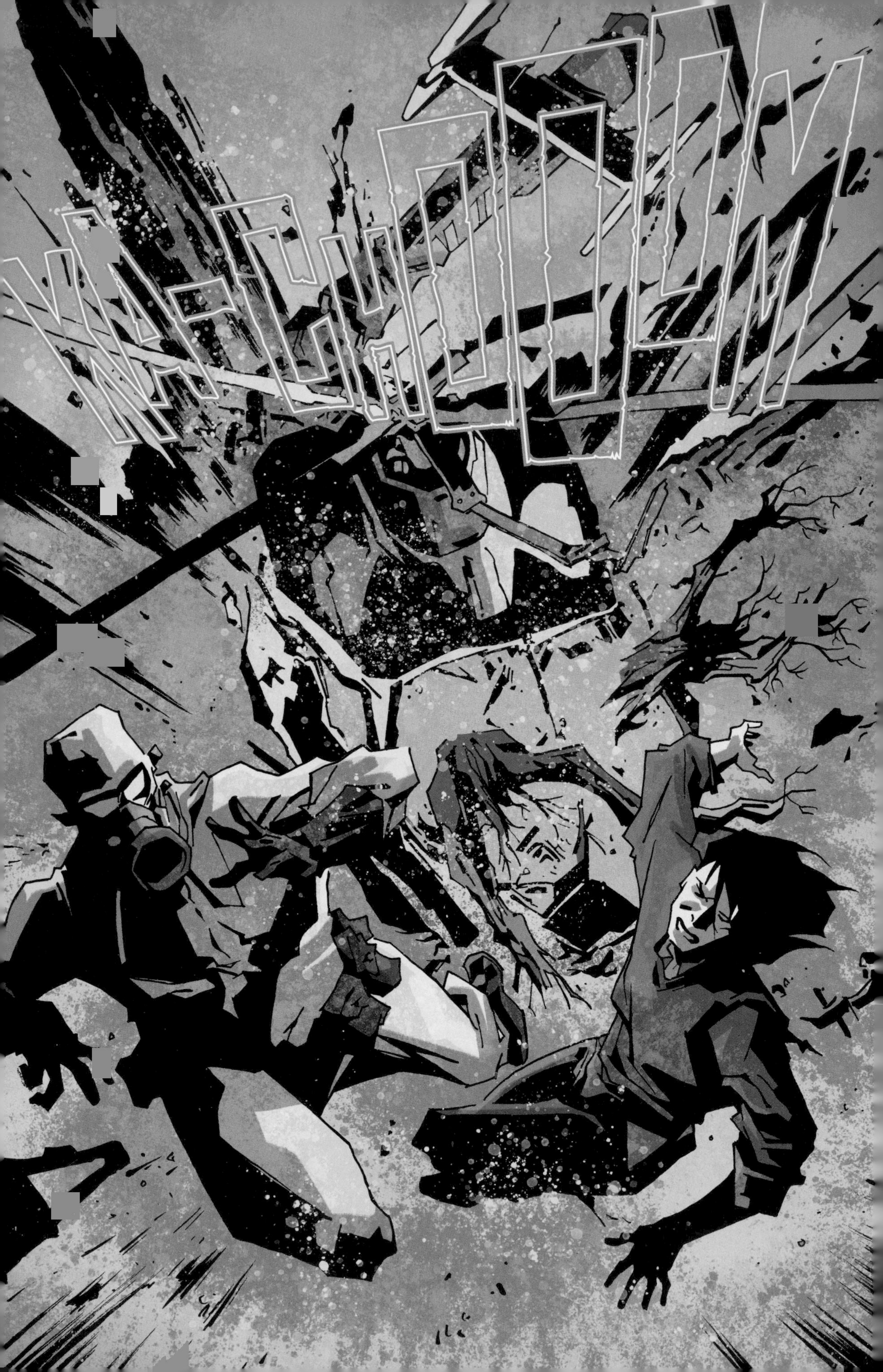
KACHOOOM

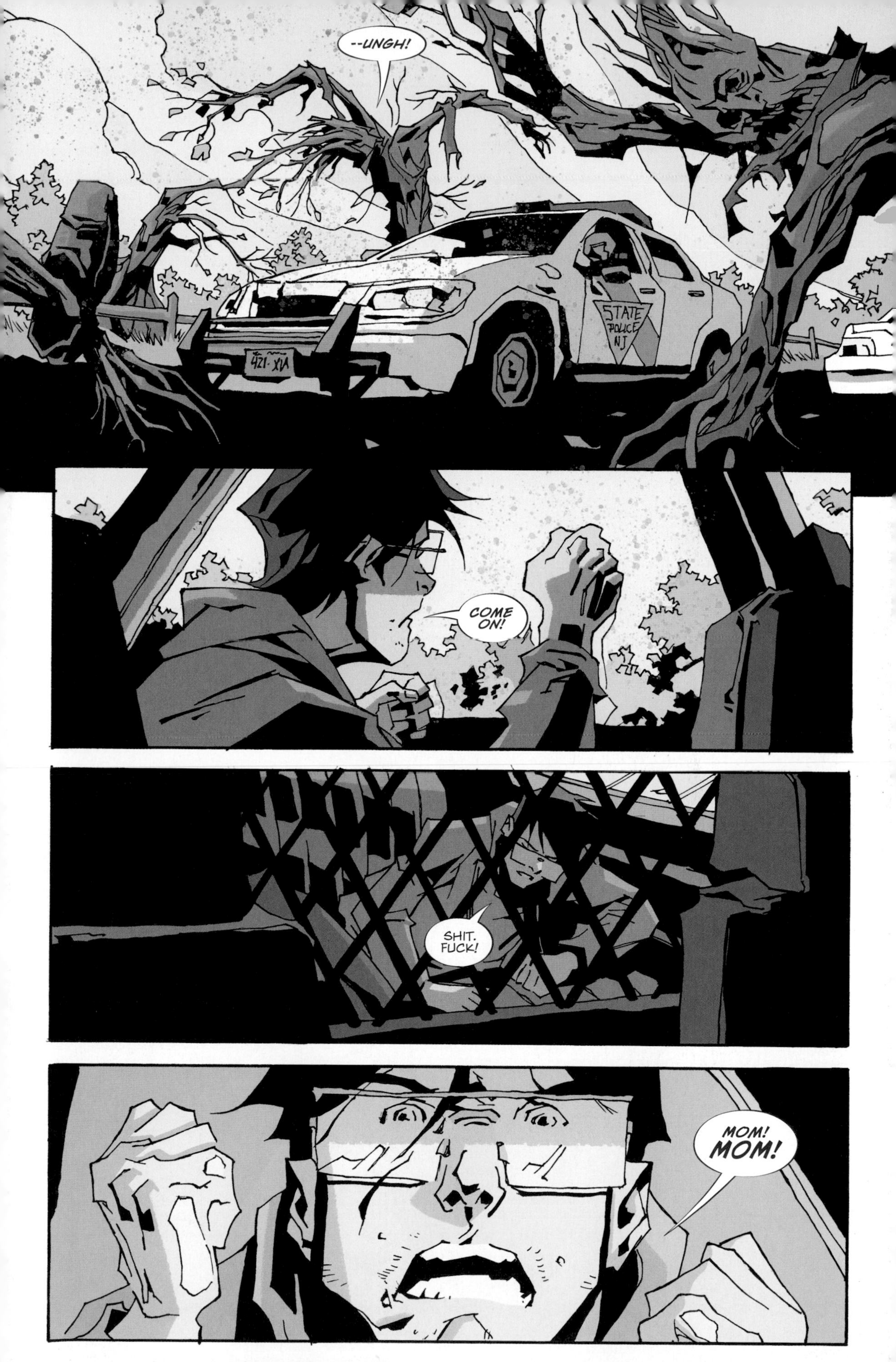
--UNGH!
STATE POLICE NJ
421·X1A
COME ON!
SHIT. FUCK!
MOM! MOM!

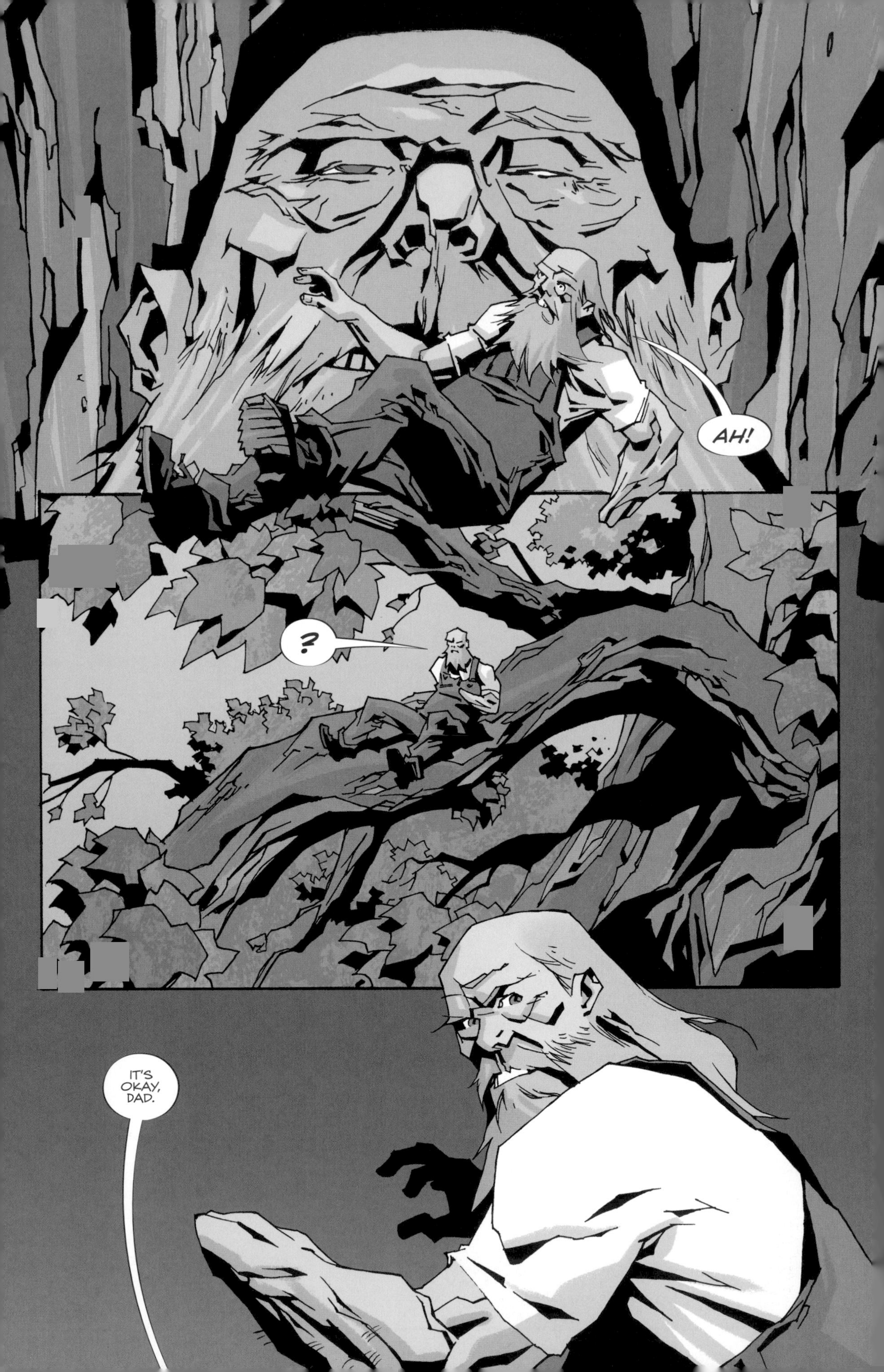
AH!
?
IT'S OKAY, DAD.

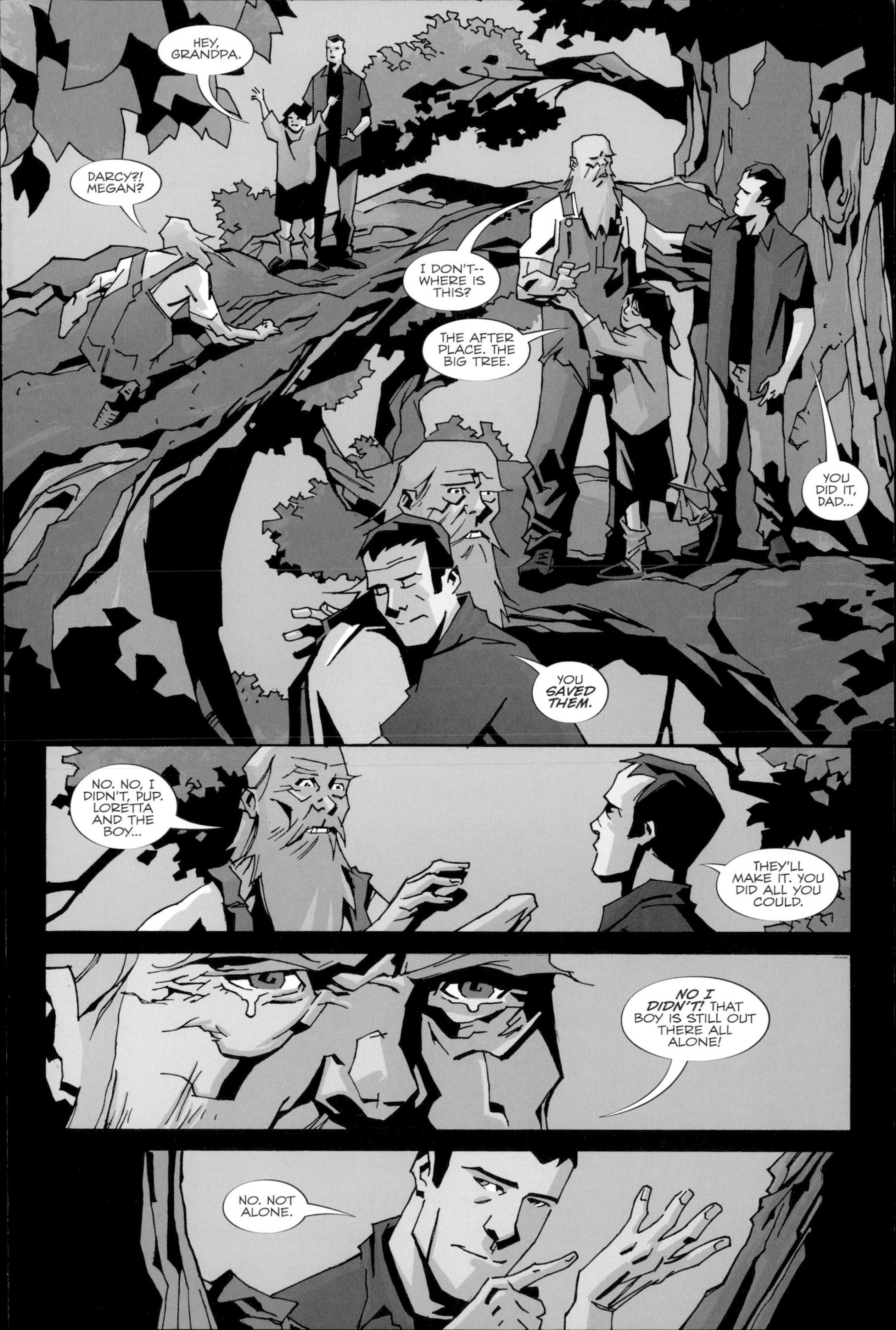
HEY, GRANDPA.
DARCY?! MEGAN?
I DON'T-- WHERE IS THIS?
THE AFTER PLACE. THE BIG TREE.
YOU DID IT, DAD...
YOU *SAVED THEM.*
NO. NO, I DIDN'T, PUP. LORETTA AND THE BOY...
THEY'LL MAKE IT. YOU DID ALL YOU COULD.
NO I DIDN'T! THAT BOY IS STILL OUT THERE ALL ALONE!
NO. NOT ALONE.

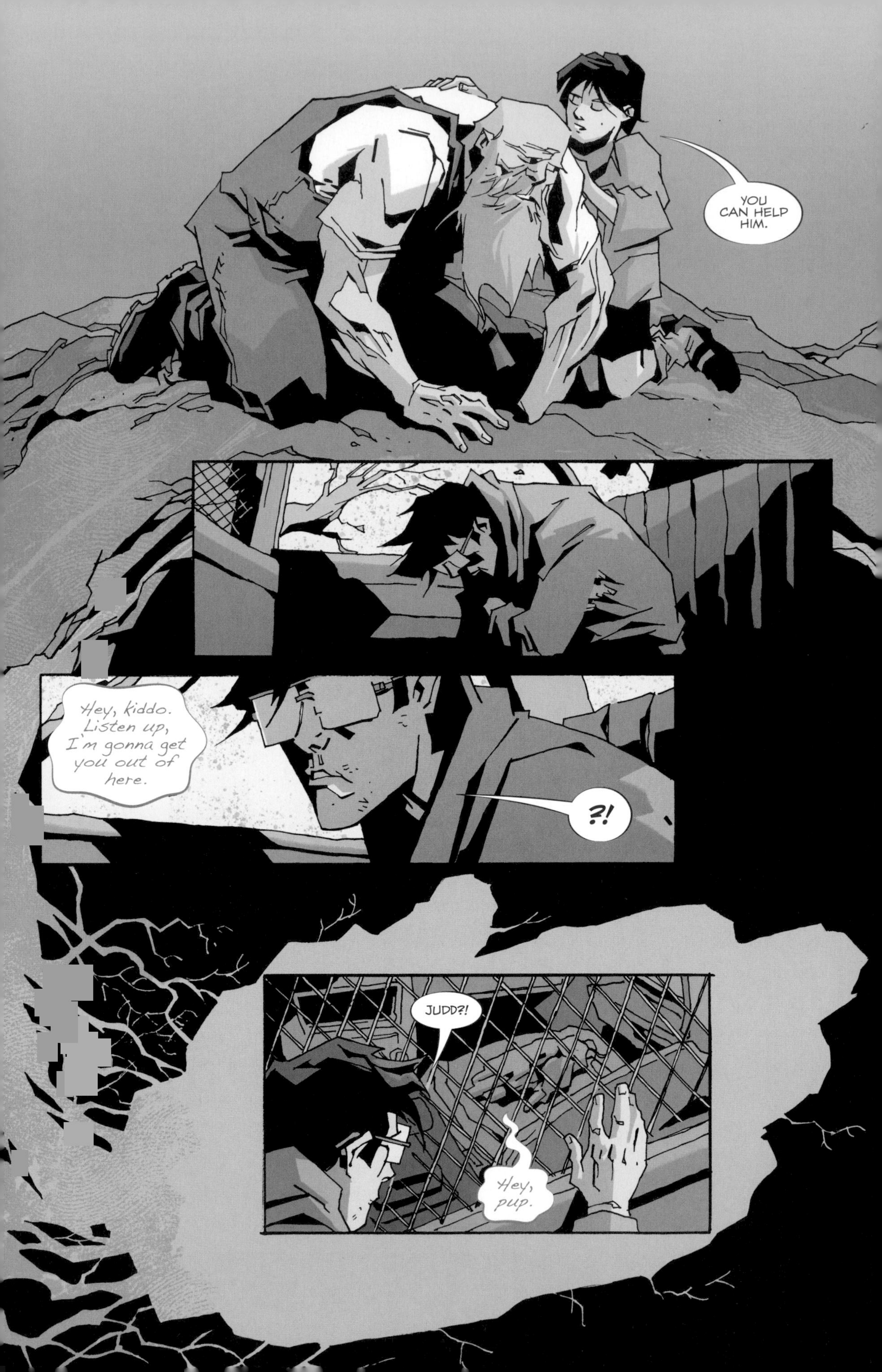
YOU CAN HELP HIM.
Hey, kiddo. Listen up, I'm gonna get you out of here.
?!
JUDD?!
Hey, pup.

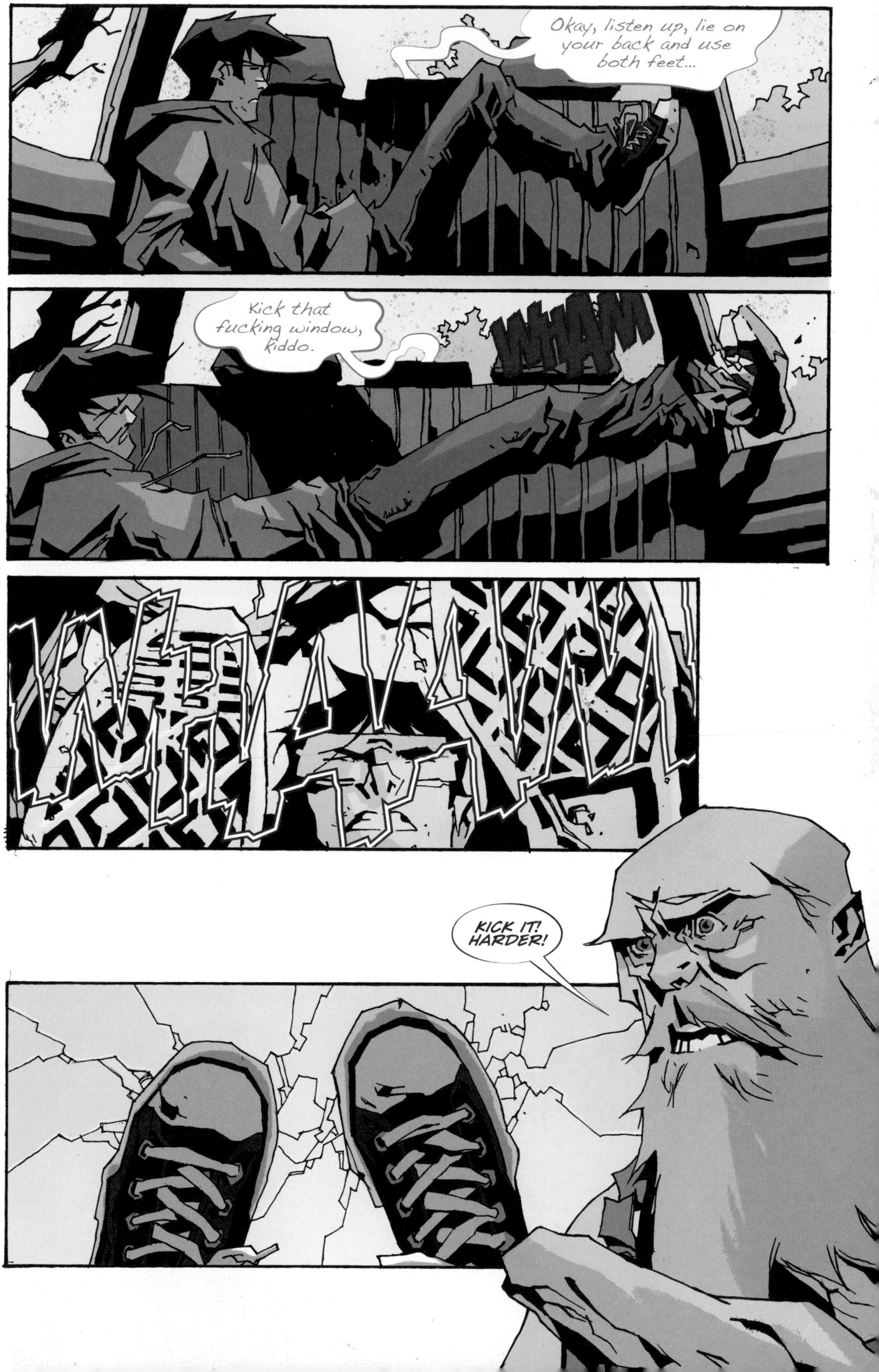
Okay, listen up, lie on your back and use both feet...
Kick that fucking window, kiddo.
WHAM
KICK IT! HARDER!

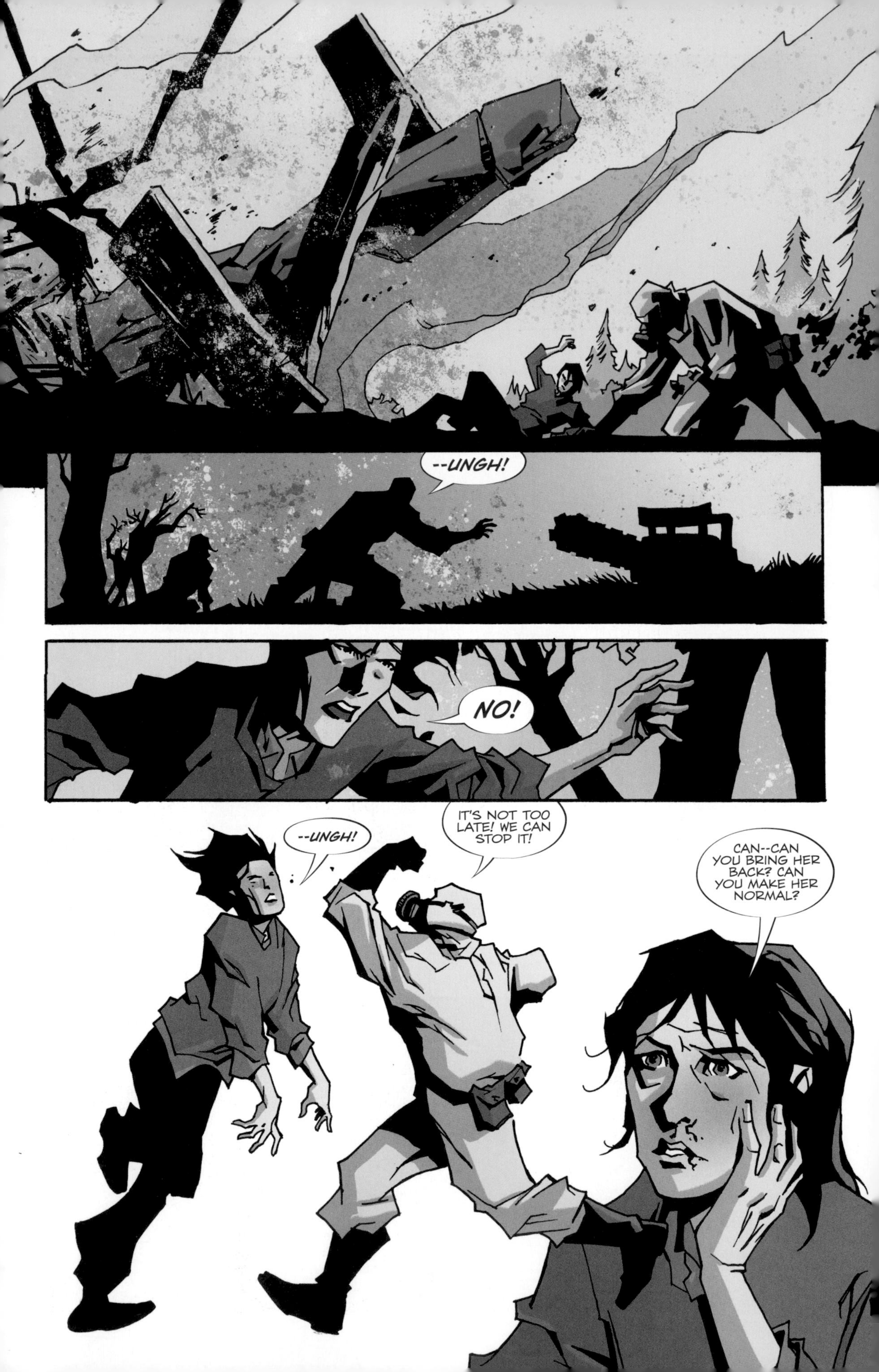
--UNGH!
NO!
--UNGH!
IT'S NOT TOO LATE! WE CAN STOP IT!
CAN--CAN YOU BRING HER BACK? CAN YOU MAKE HER NORMAL?

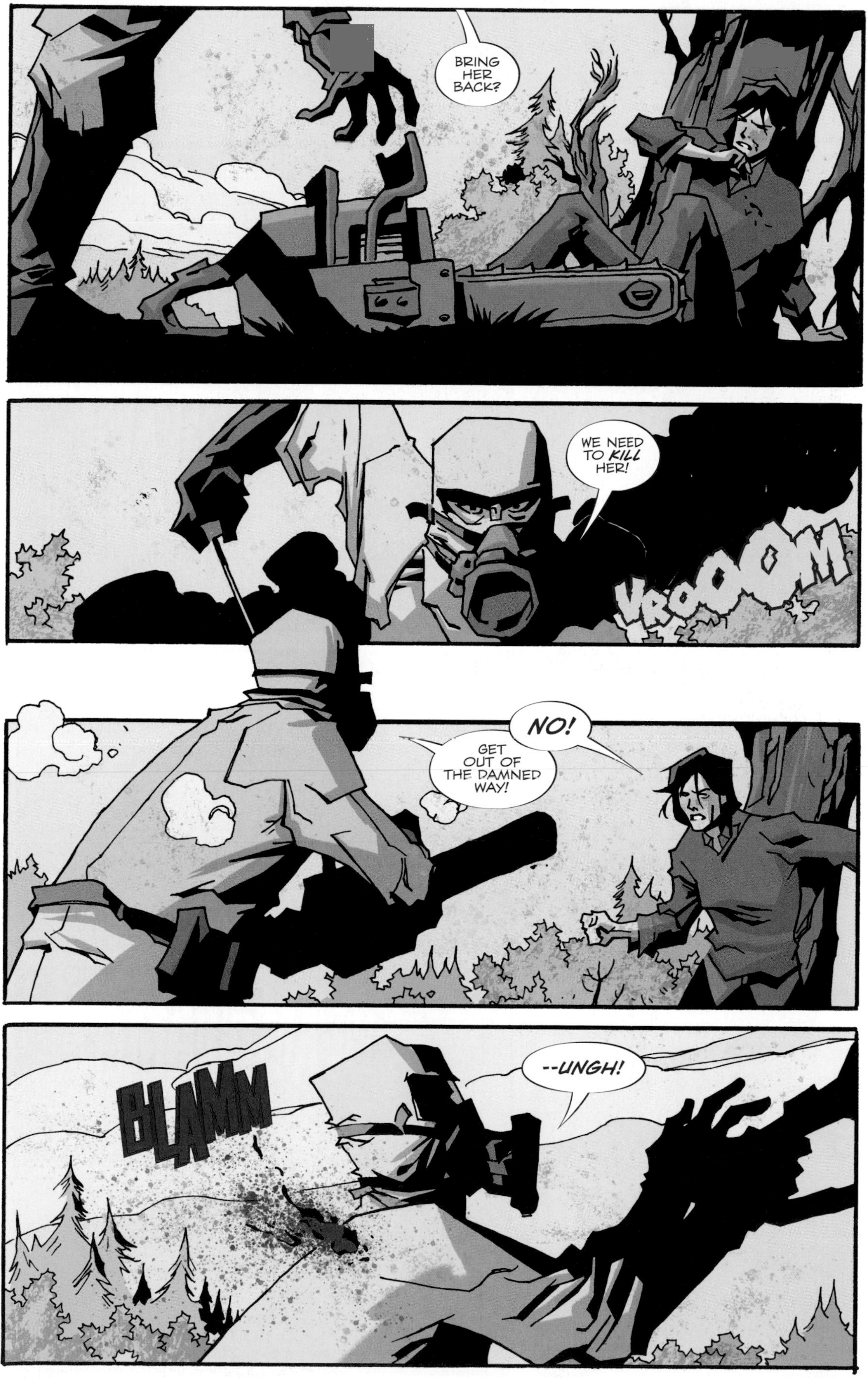
BRING HER BACK?
WE NEED TO KILL HER!
VROOOM
NO!
GET OUT OF THE DAMNED WAY!
BLAMM
--UNGH!

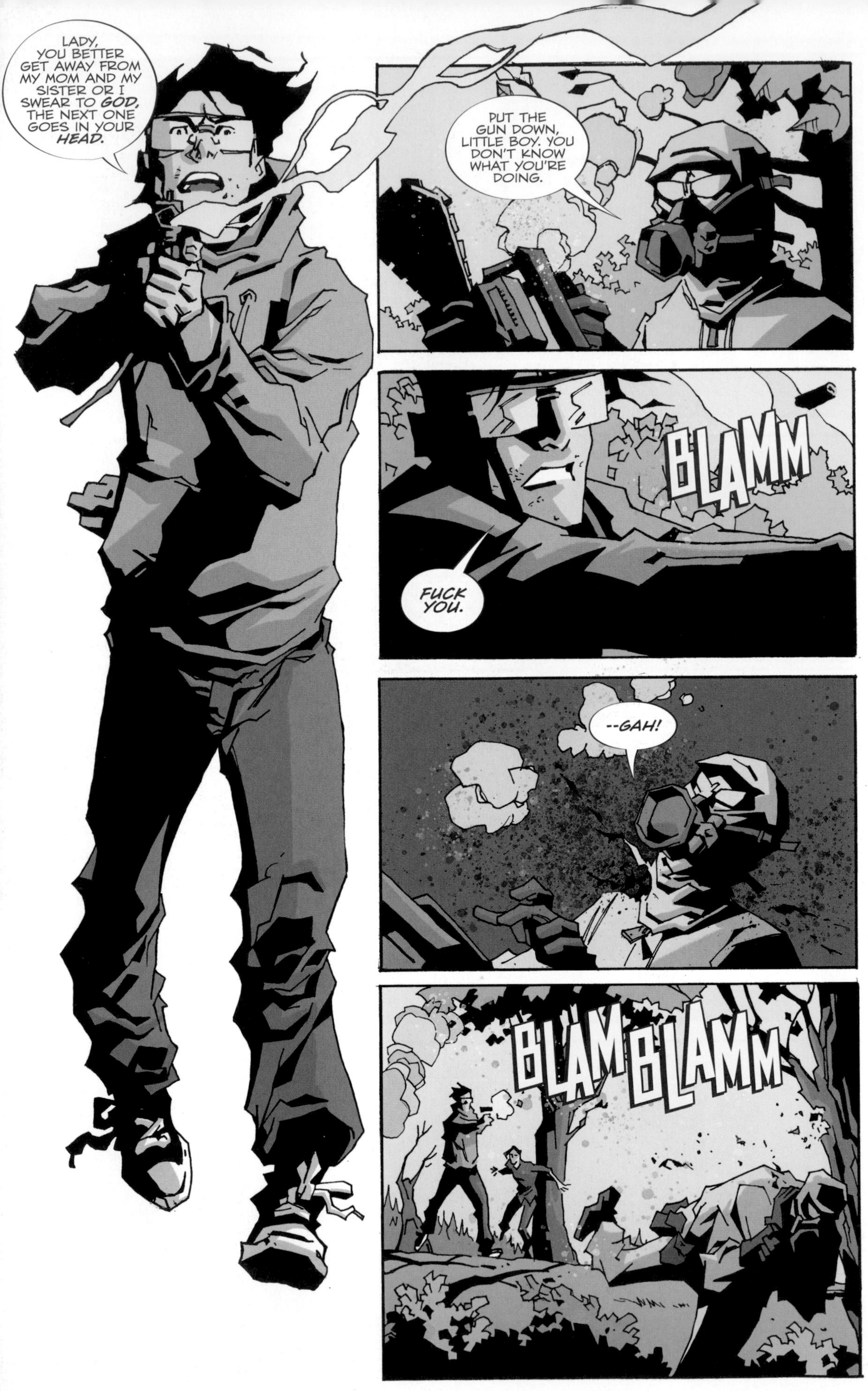
LADY, YOU BETTER GET AWAY FROM MY MOM AND MY SISTER OR I SWEAR TO *GOD*, THE NEXT ONE GOES IN YOUR *HEAD*.
PUT THE GUN DOWN, LITTLE BOY. YOU DON'T KNOW WHAT YOU'RE DOING.
BLAMM
FUCK YOU.
--*GAH!*
BLAM BLAMM

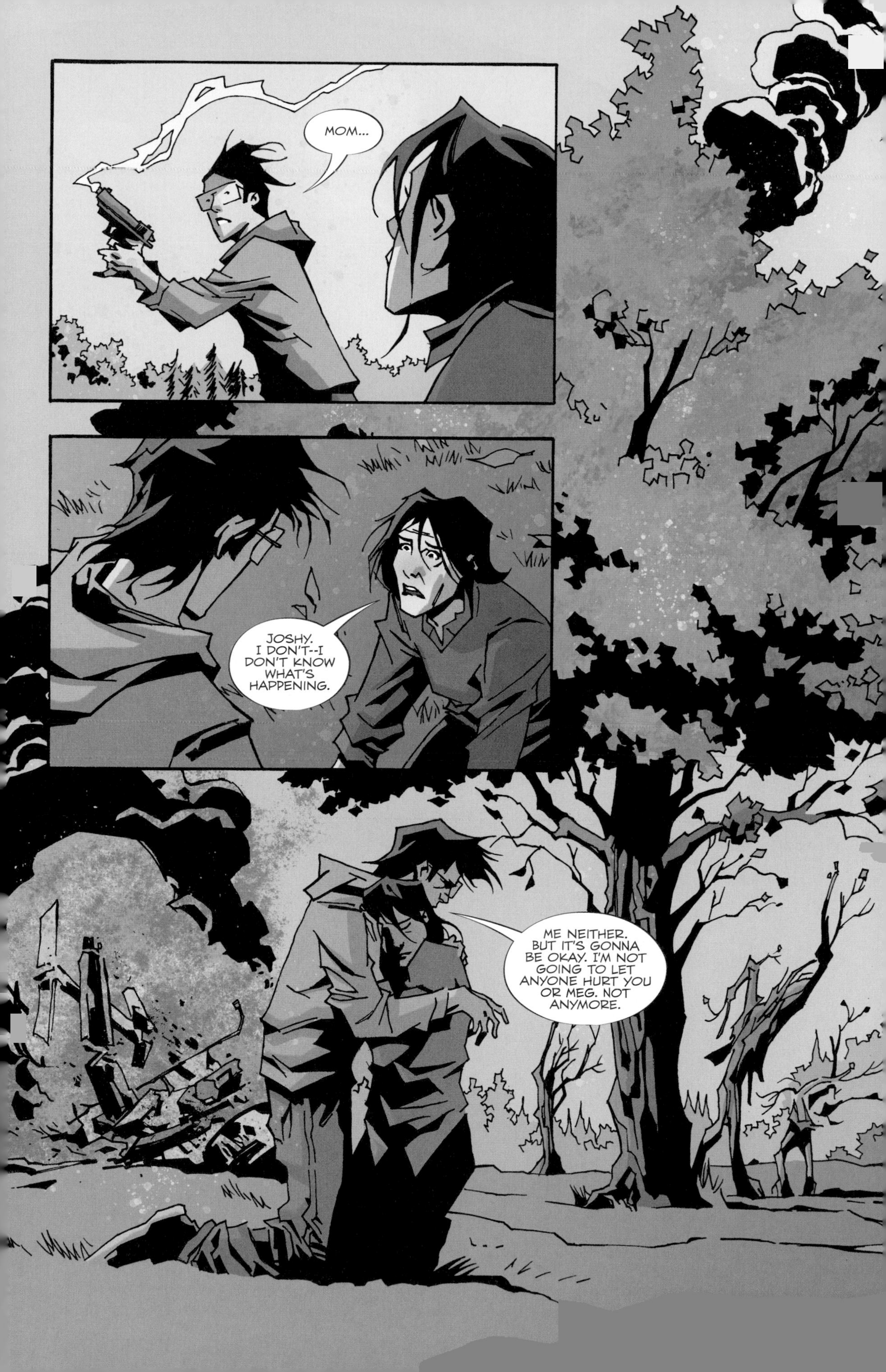
MOM...
JOSHY. I DON'T--I DON'T KNOW WHAT'S HAPPENING.
ME NEITHER. BUT IT'S GONNA BE OKAY. I'M NOT GOING TO LET ANYONE HURT YOU OR MEG. NOT ANYMORE.

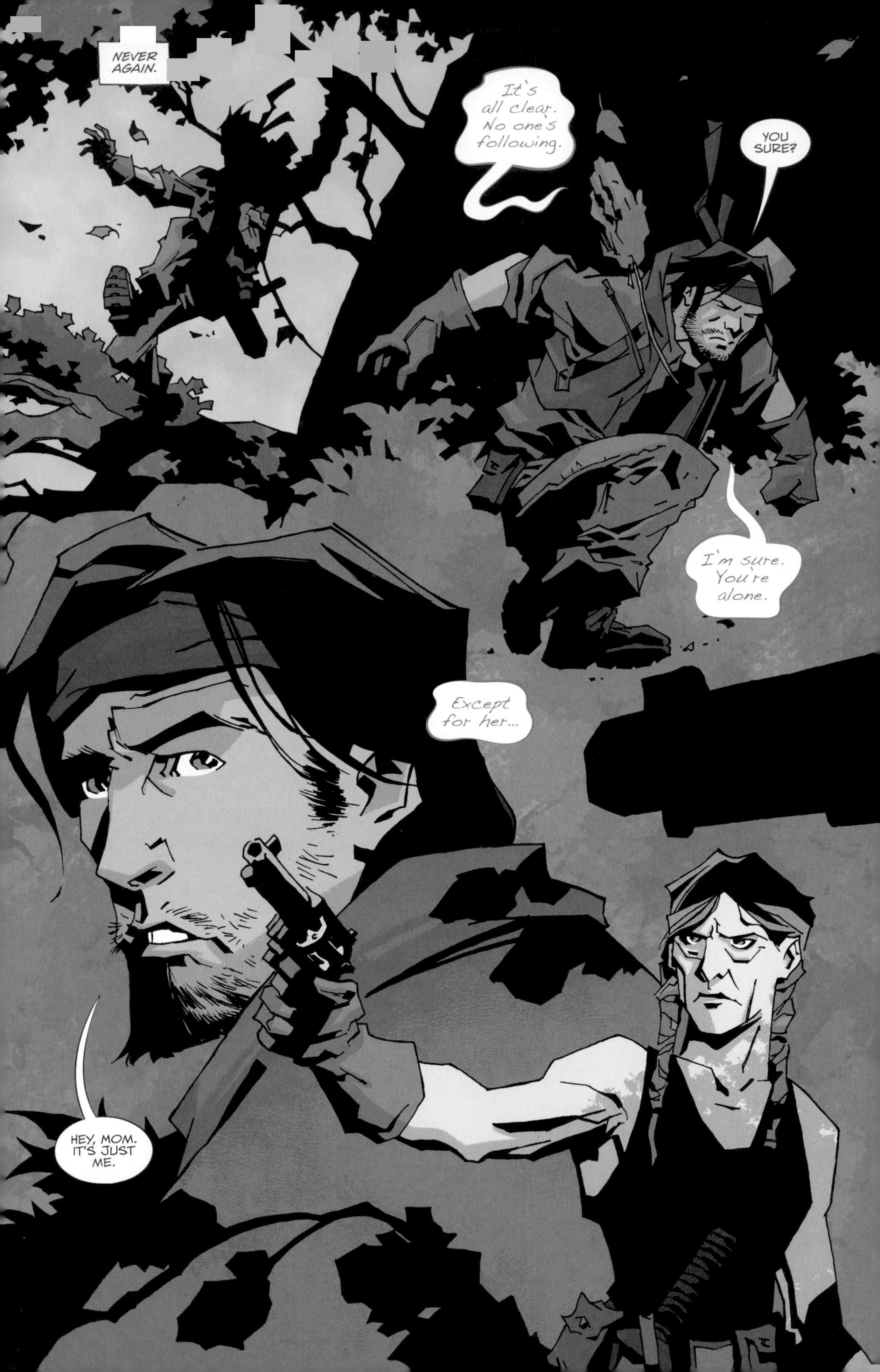
NEVER AGAIN.
It's all clear. No one's following.
YOU SURE?
I'm sure. You're alone.
Except for her...
HEY, MOM. IT'S JUST ME.

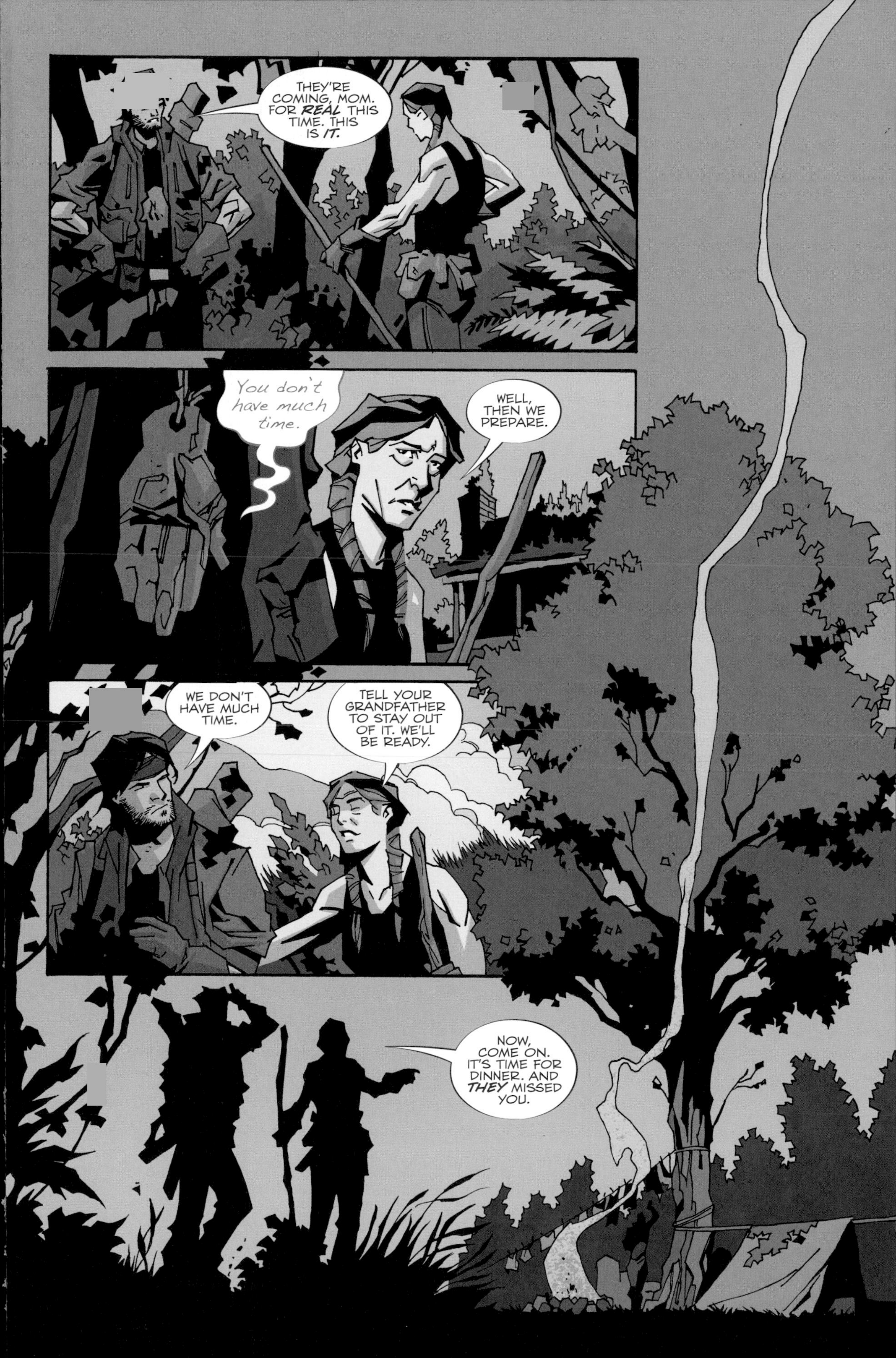
THEY'RE COMING, MOM. FOR REAL THIS TIME. THIS IS IT.
You don't have much time.
WELL, THEN WE PREPARE.
WE DON'T HAVE MUCH TIME.
TELL YOUR GRANDFATHER TO STAY OUT OF IT. WE'LL BE READY.
NOW, COME ON. IT'S TIME FOR DINNER. AND THEY MISSED YOU.

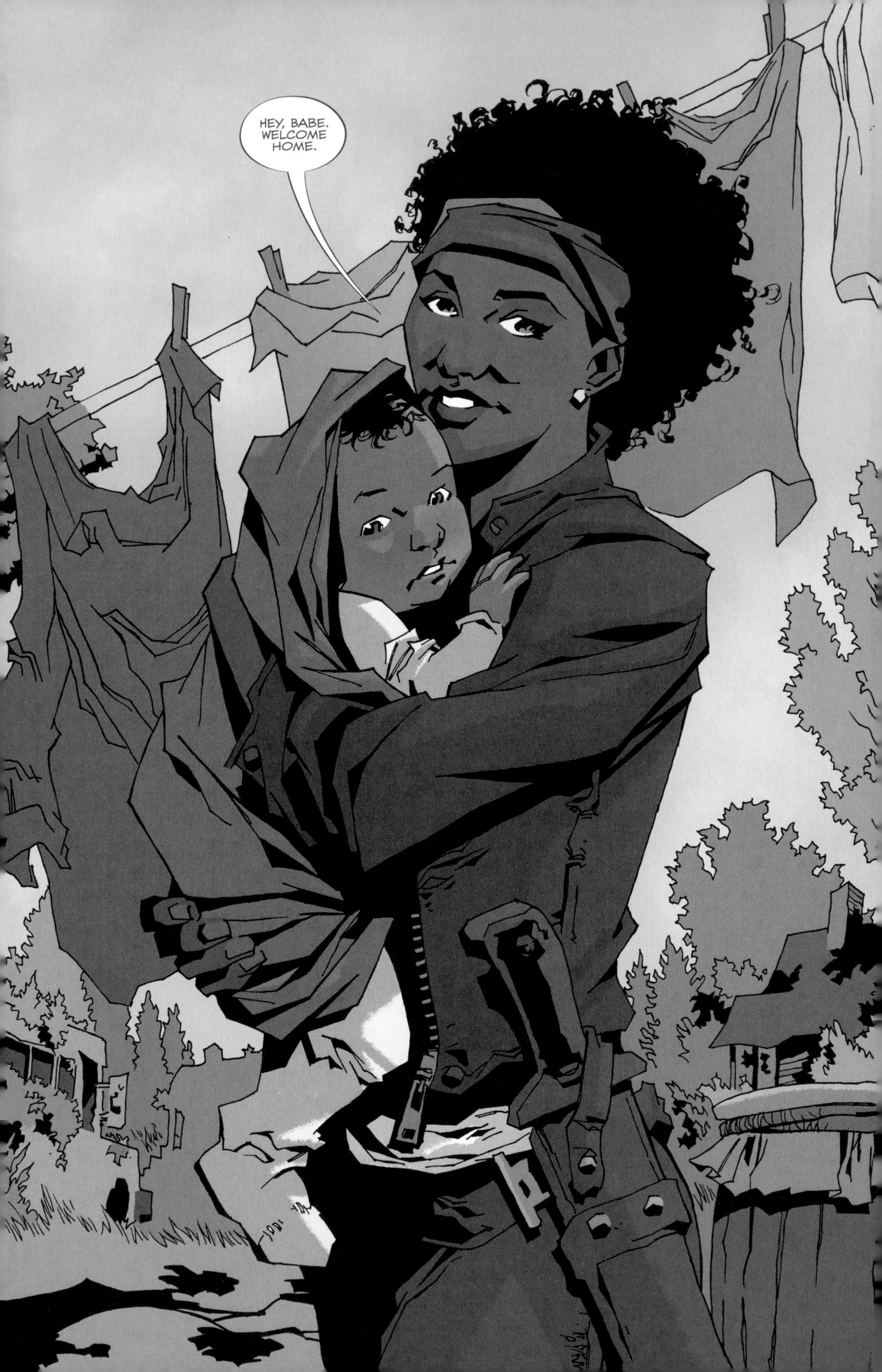
HEY, BABE. WELCOME HOME.

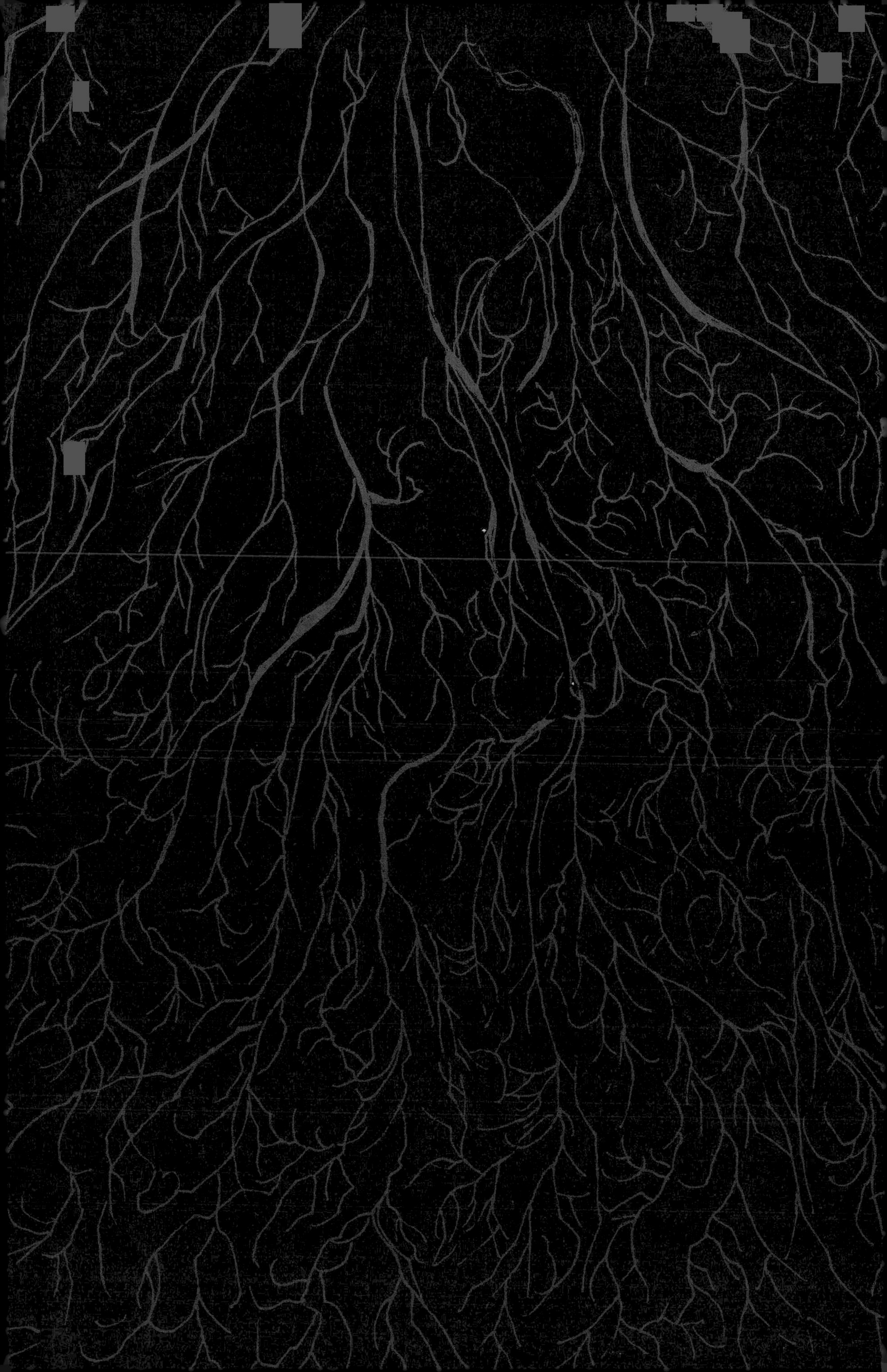

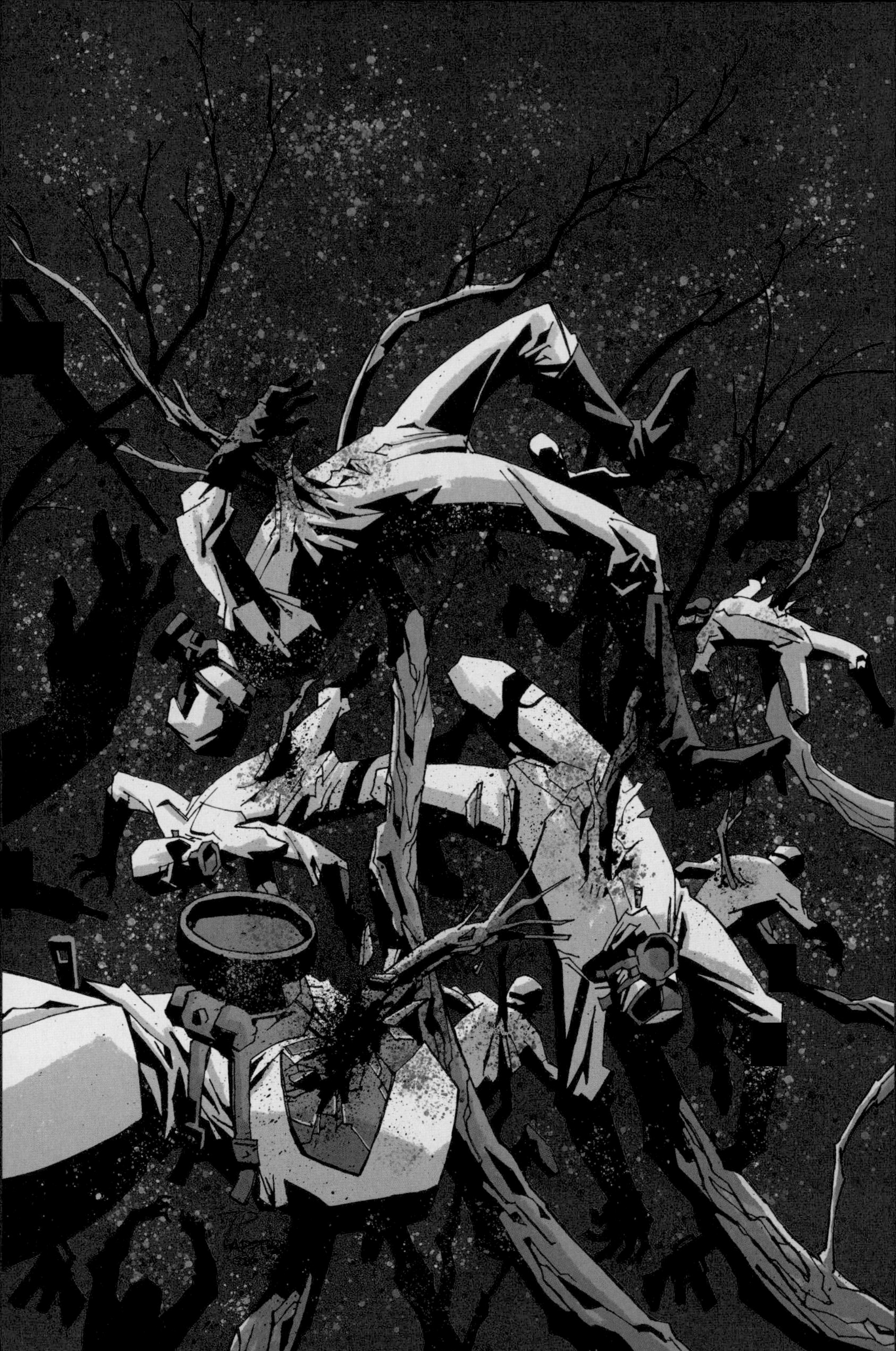

CHAPTER TEN

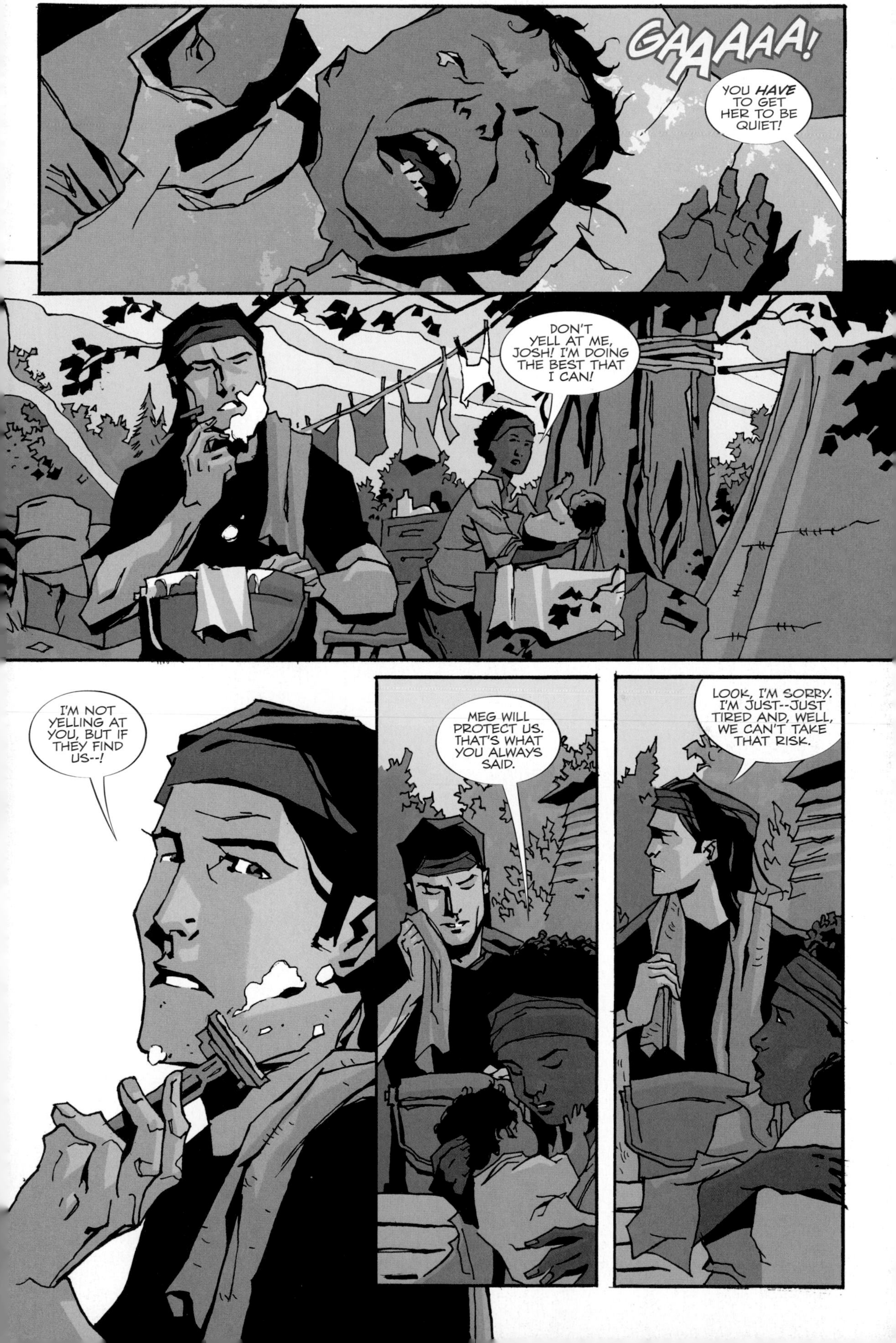
GAAAAA!
YOU HAVE TO GET HER TO BE QUIET!
DON'T YELL AT ME, JOSH! I'M DOING THE BEST THAT I CAN!
I'M NOT YELLING AT YOU, BUT IF THEY FIND US--!
MEG WILL PROTECT US. THAT'S WHAT YOU ALWAYS SAID.
LOOK, I'M SORRY. I'M JUST--JUST TIRED AND, WELL, WE CAN'T TAKE THAT RISK.

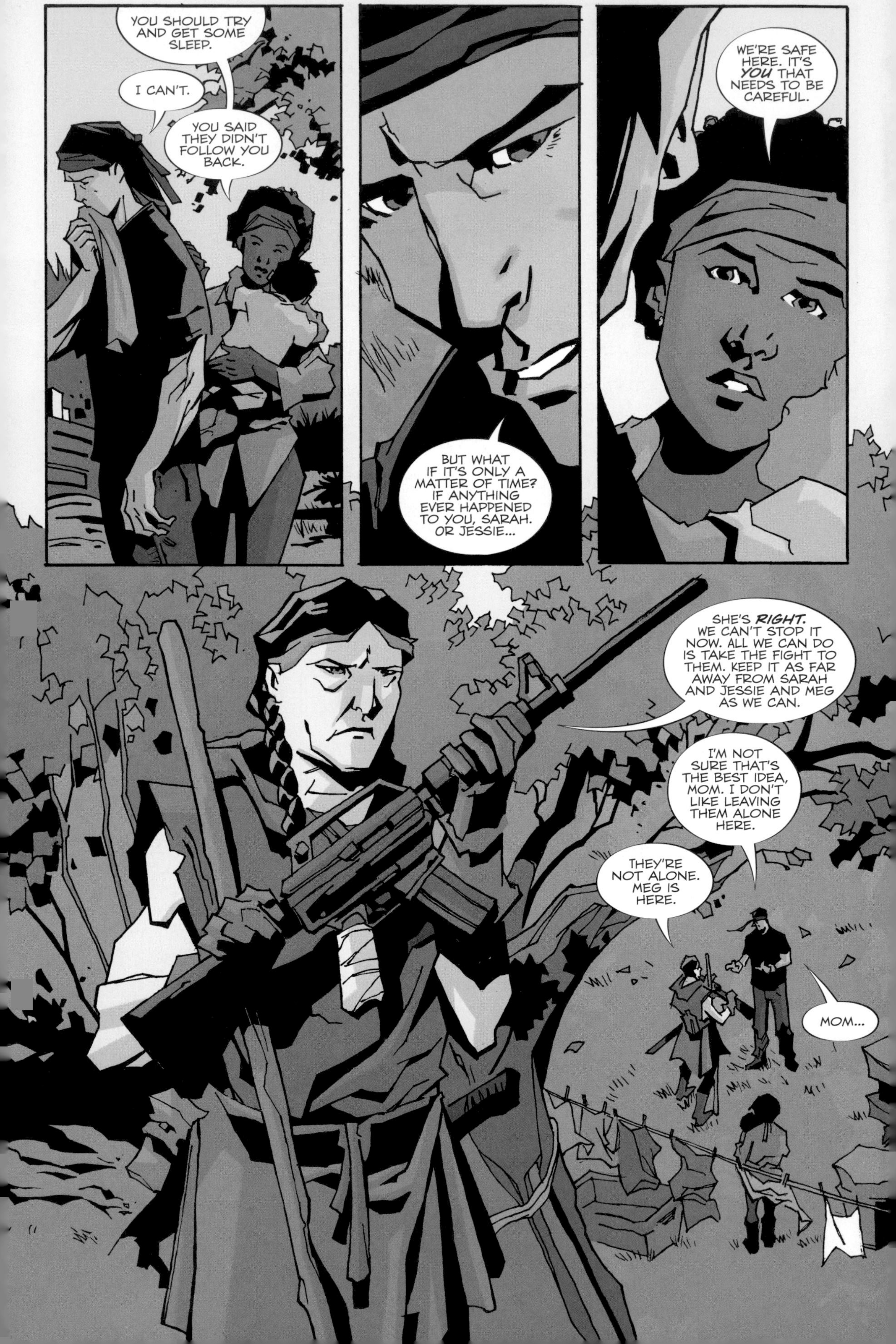

YOU SHOULD TRY AND GET SOME SLEEP.
I CAN'T.
YOU SAID THEY DIDN'T FOLLOW YOU BACK.
BUT WHAT IF IT'S ONLY A MATTER OF TIME? IF ANYTHING EVER HAPPENED TO YOU, SARAH. OR JESSIE...
WE'RE SAFE HERE. IT'S YOU THAT NEEDS TO BE CAREFUL.
SHE'S RIGHT. WE CAN'T STOP IT NOW. ALL WE CAN DO IS TAKE THE FIGHT TO THEM. KEEP IT AS FAR AWAY FROM SARAH AND JESSIE AND MEG AS WE CAN.
I'M NOT SURE THAT'S THE BEST IDEA, MOM. I DON'T LIKE LEAVING THEM ALONE HERE.
THEY'RE NOT ALONE. MEG IS HERE.
MOM...

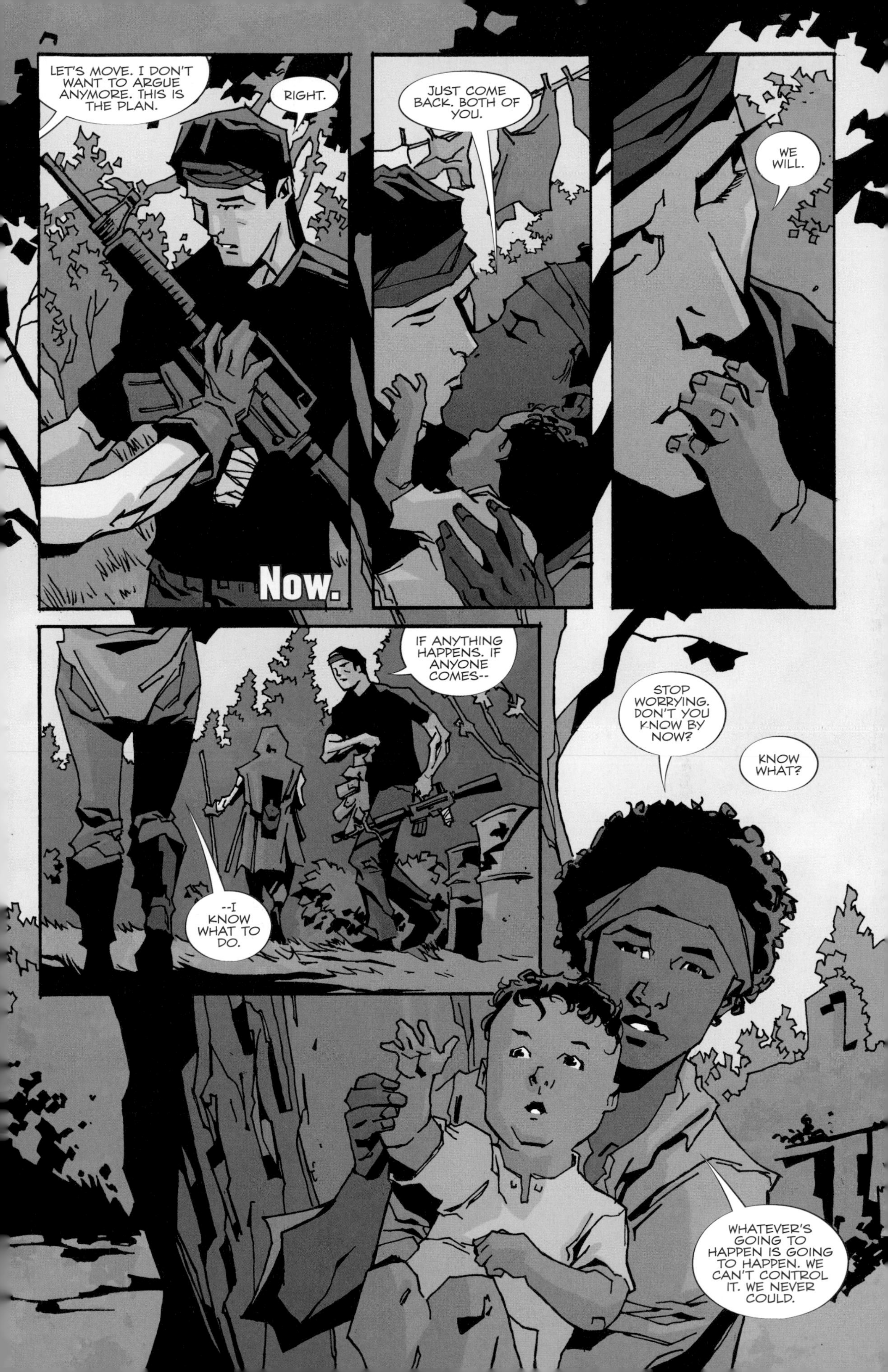
LET'S MOVE. I DON'T WANT TO ARGUE ANYMORE. THIS IS THE PLAN.
RIGHT.
Now.
JUST COME BACK. BOTH OF YOU.
WE WILL.
IF ANYTHING HAPPENS. IF ANYONE COMES--
--I KNOW WHAT TO DO.
STOP WORRYING. DON'T YOU KNOW BY NOW?
KNOW WHAT?
WHATEVER'S GOING TO HAPPEN IS GOING TO HAPPEN. WE CAN'T CONTROL IT. WE NEVER COULD.

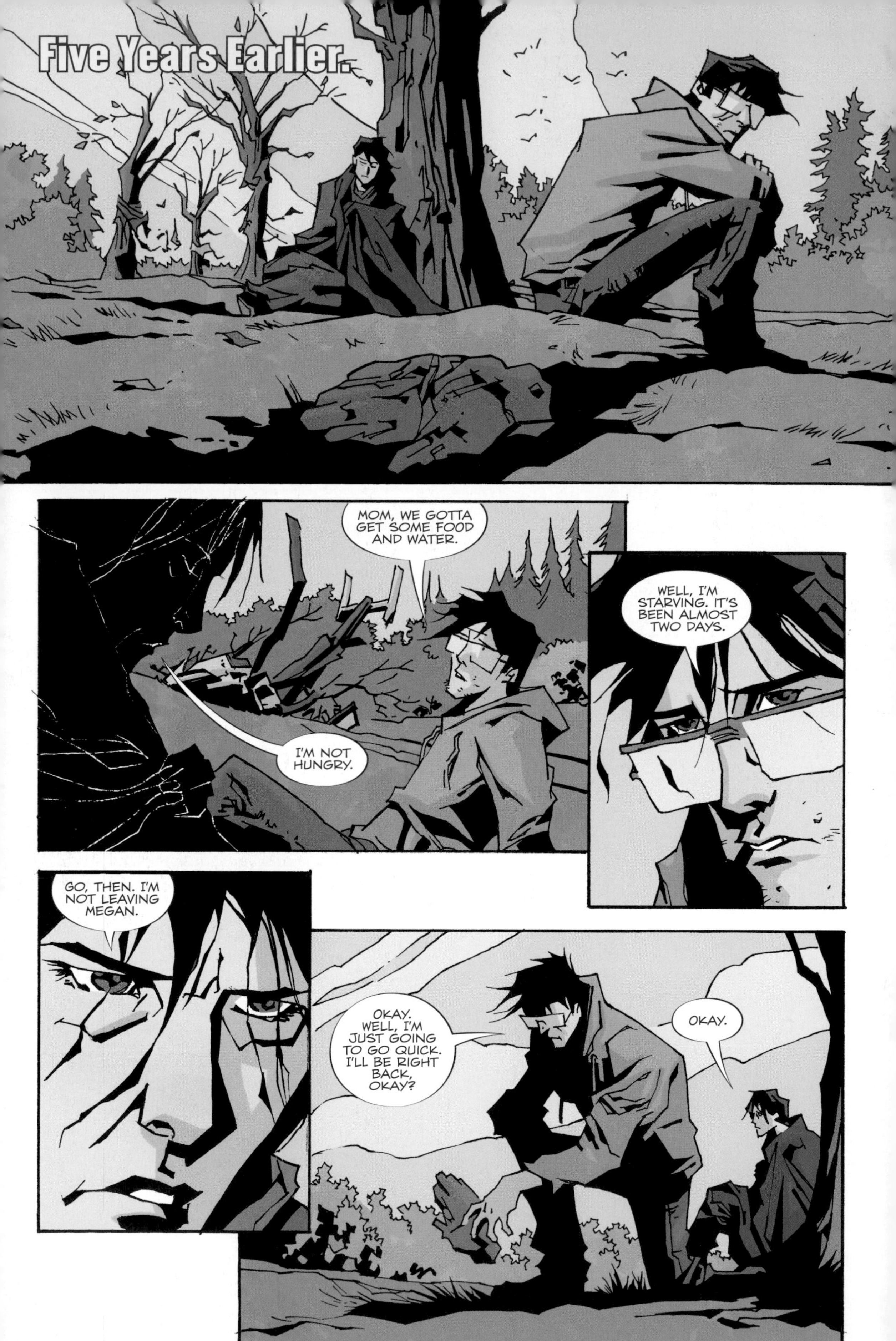
Five Years Earlier.
MOM, WE GOTTA GET SOME FOOD AND WATER.
I'M NOT HUNGRY.
WELL, I'M STARVING. IT'S BEEN ALMOST TWO DAYS.
GO, THEN. I'M NOT LEAVING MEGAN.
OKAY. WELL, I'M JUST GOING TO GO QUICK. I'LL BE RIGHT BACK, OKAY?
OKAY.

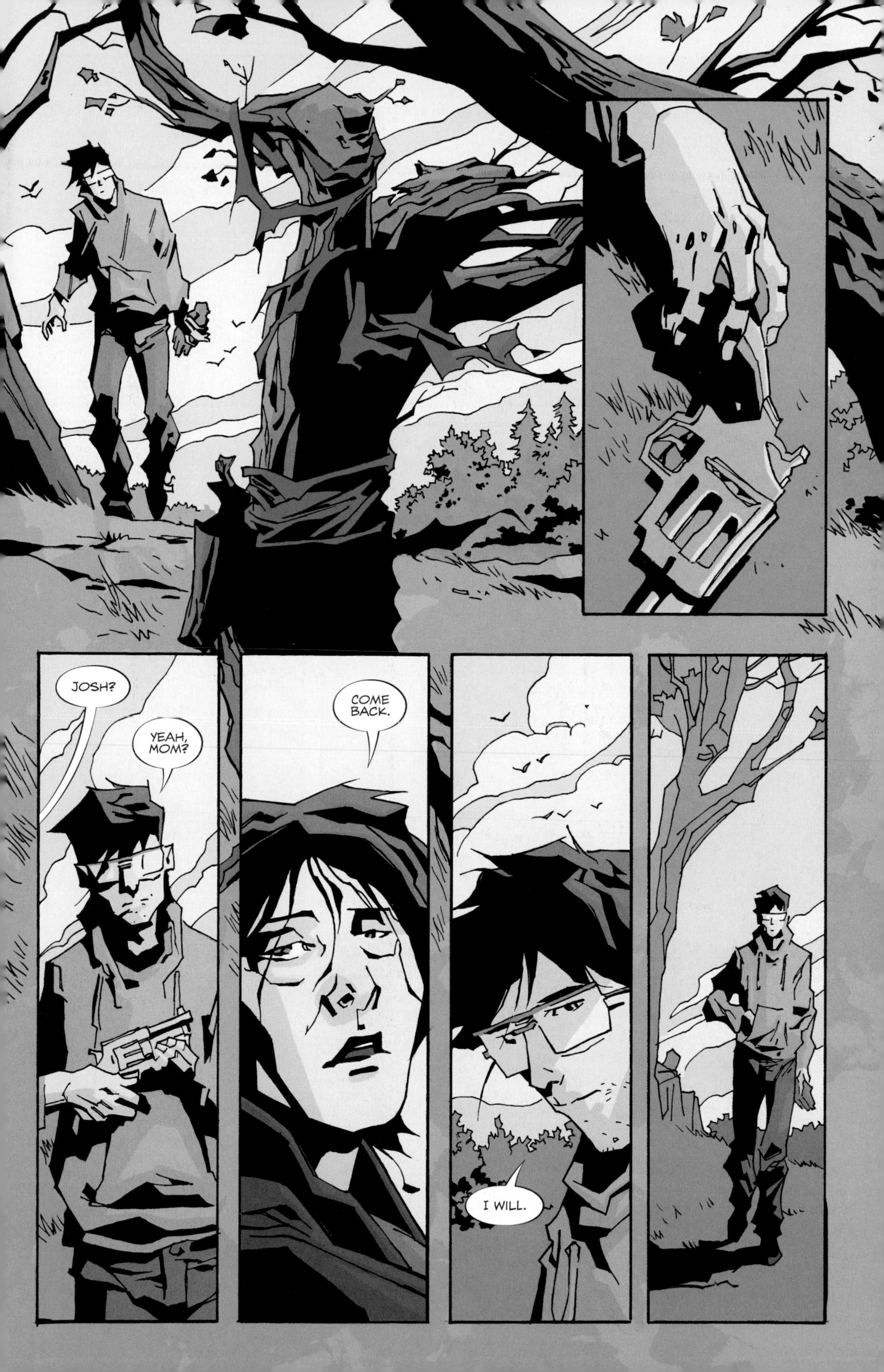
JOSH?
YEAH, MOM?
COME BACK.
I WILL.

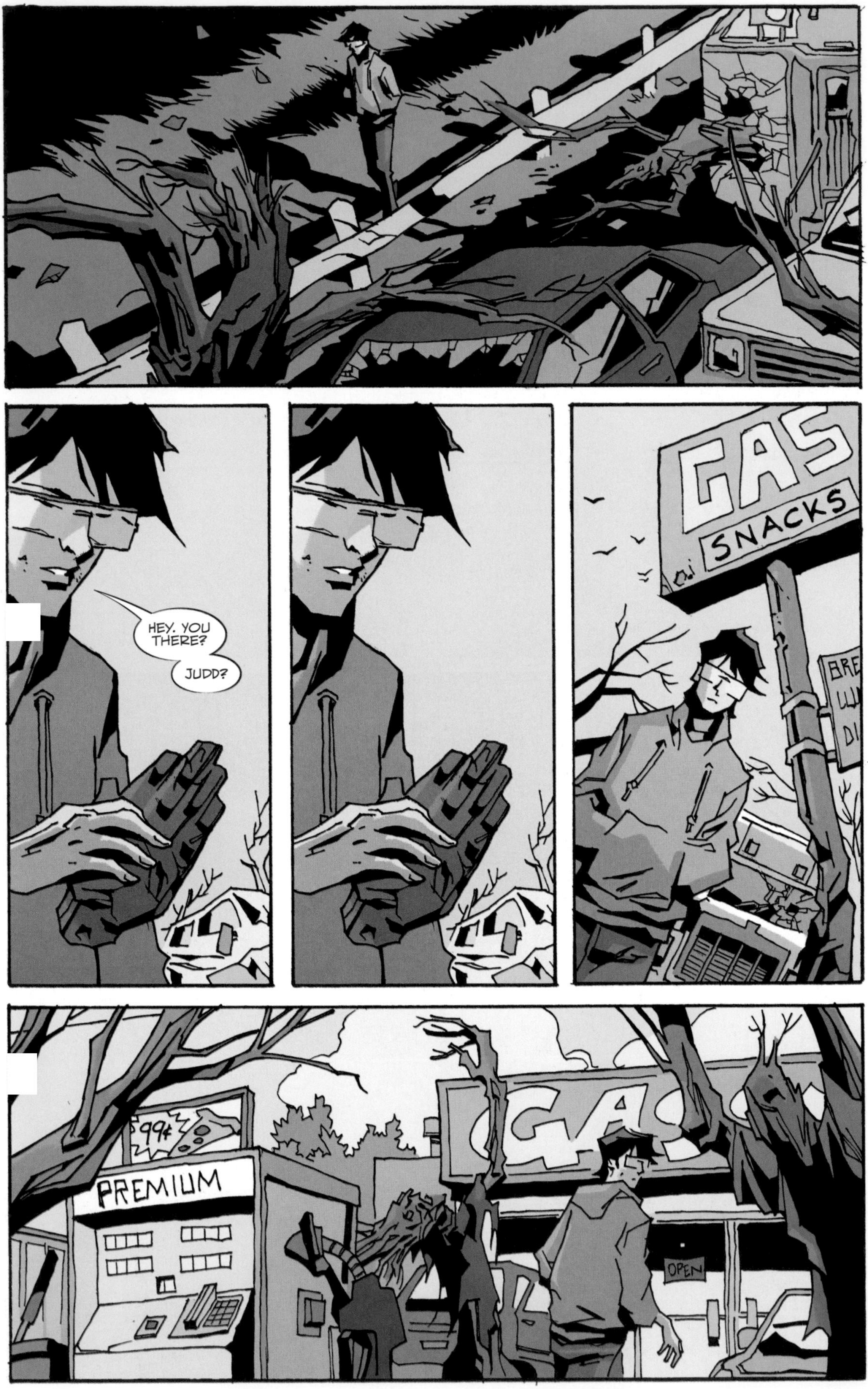
HEY. YOU THERE?
JUDD?
GAS
SNACKS
PREMIUM
99¢
GAS
OPEN

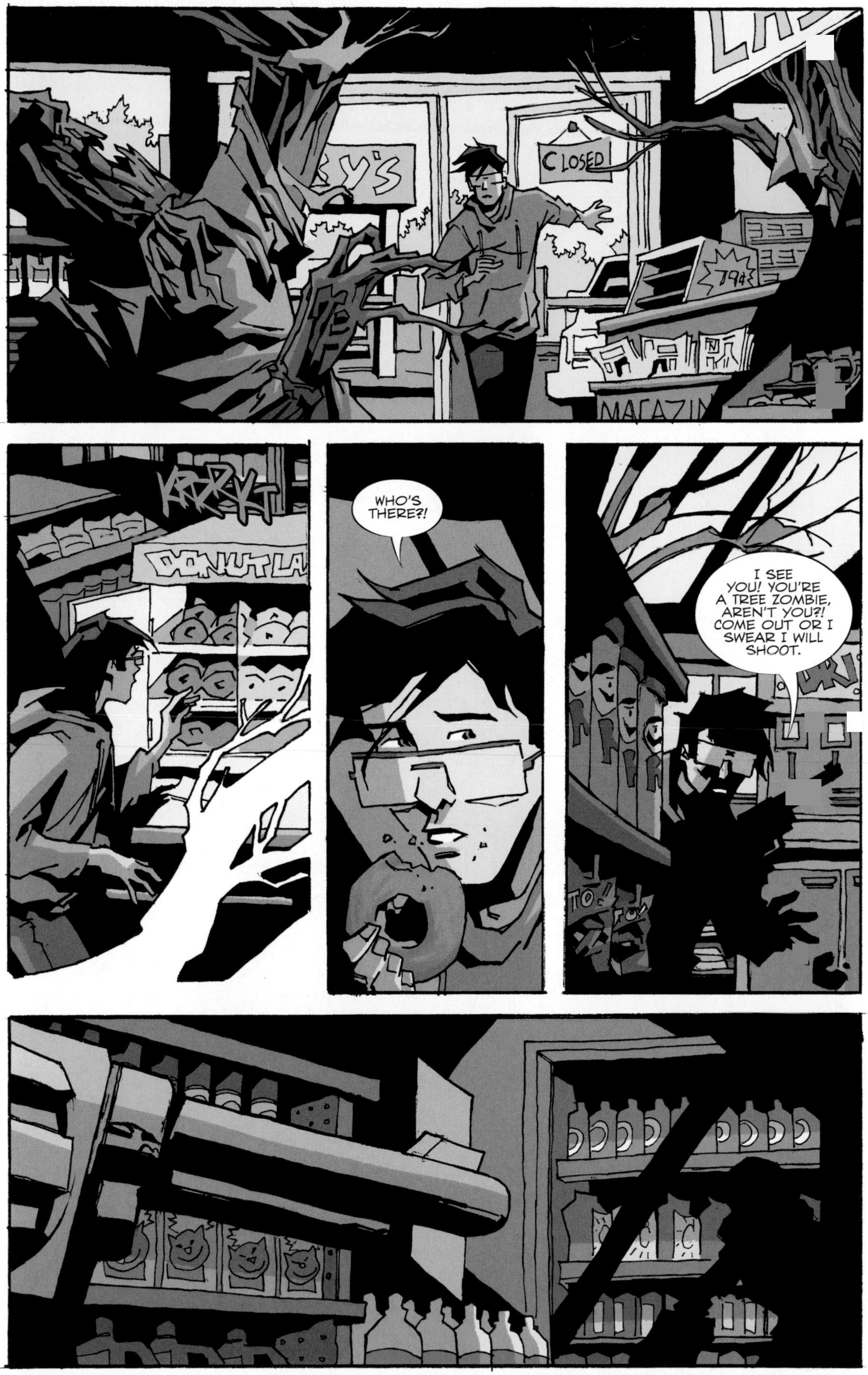

Y'S
CLOSED
79¢
MAGAZIN
KRDRKT
DONUT LA
WHO'S THERE?!
I SEE YOU! YOU'RE A TREE ZOMBIE, AREN'T YOU?! COME OUT OR I SWEAR I WILL SHOOT.

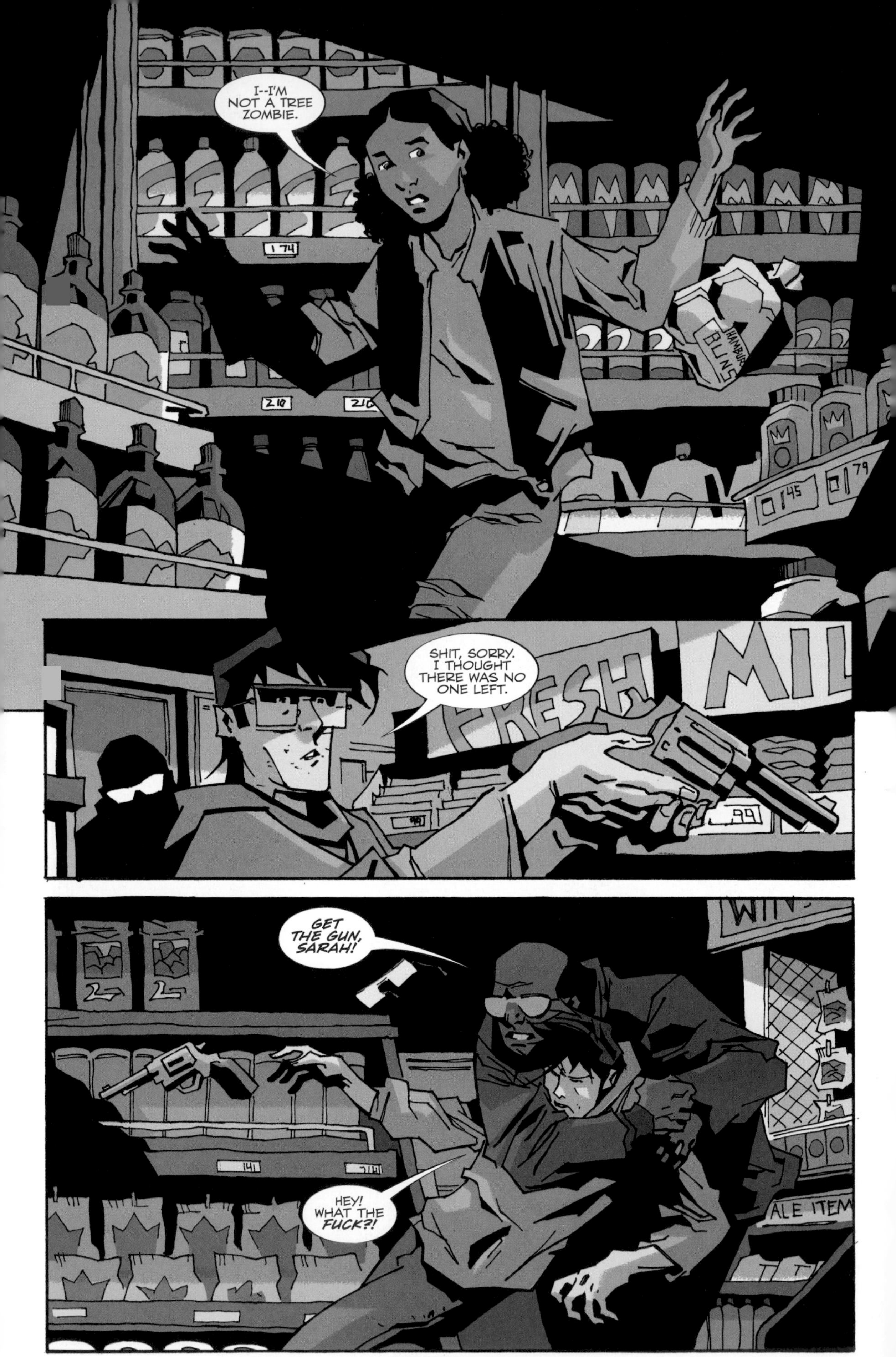
I--I'M NOT A TREE ZOMBIE.
HAMBURGER BUNS
SHIT, SORRY. I THOUGHT THERE WAS NO ONE LEFT.
FRESH
GET THE GUN, SARAH!
HEY! WHAT THE FUCK?!
ALE ITEM

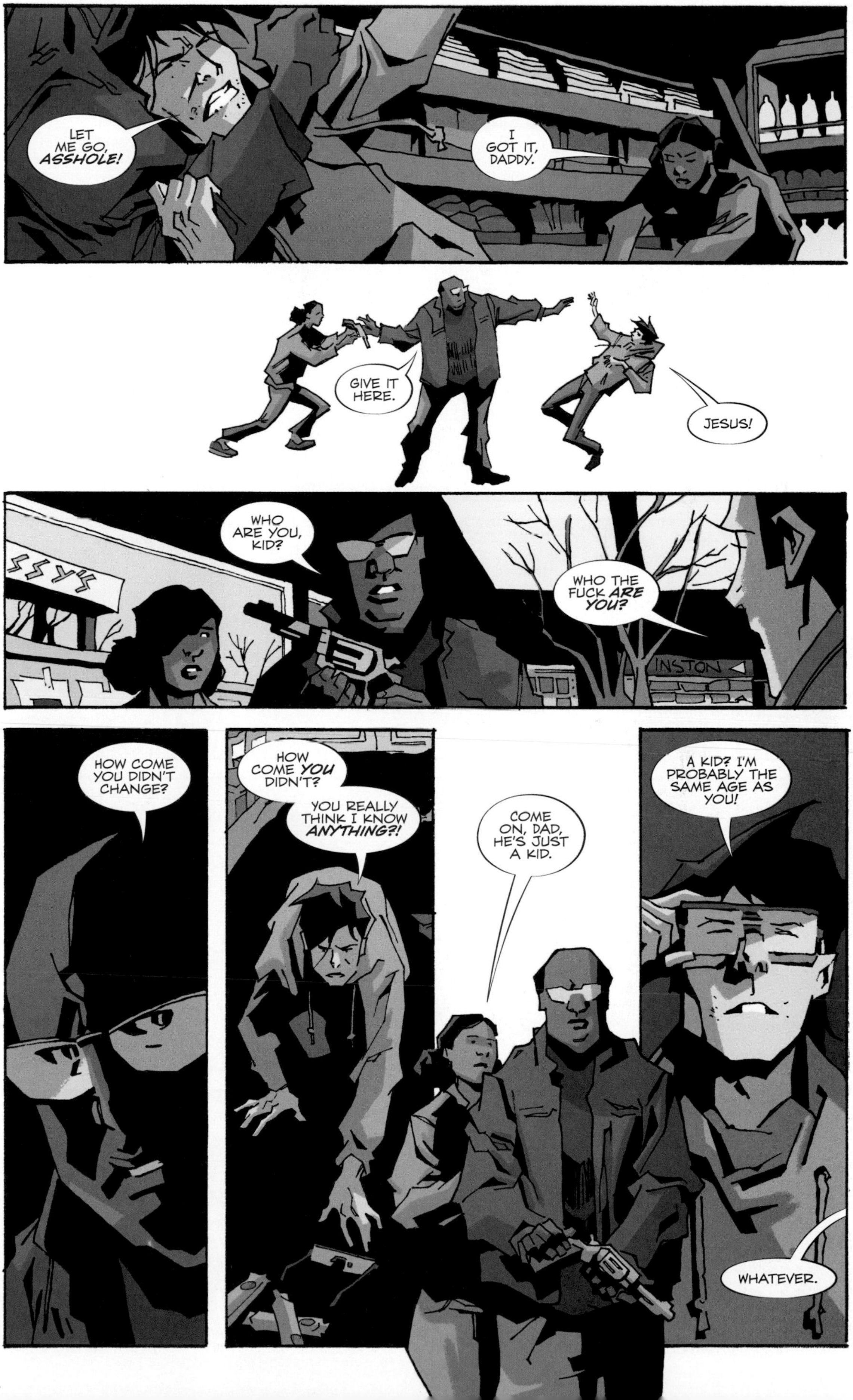
LET ME GO, ASSHOLE!
I GOT IT, DADDY.
GIVE IT HERE.
JESUS!
WHO ARE YOU, KID?
WHO THE FUCK ARE YOU?
INSTON
HOW COME YOU DIDN'T CHANGE?
HOW COME YOU DIDN'T?
YOU REALLY THINK I KNOW ANYTHING?!
COME ON, DAD, HE'S JUST A KID.
A KID? I'M PROBABLY THE SAME AGE AS YOU!
WHATEVER.

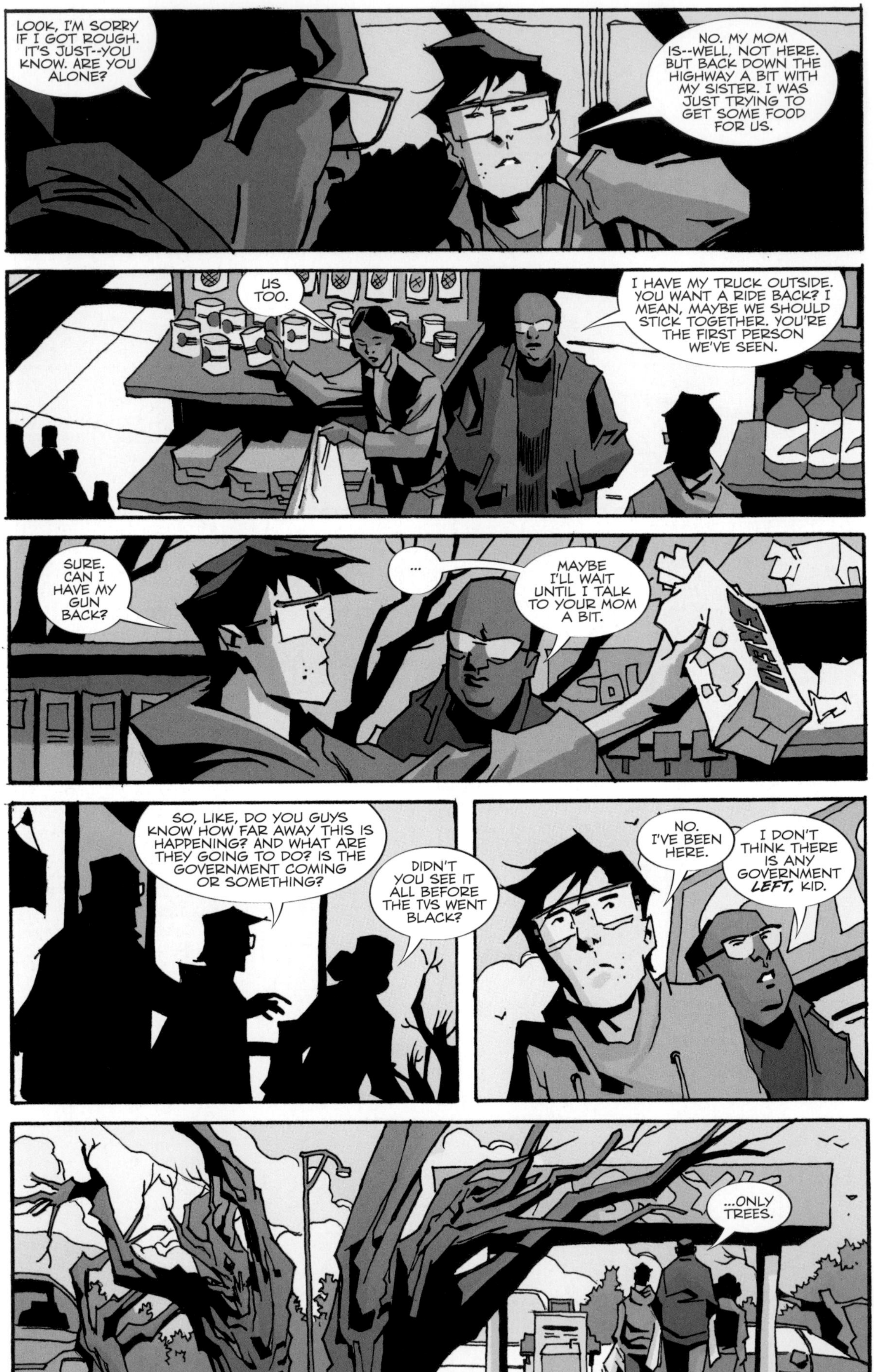
LOOK, I'M SORRY IF I GOT ROUGH. IT'S JUST--YOU KNOW. ARE YOU ALONE?
NO. MY MOM IS--WELL, NOT HERE. BUT BACK DOWN THE HIGHWAY A BIT WITH MY SISTER. I WAS JUST TRYING TO GET SOME FOOD FOR US.
US TOO.
I HAVE MY TRUCK OUTSIDE. YOU WANT A RIDE BACK? I MEAN, MAYBE WE SHOULD STICK TOGETHER. YOU'RE THE FIRST PERSON WE'VE SEEN.
SURE. CAN I HAVE MY GUN BACK?
...
MAYBE I'LL WAIT UNTIL I TALK TO YOUR MOM A BIT.
SO, LIKE, DO YOU GUYS KNOW HOW FAR AWAY THIS IS HAPPENING? AND WHAT ARE THEY GOING TO DO? IS THE GOVERNMENT COMING OR SOMETHING?
DIDN'T YOU SEE IT ALL BEFORE THE TVS WENT BLACK?
NO. I'VE BEEN HERE.
I DON'T THINK THERE IS ANY GOVERNMENT ***LEFT,*** KID.
...ONLY TREES.

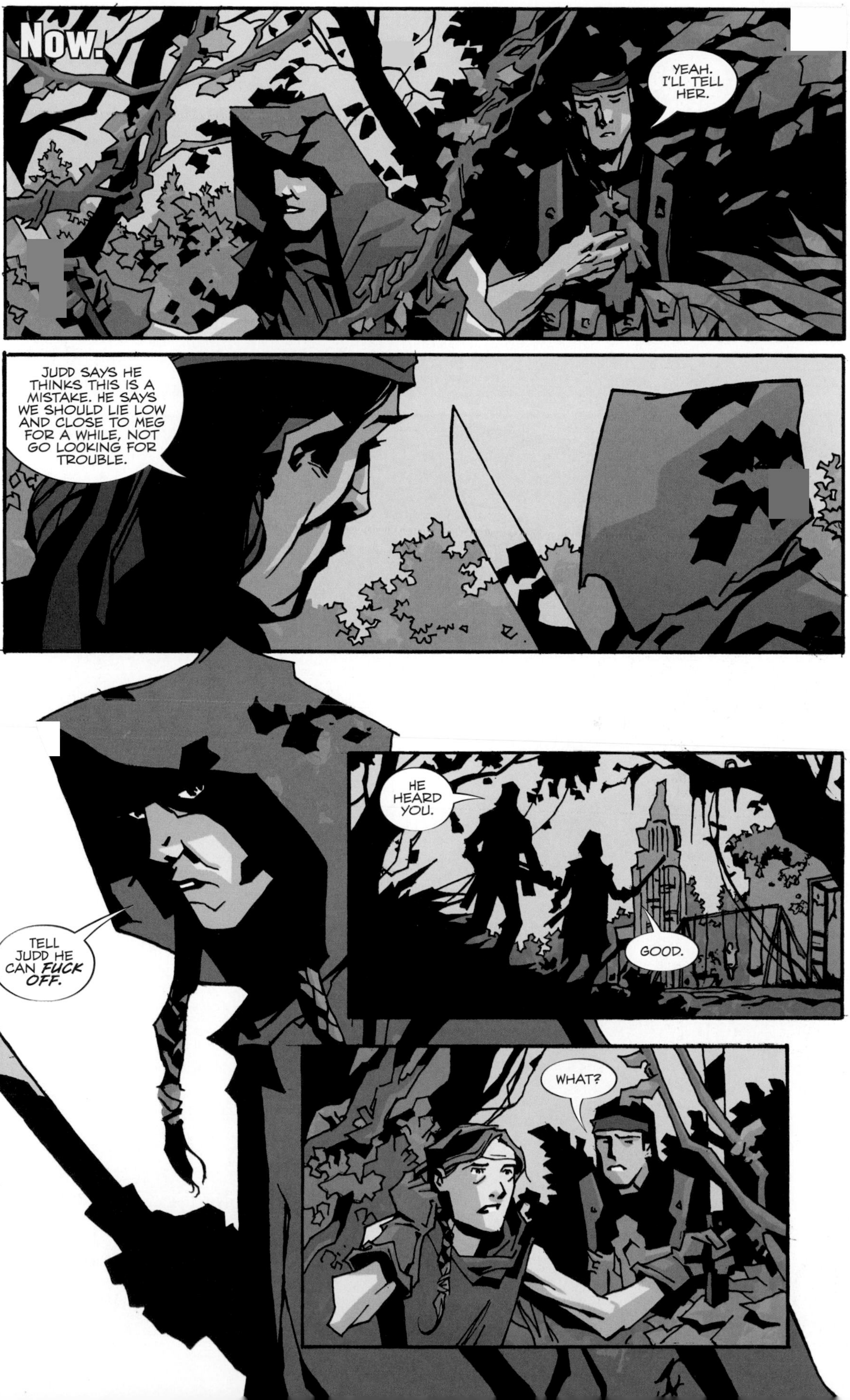
Now.
YEAH. I'LL TELL HER.
JUDD SAYS HE THINKS THIS IS A MISTAKE. HE SAYS WE SHOULD LIE LOW AND CLOSE TO MEG FOR A WHILE, NOT GO LOOKING FOR TROUBLE.
TELL JUDD HE CAN FUCK OFF.
HE HEARD YOU.
GOOD.
WHAT?

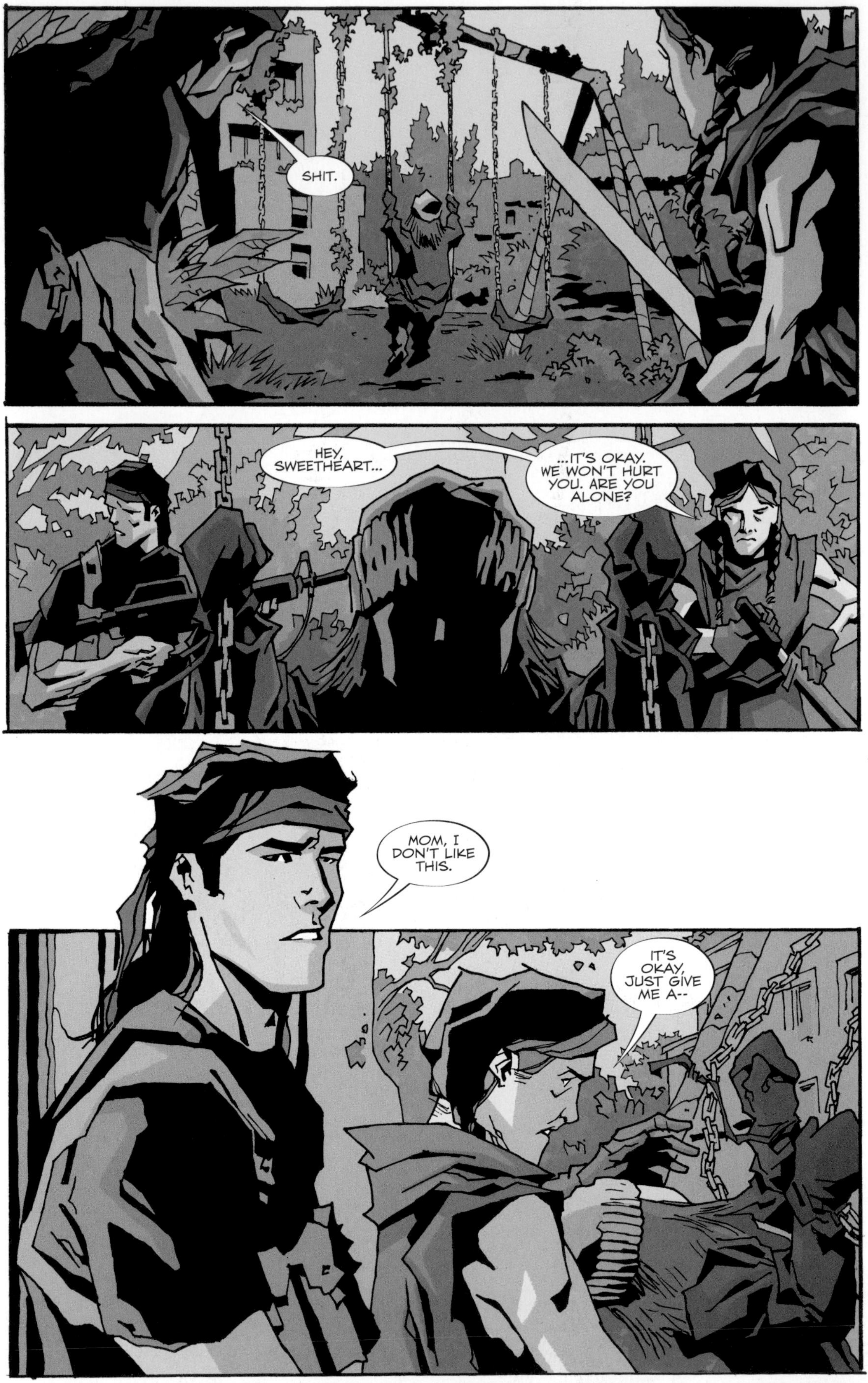
SHIT.
HEY, SWEETHEART...
...IT'S OKAY. WE WON'T HURT YOU. ARE YOU ALONE?
MOM, I DON'T LIKE THIS.
IT'S OKAY, JUST GIVE ME A--

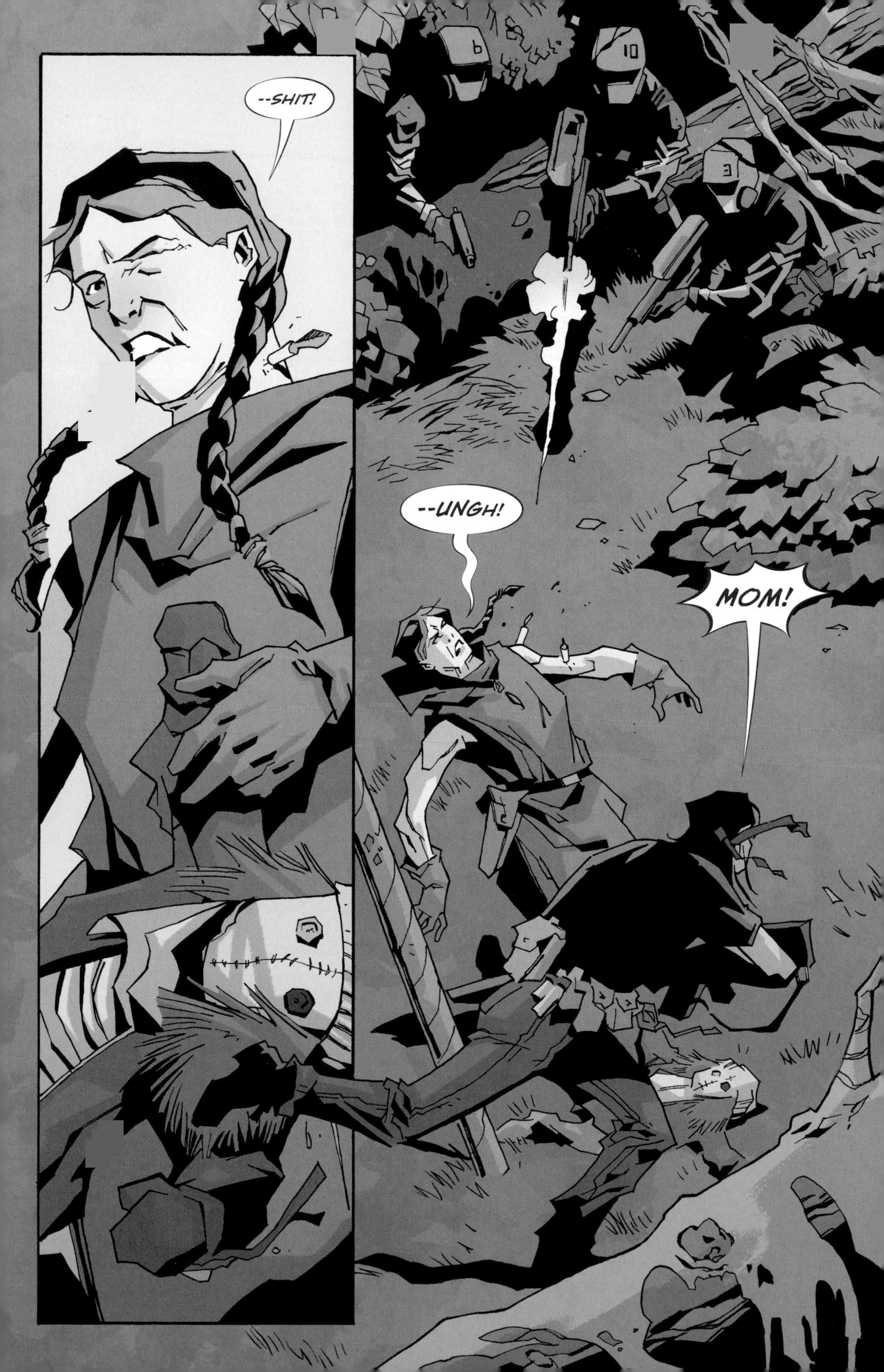
--SHIT!
--UNGH!
MOM!

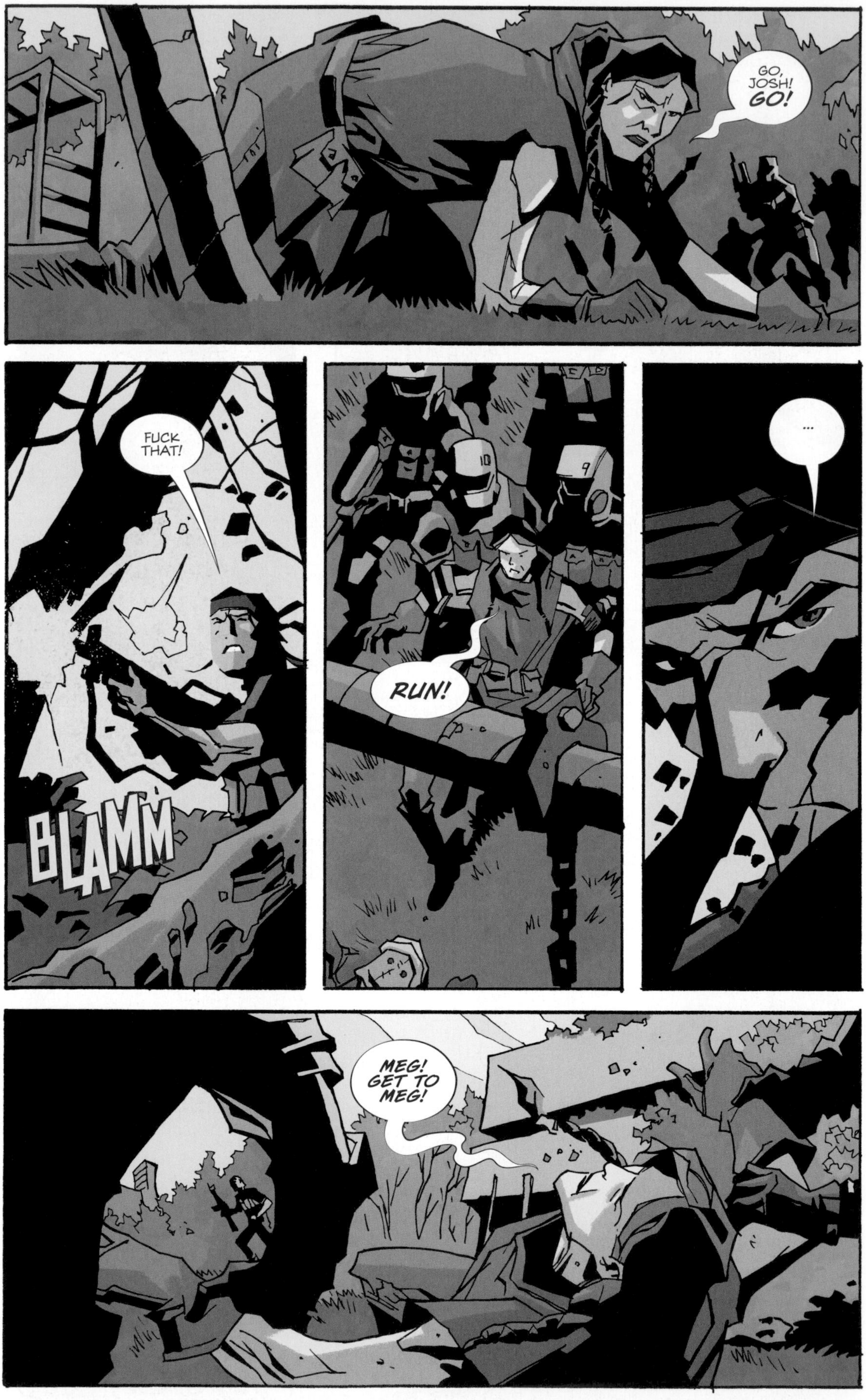
GO, JOSH! GO!
FUCK THAT!
BLAMM
RUN!
...
MEG! GET TO MEG!

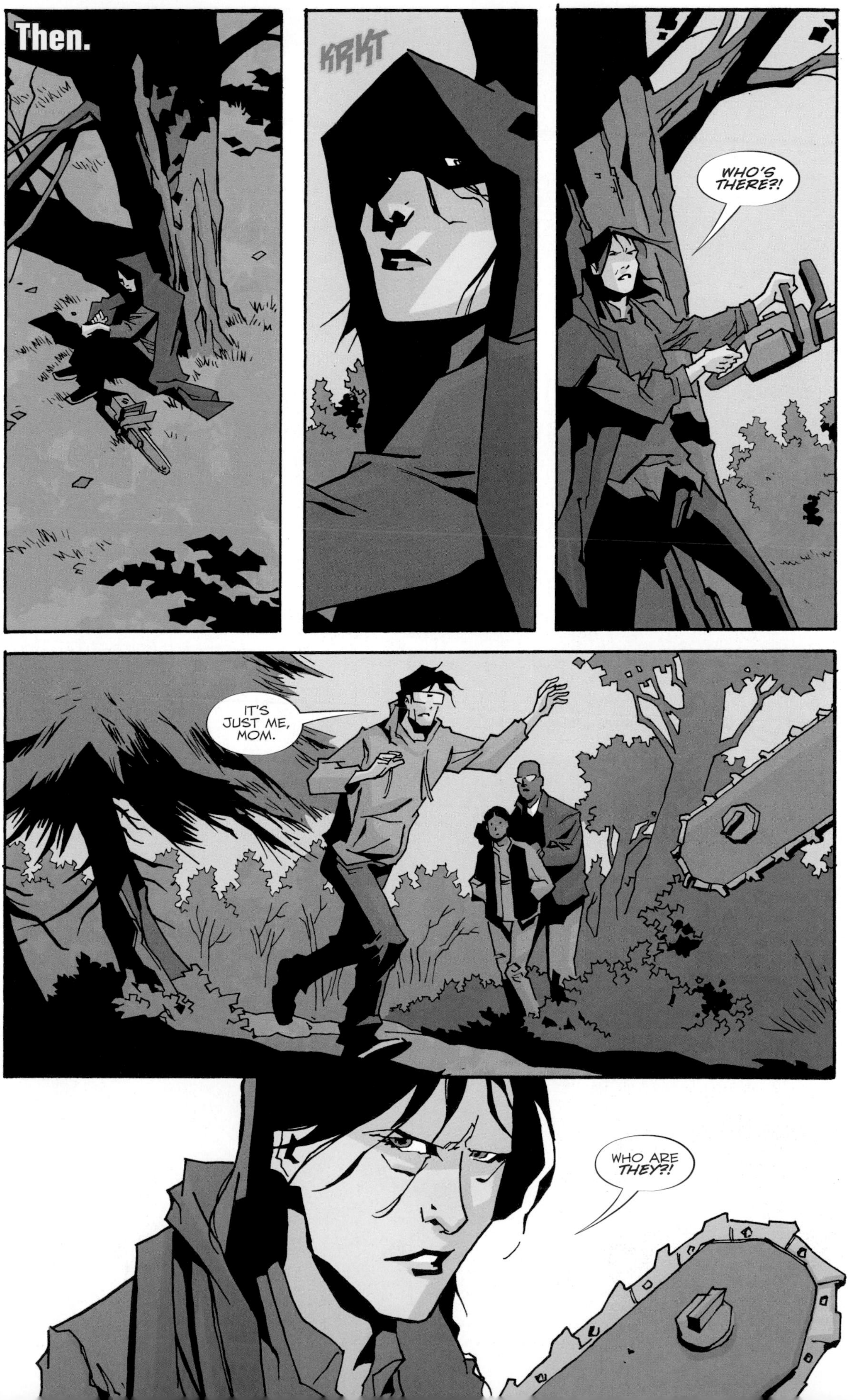
Then.
KRKT
WHO'S THERE?!
IT'S JUST ME, MOM.
WHO ARE THEY?!

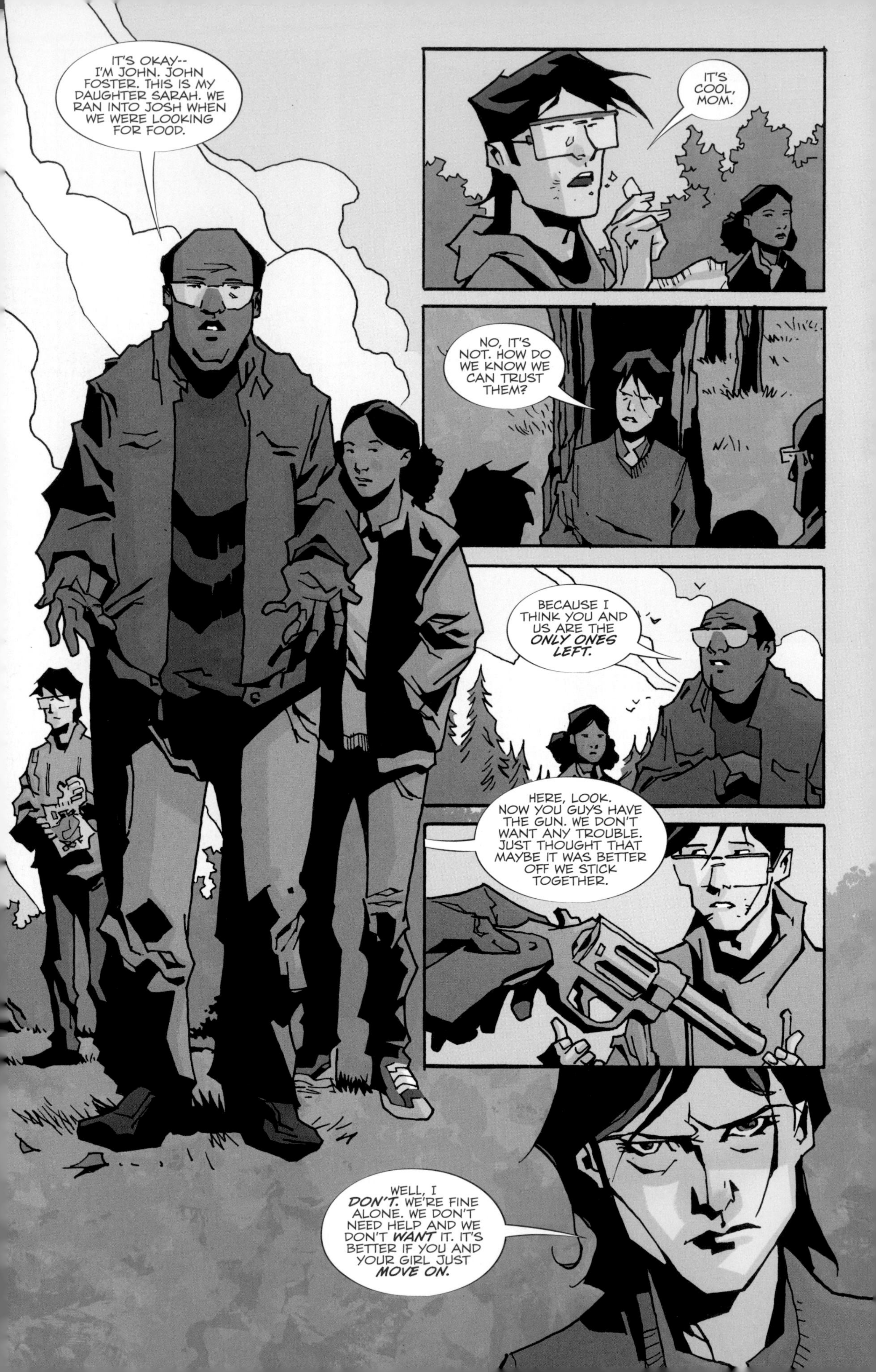
IT'S OKAY-- I'M JOHN. JOHN FOSTER. THIS IS MY DAUGHTER SARAH. WE RAN INTO JOSH WHEN WE WERE LOOKING FOR FOOD.
IT'S COOL, MOM.
NO, IT'S NOT. HOW DO WE KNOW WE CAN TRUST THEM?
BECAUSE I THINK YOU AND US ARE THE ONLY ONES LEFT.
HERE, LOOK. NOW YOU GUYS HAVE THE GUN. WE DON'T WANT ANY TROUBLE. JUST THOUGHT THAT MAYBE IT WAS BETTER OFF WE STICK TOGETHER.
WELL, I DON'T. WE'RE FINE ALONE. WE DON'T NEED HELP AND WE DON'T WANT IT. IT'S BETTER IF YOU AND YOUR GIRL JUST MOVE ON.

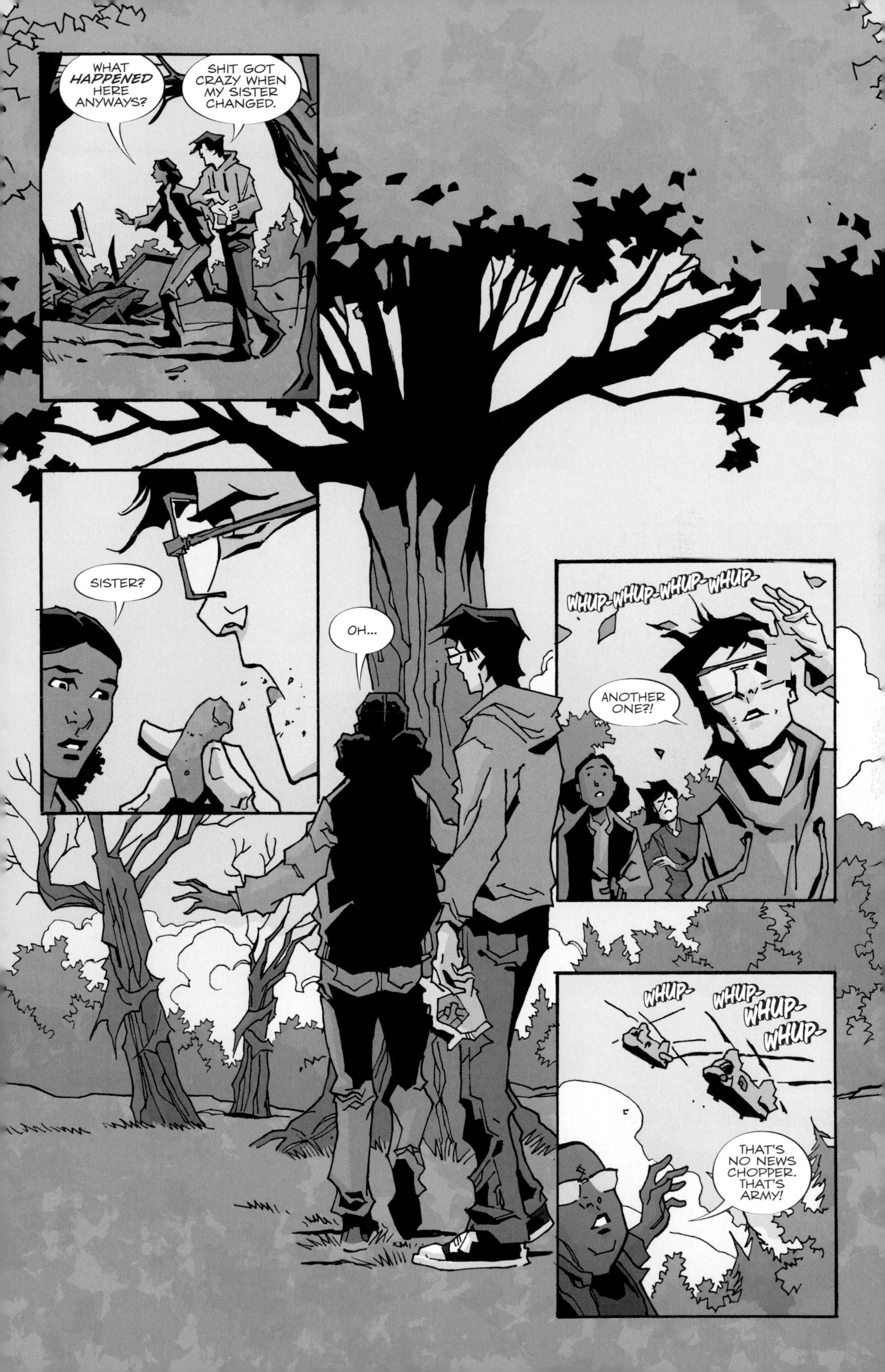
WHAT *HAPPENED* HERE ANYWAYS?
SHIT GOT CRAZY WHEN MY SISTER CHANGED.
SISTER?
OH...
WHUP-WHUP-WHUP-WHUP-
ANOTHER ONE?!
WHUP-
WHUP-
WHUP-
WHUP-
THAT'S NO NEWS CHOPPER. THAT'S ARMY!

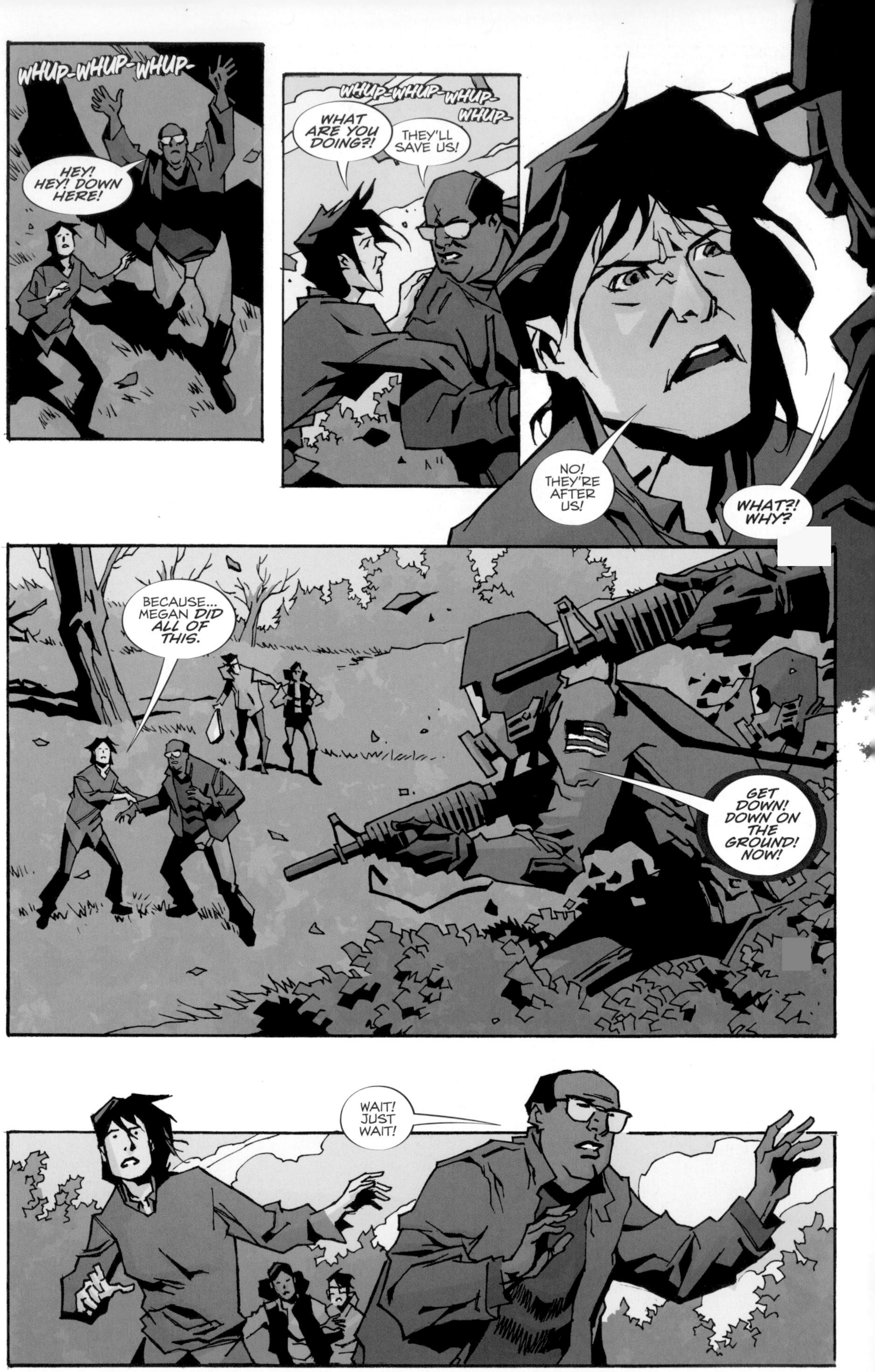
WHUP-WHUP-WHUP-
HEY! HEY! DOWN HERE!
WHUP-WHUP-WHUP-WHUP-
WHAT ARE YOU DOING?!
THEY'LL SAVE US!
NO! THEY'RE AFTER US!
WHAT?! WHY?
BECAUSE... MEGAN DID ALL OF THIS.
GET DOWN! DOWN ON THE GROUND! NOW!
WAIT! JUST WAIT!

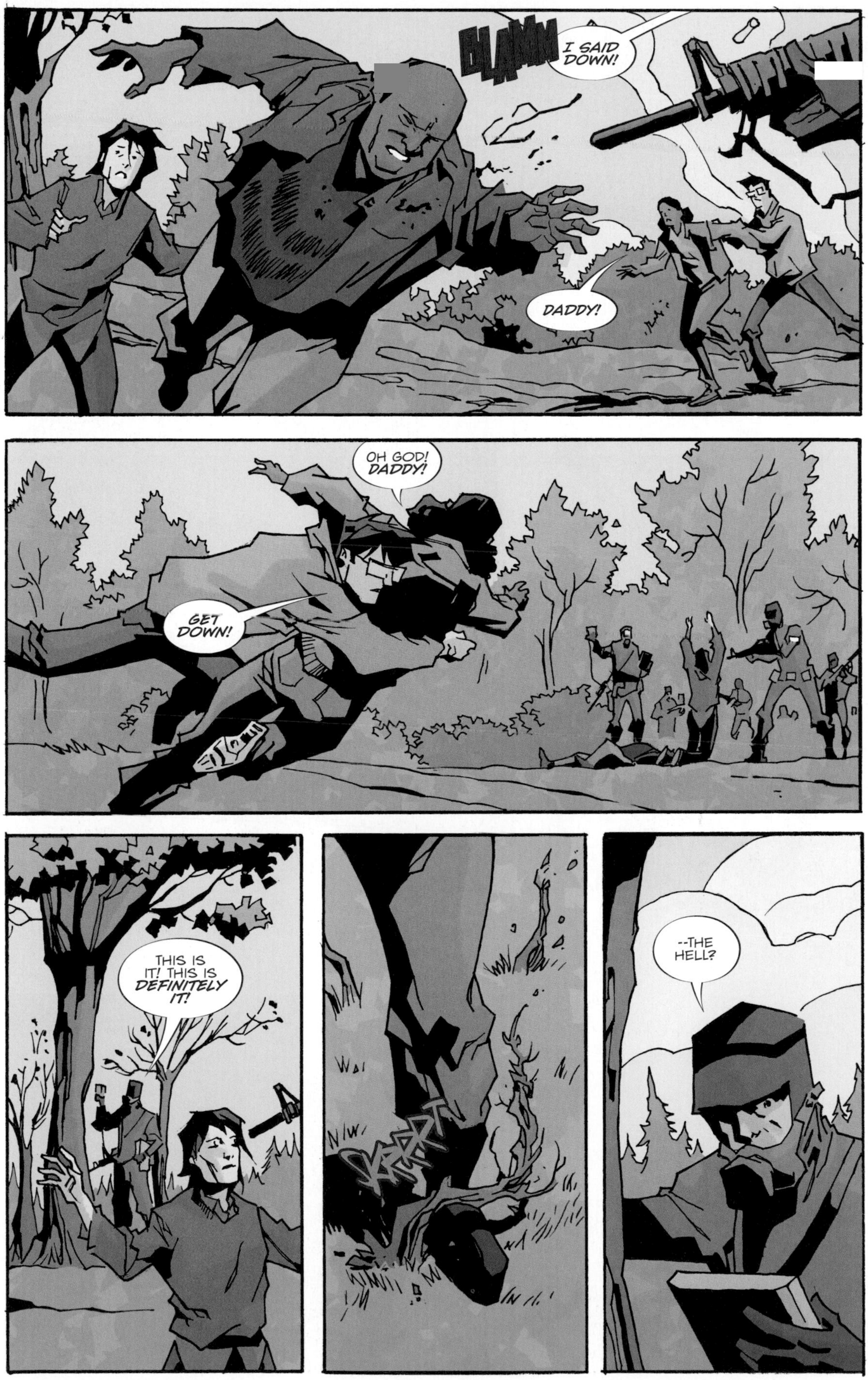
BLAMM
I SAID DOWN!
DADDY!
OH GOD! DADDY!
GET DOWN!
THIS IS IT! THIS IS DEFINITELY IT!
--THE HELL?

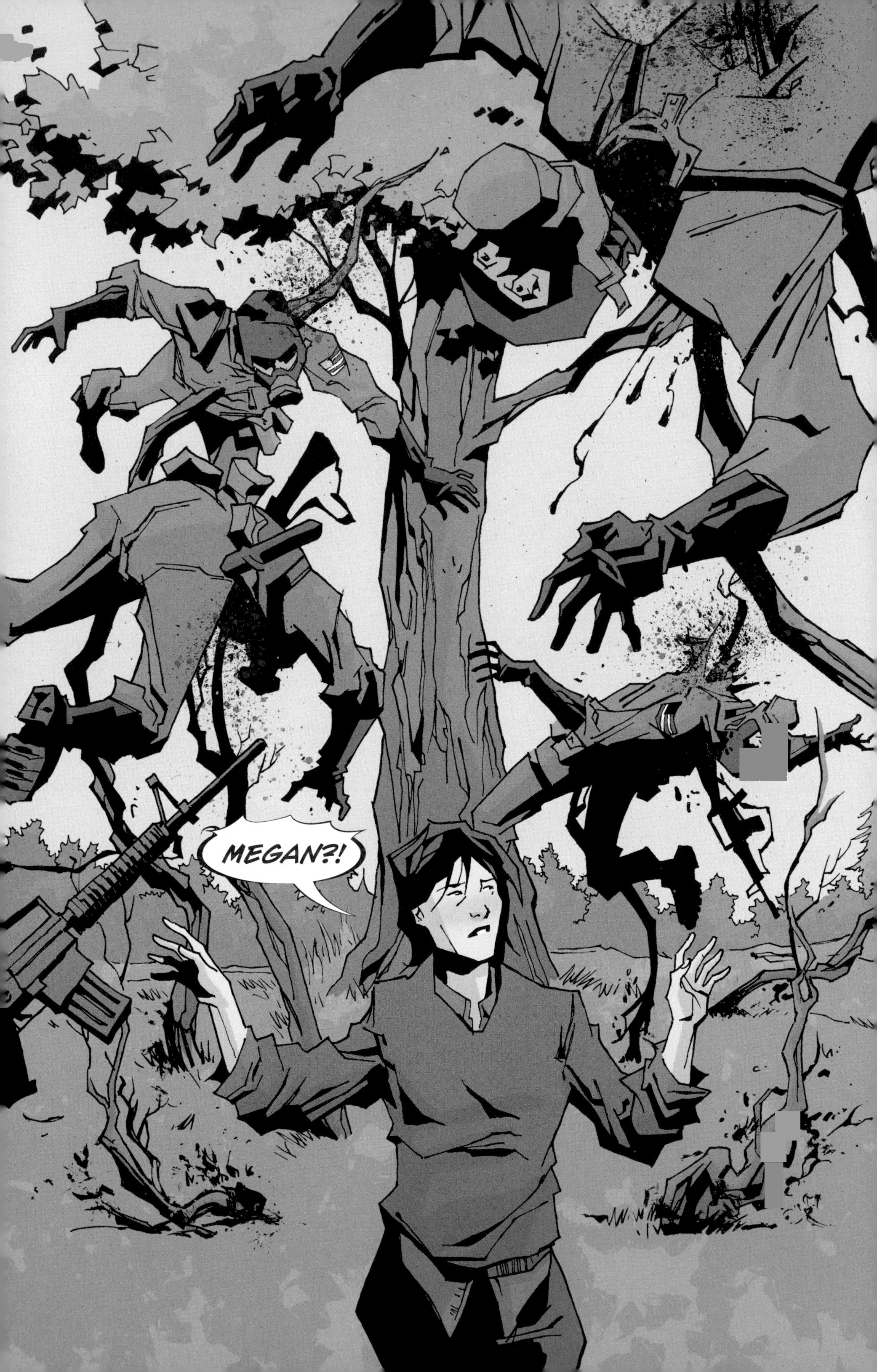
MEGAN?!

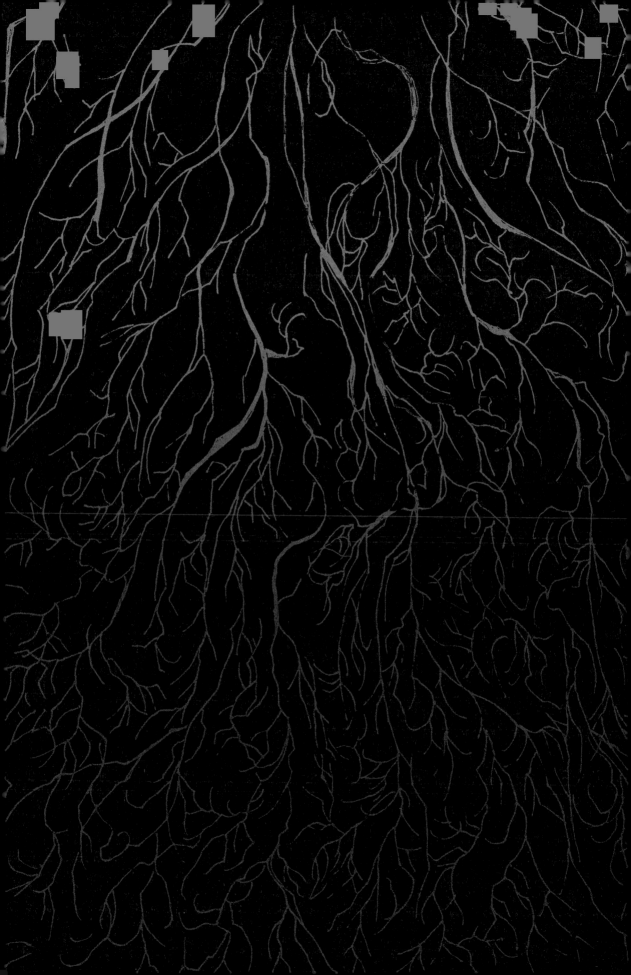

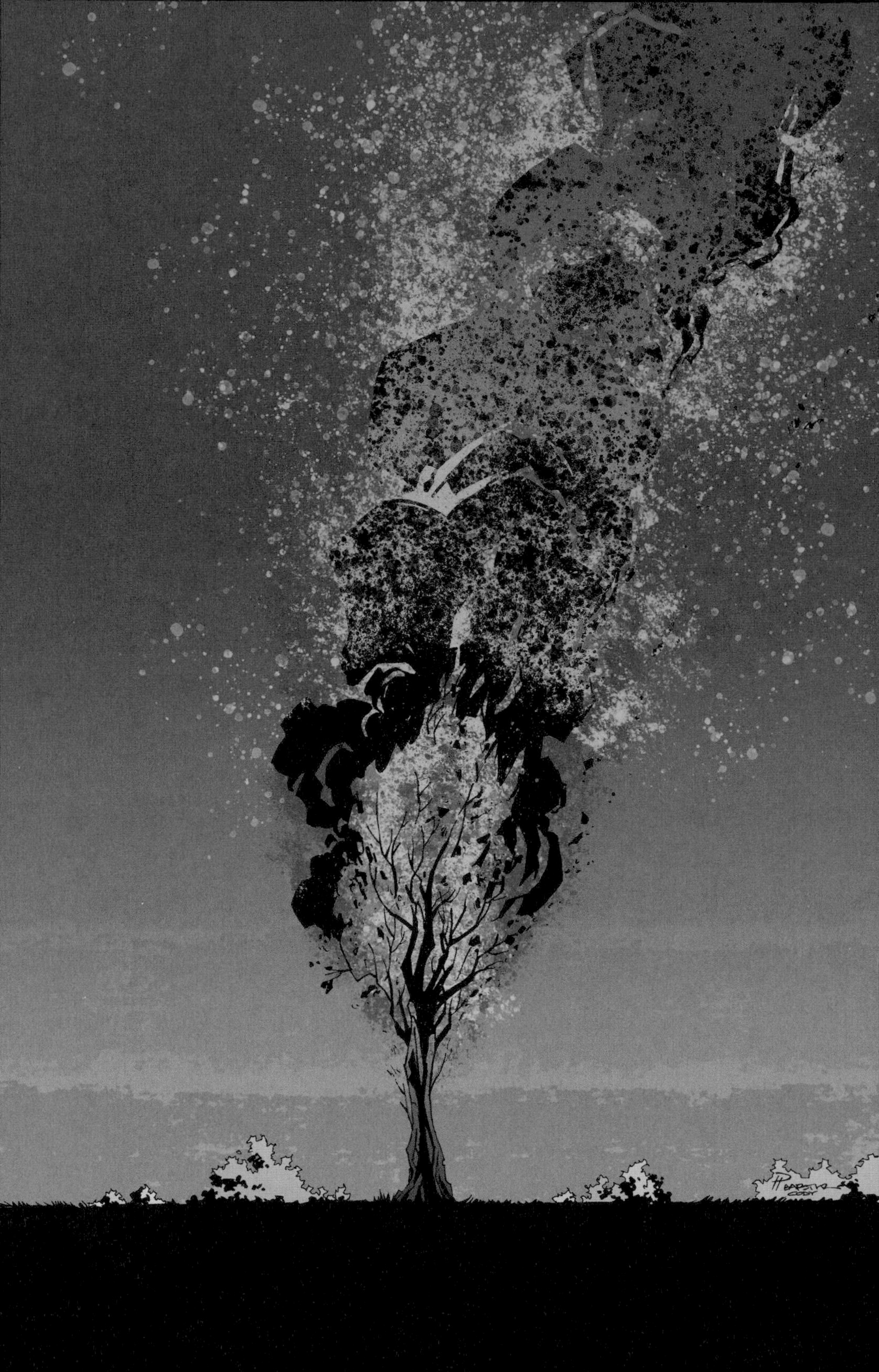

CHAPTER
ELEVEN

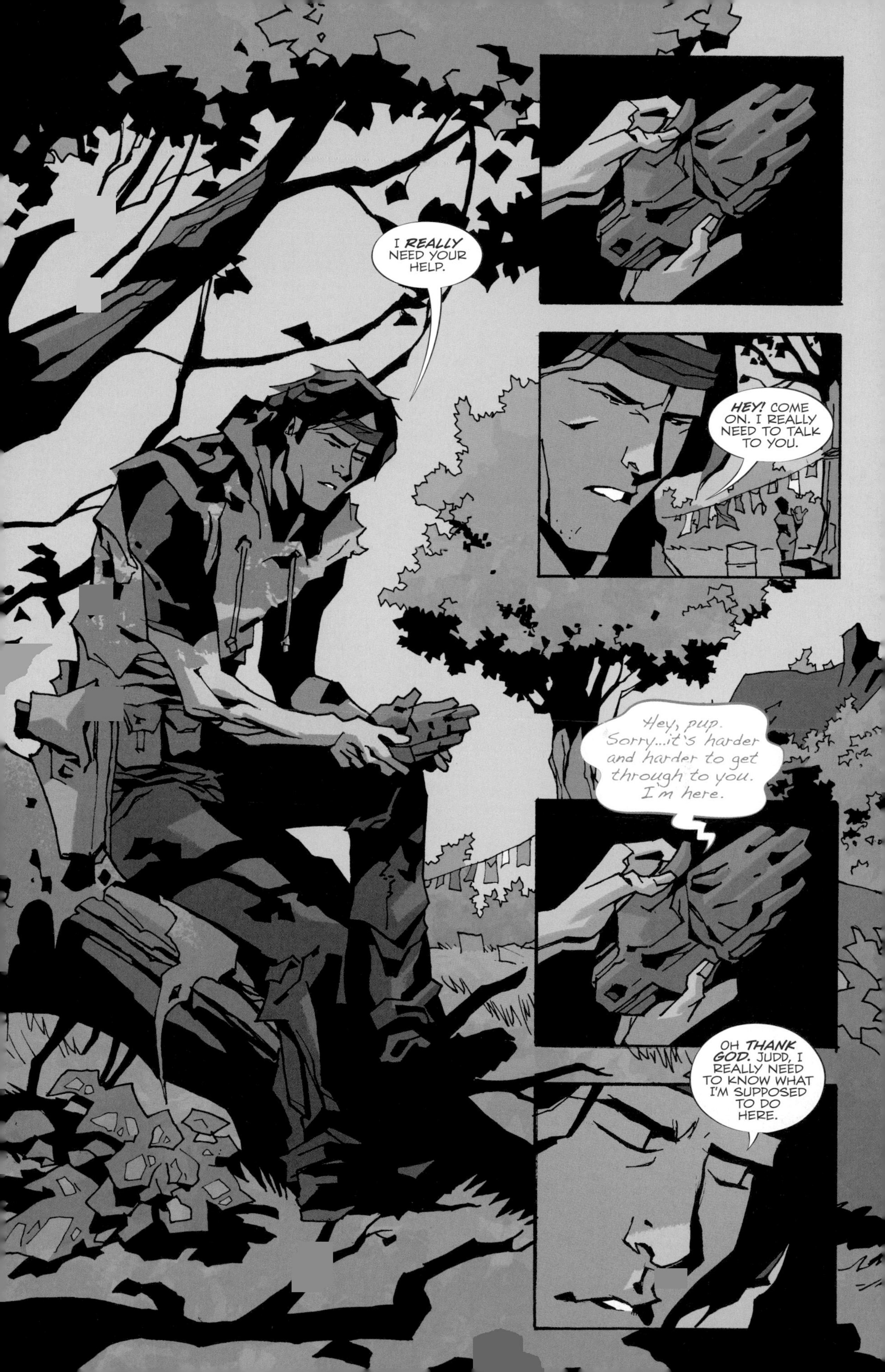
I REALLY NEED YOUR HELP.
HEY! COME ON. I REALLY NEED TO TALK TO YOU.
Hey, pup. Sorry...it's harder and harder to get through to you. I'm here.
OH THANK GOD. JUDD, I REALLY NEED TO KNOW WHAT I'M SUPPOSED TO DO HERE.

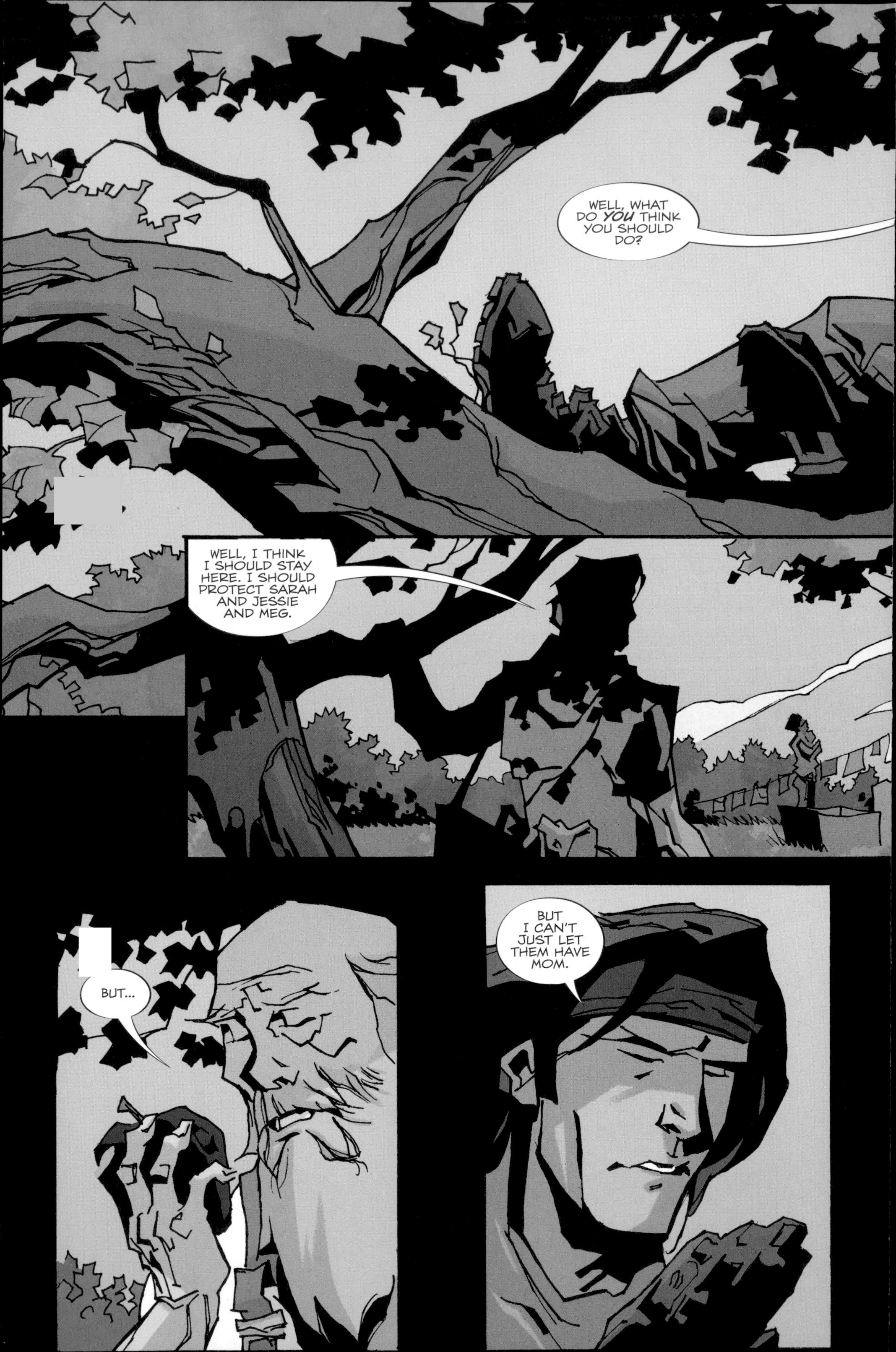
WELL, WHAT DO *YOU* THINK YOU SHOULD DO?
WELL, I THINK I SHOULD STAY HERE. I SHOULD PROTECT SARAH AND JESSIE AND MEG.
BUT...
BUT I CAN'T JUST LET THEM HAVE MOM.

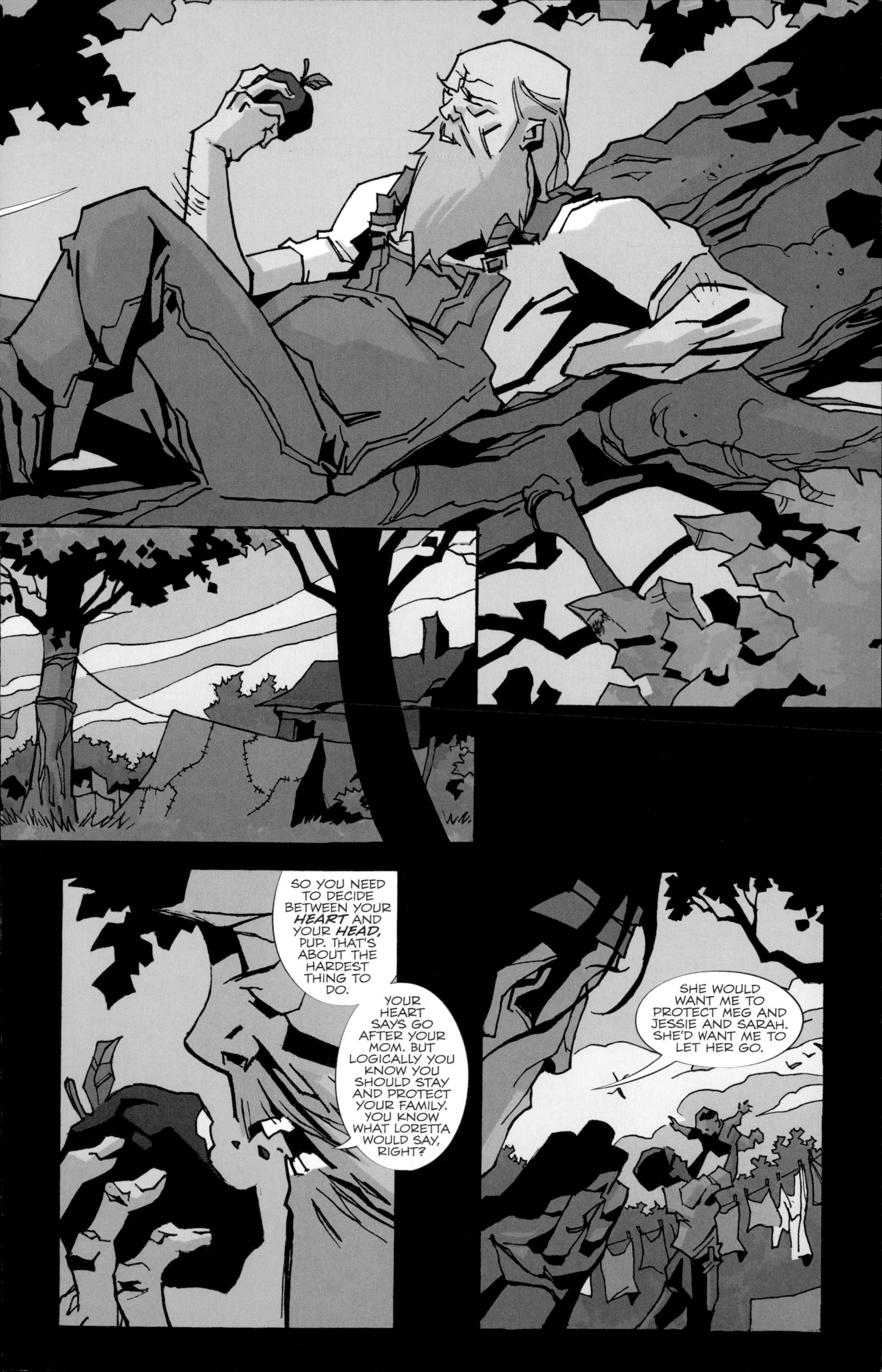
SO YOU NEED TO DECIDE BETWEEN YOUR **HEART** AND YOUR **HEAD,** PUP. THAT'S ABOUT THE HARDEST THING TO DO.
YOUR HEART SAYS GO AFTER YOUR MOM. BUT LOGICALLY YOU KNOW YOU SHOULD STAY AND PROTECT YOUR FAMILY. YOU KNOW WHAT LORETTA WOULD SAY, RIGHT?
SHE WOULD WANT ME TO PROTECT MEG AND JESSIE AND SARAH. SHE'D WANT ME TO LET HER GO.

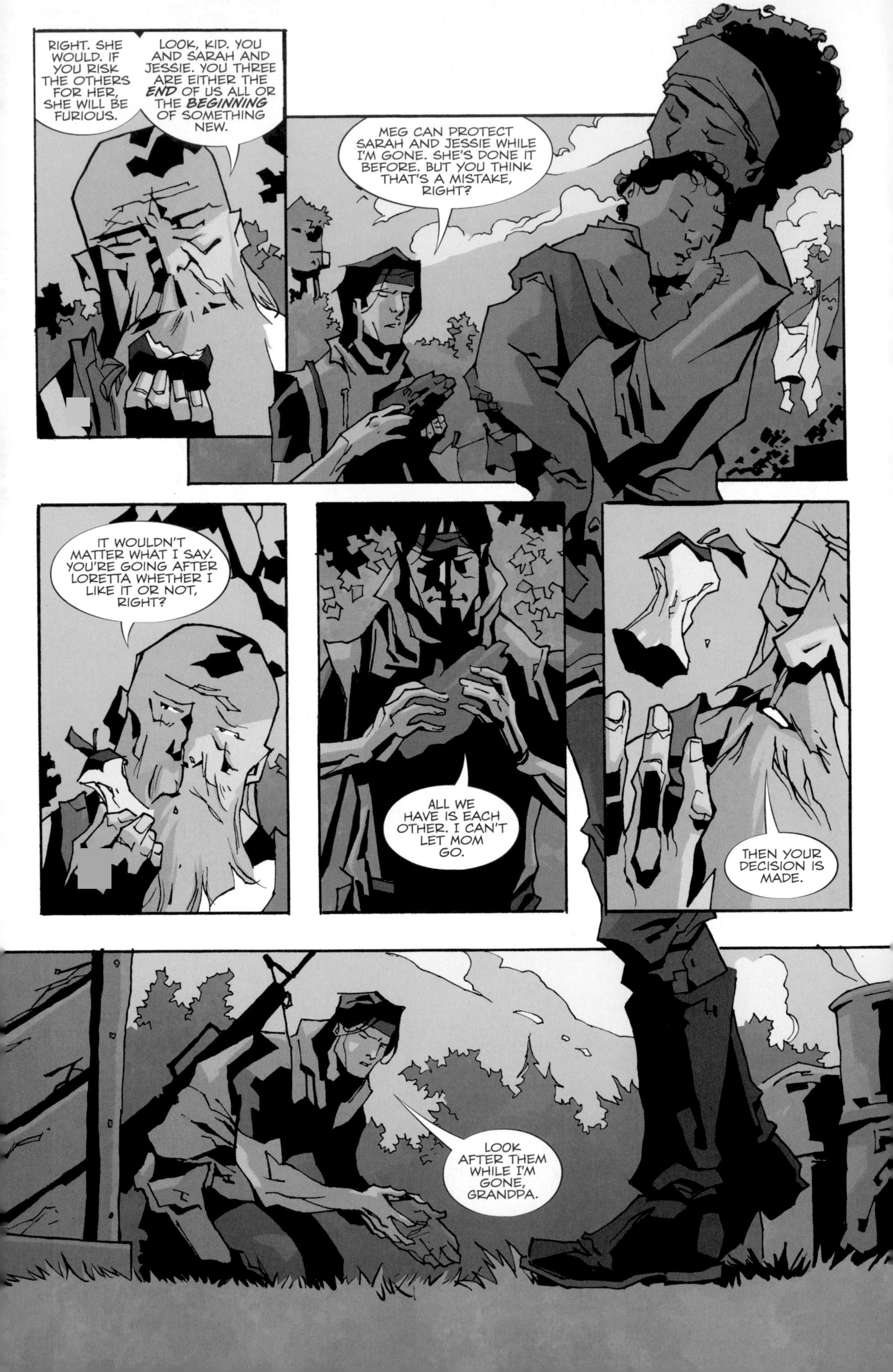
RIGHT. SHE WOULD. IF YOU RISK THE OTHERS FOR HER, SHE WILL BE FURIOUS.
LOOK, KID. YOU AND SARAH AND JESSIE. YOU THREE ARE EITHER THE END OF US ALL OR THE BEGINNING OF SOMETHING NEW.
MEG CAN PROTECT SARAH AND JESSIE WHILE I'M GONE. SHE'S DONE IT BEFORE. BUT YOU THINK THAT'S A MISTAKE, RIGHT?
IT WOULDN'T MATTER WHAT I SAY. YOU'RE GOING AFTER LORETTA WHETHER I LIKE IT OR NOT, RIGHT?
ALL WE HAVE IS EACH OTHER. I CAN'T LET MOM GO.
THEN YOUR DECISION IS MADE.
LOOK AFTER THEM WHILE I'M GONE, GRANDPA.

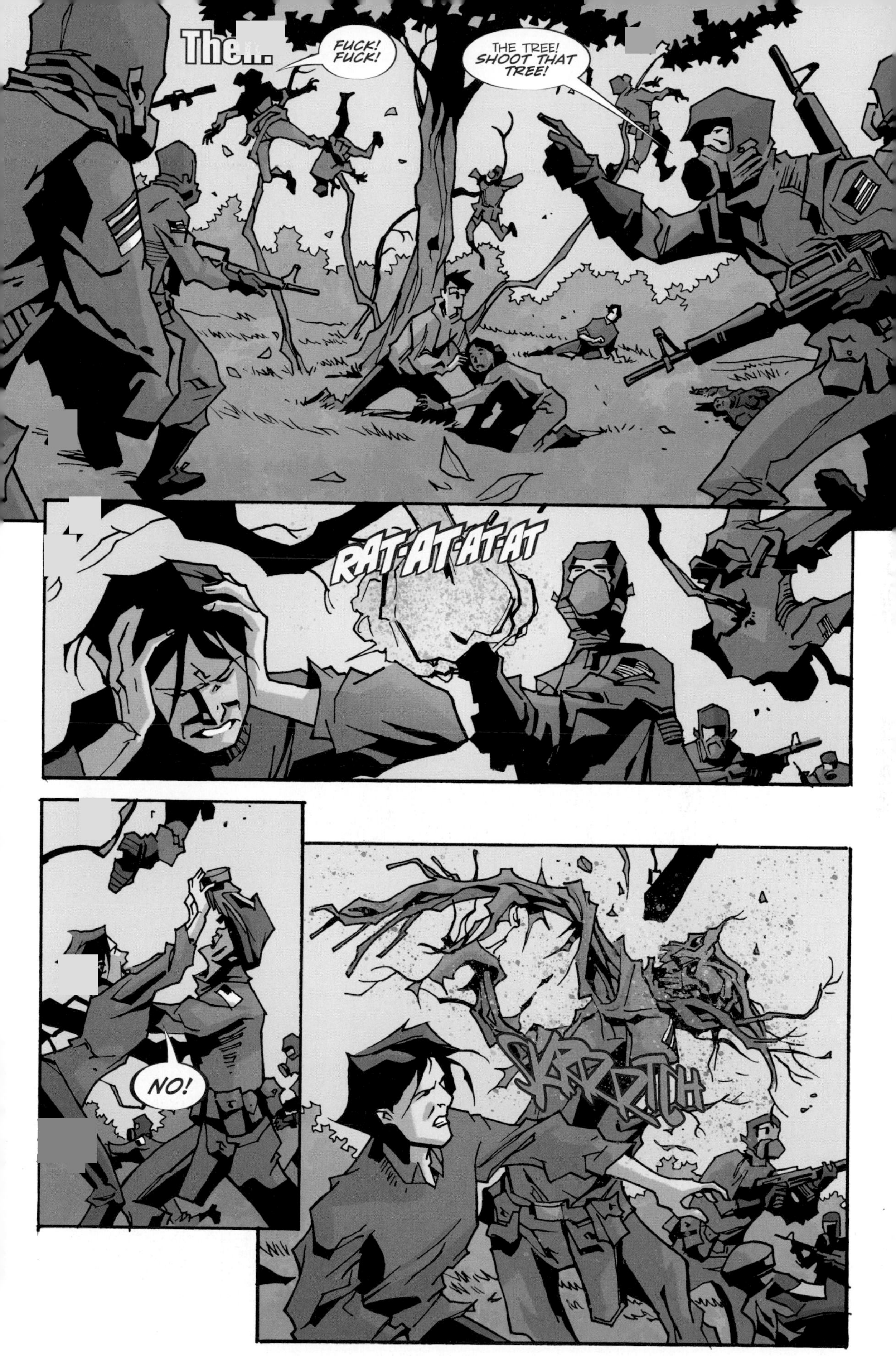
Then.
FUCK! FUCK!
THE TREE! SHOOT THAT TREE!
RAT-AT-AT-AT
NO!

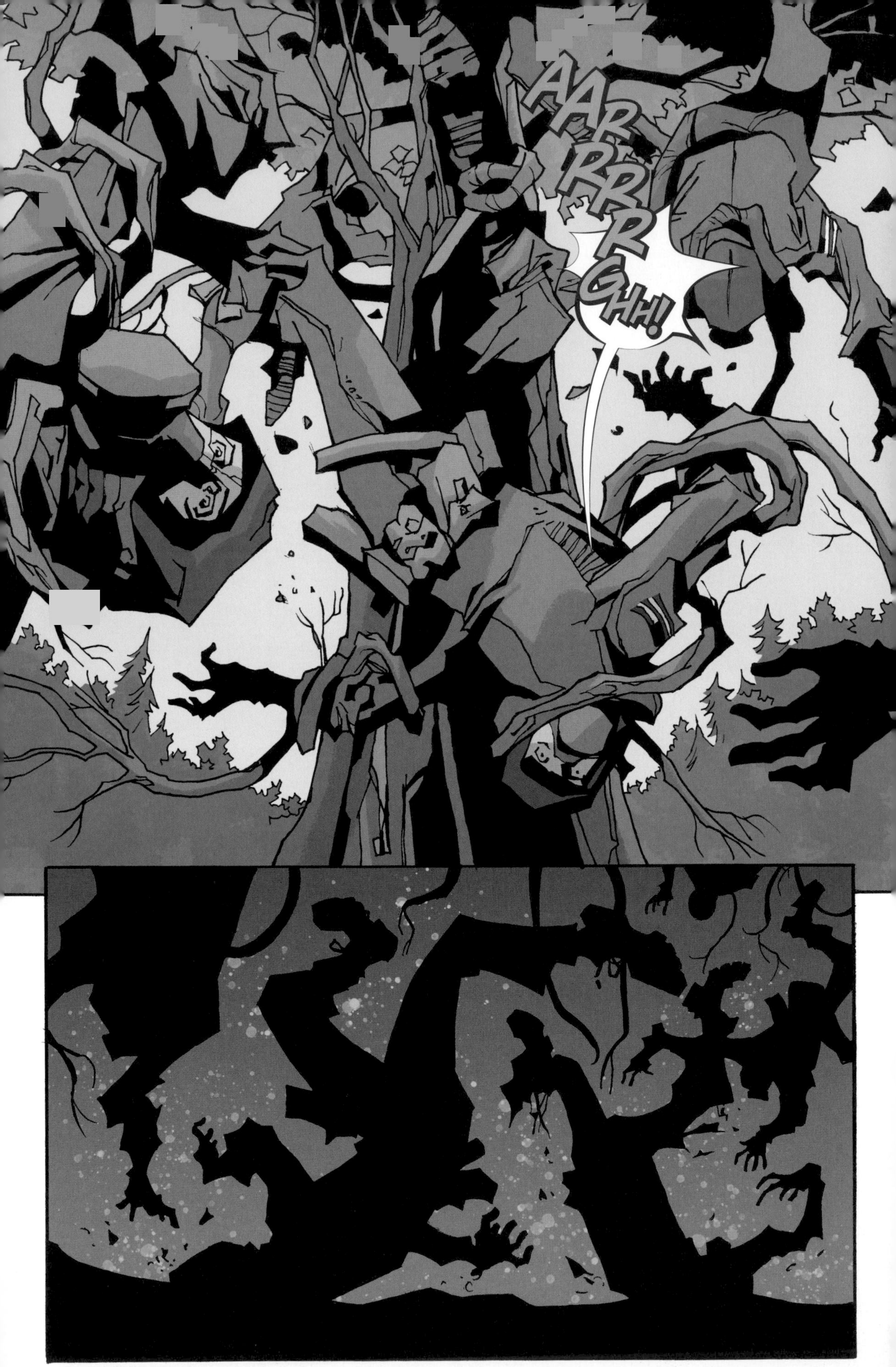
AARRRRGHH!

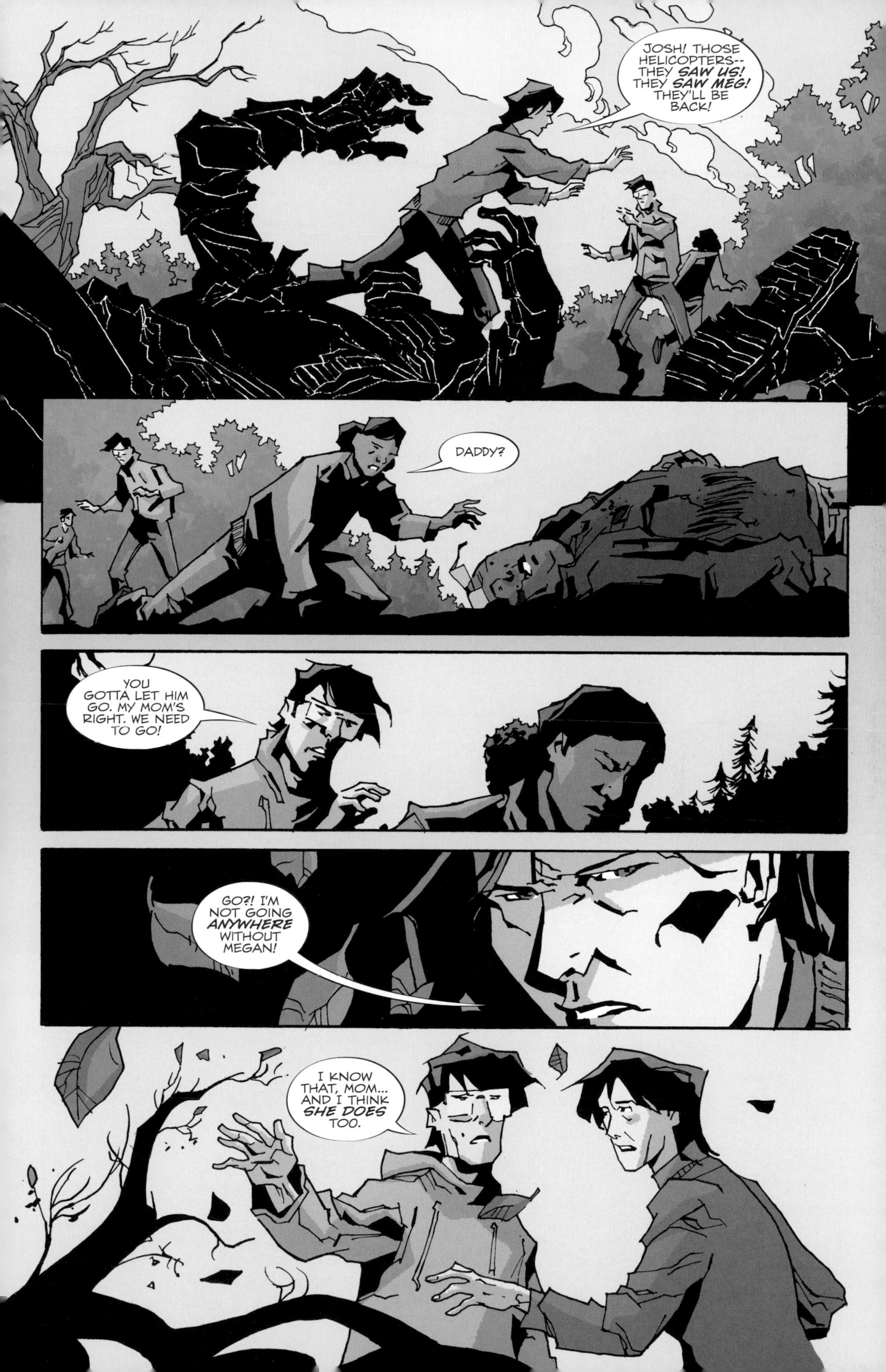
JOSH! THOSE HELICOPTERS-- THEY SAW US! THEY SAW MEG! THEY'LL BE BACK!
DADDY?
YOU GOTTA LET HIM GO. MY MOM'S RIGHT. WE NEED TO GO!
GO?! I'M NOT GOING ANYWHERE WITHOUT MEGAN!
I KNOW THAT, MOM... AND I THINK SHE DOES TOO.

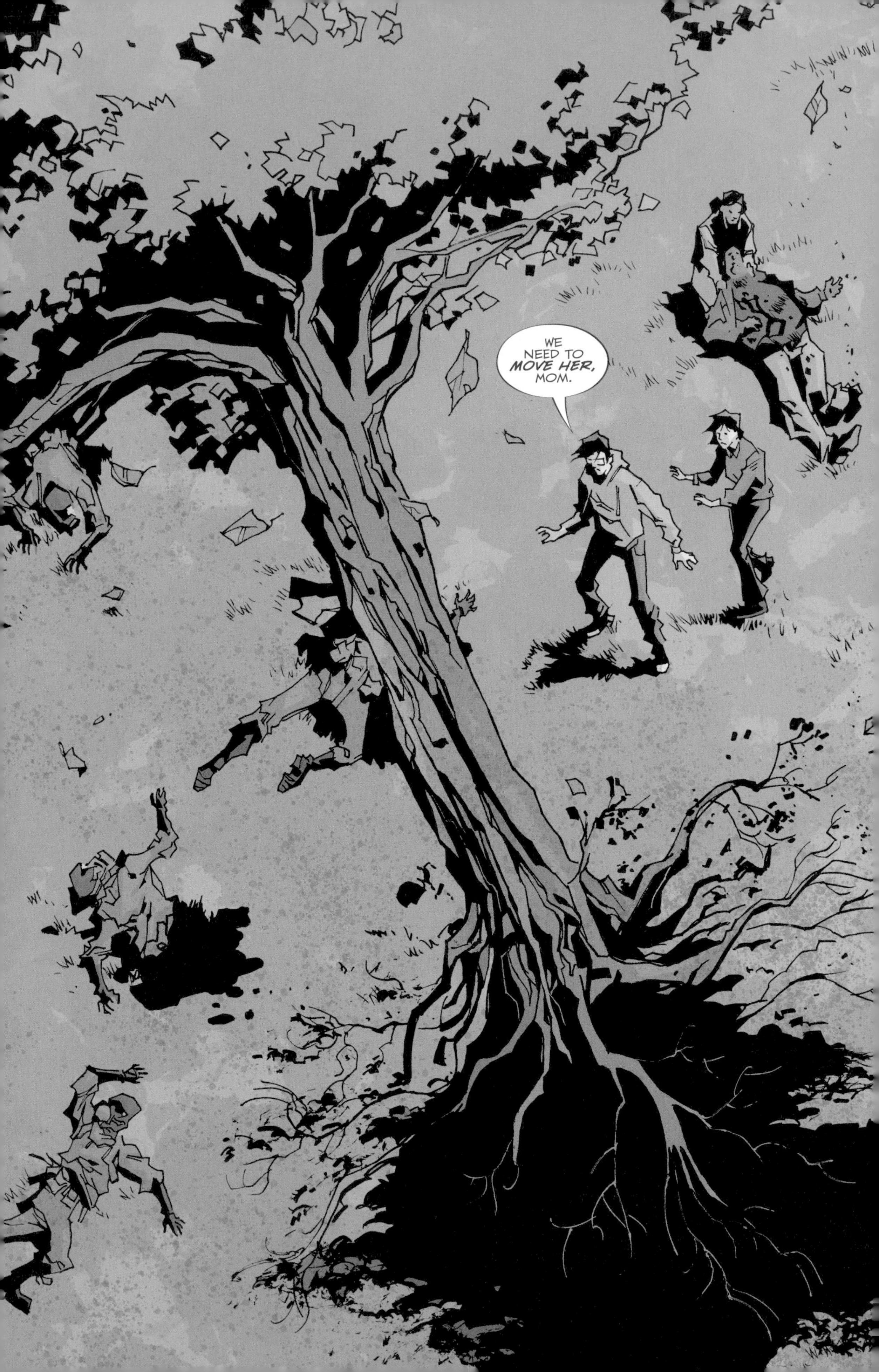
WE NEED TO MOVE HER, MOM.

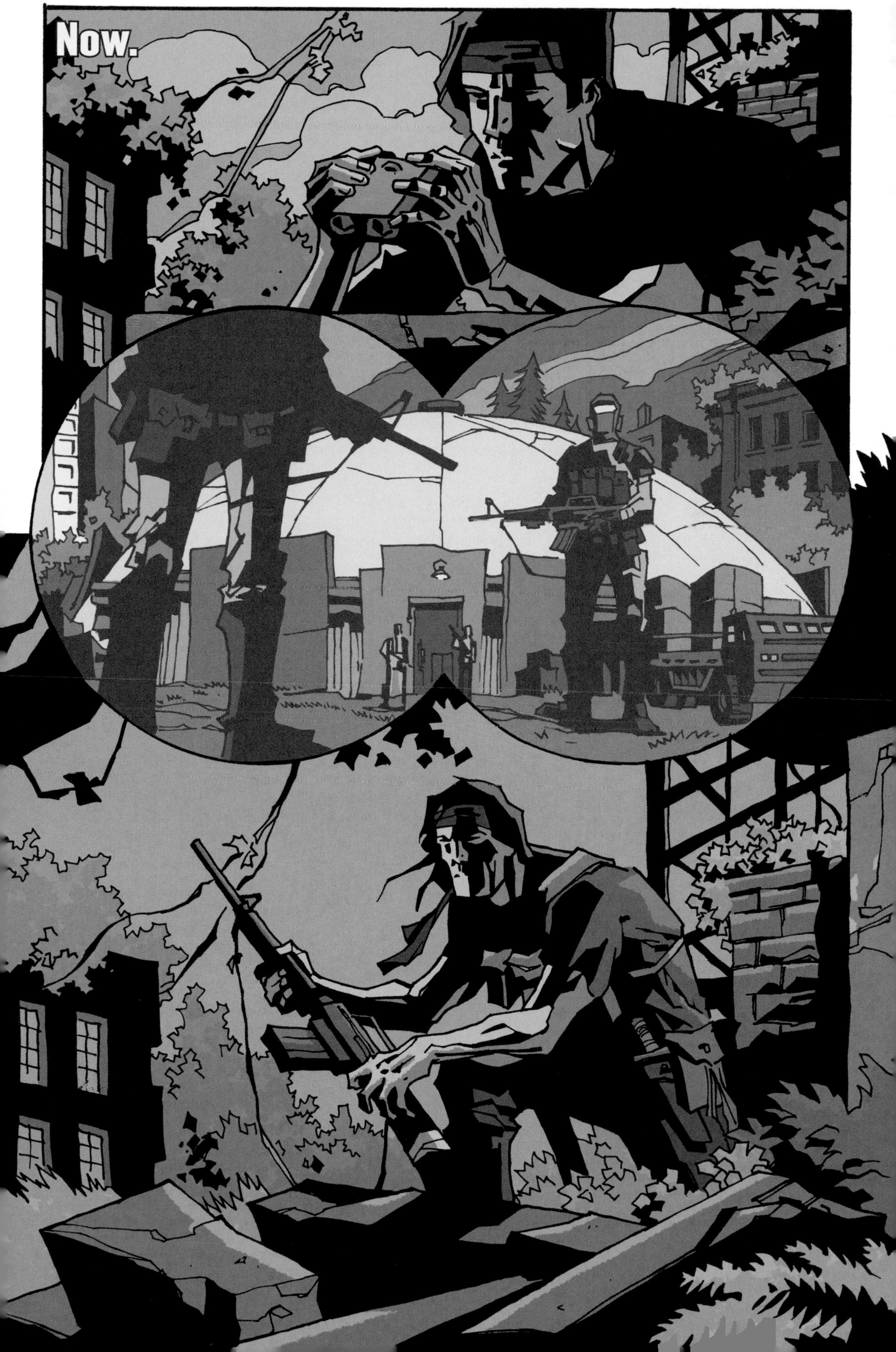
Now.

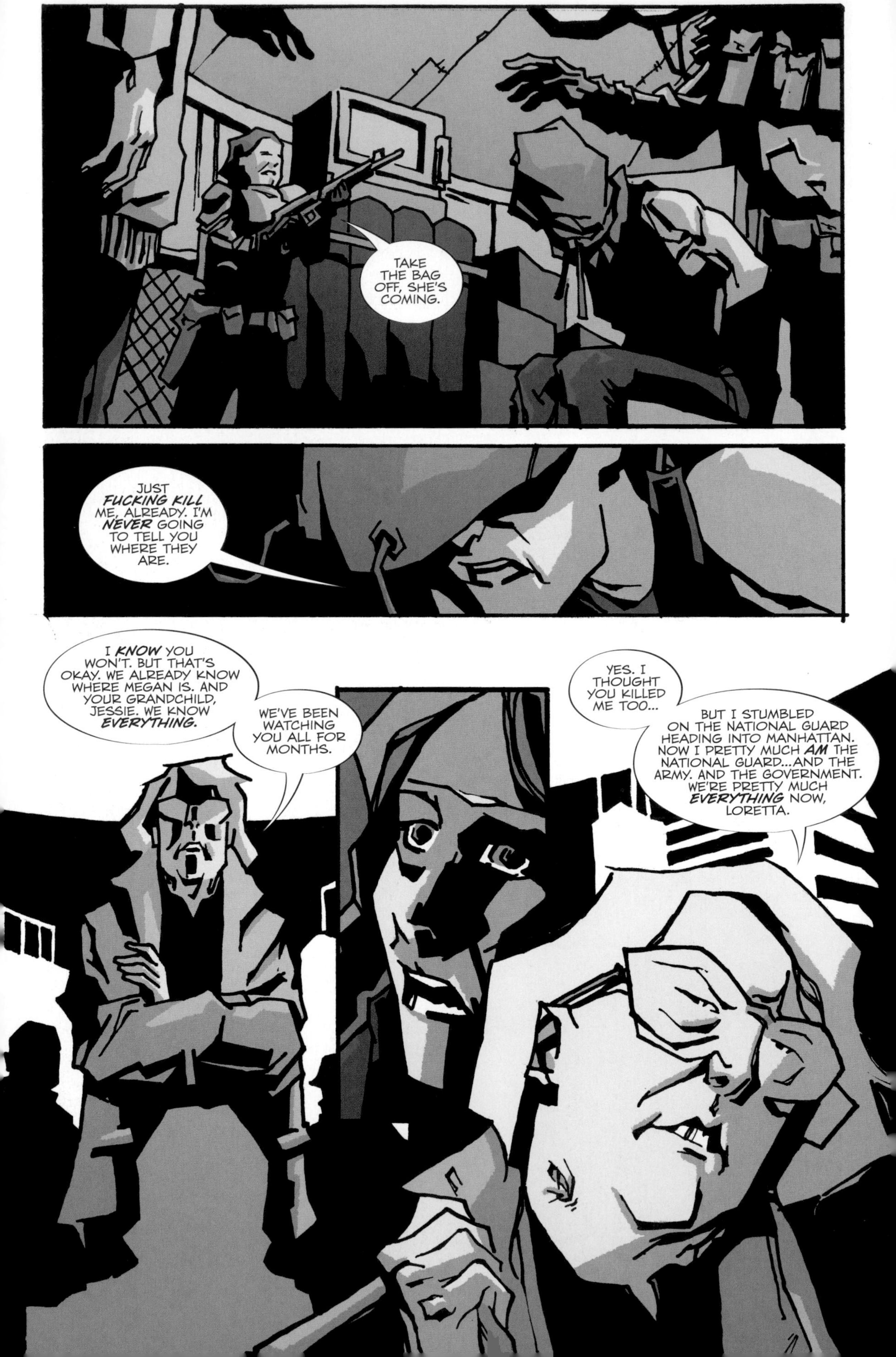
TAKE THE BAG OFF, SHE'S COMING.
JUST FUCKING KILL ME, ALREADY. I'M NEVER GOING TO TELL YOU WHERE THEY ARE.
I KNOW YOU WON'T. BUT THAT'S OKAY. WE ALREADY KNOW WHERE MEGAN IS. AND YOUR GRANDCHILD, JESSIE. WE KNOW EVERYTHING.
WE'VE BEEN WATCHING YOU ALL FOR MONTHS.
YES. I THOUGHT YOU KILLED ME TOO...
BUT I STUMBLED ON THE NATIONAL GUARD HEADING INTO MANHATTAN. NOW I PRETTY MUCH AM THE NATIONAL GUARD...AND THE ARMY. AND THE GOVERNMENT. WE'RE PRETTY MUCH EVERYTHING NOW, LORETTA.

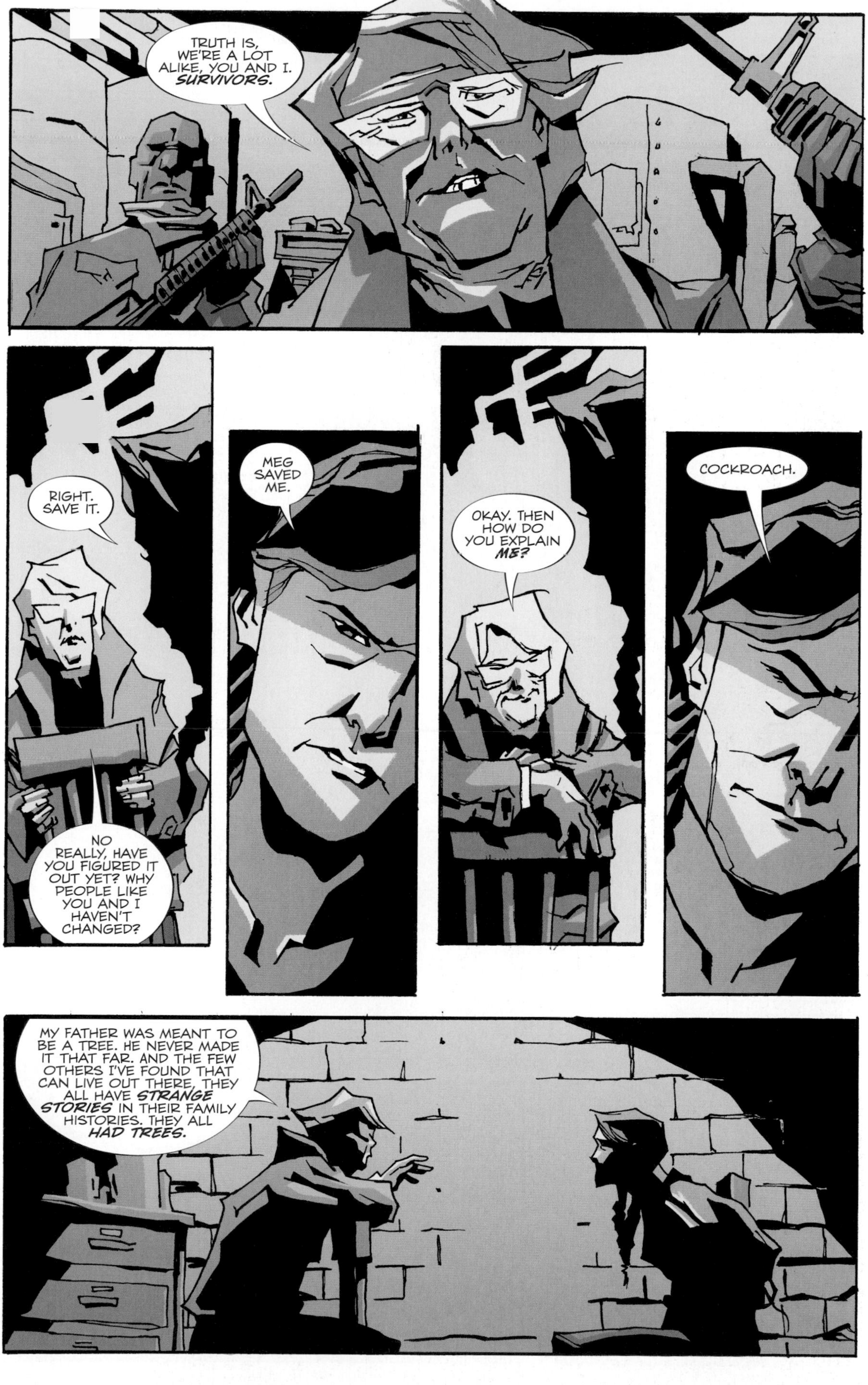
TRUTH IS, WE'RE A LOT ALIKE, YOU AND I. SURVIVORS.
RIGHT. SAVE IT.
NO REALLY, HAVE YOU FIGURED IT OUT YET? WHY PEOPLE LIKE YOU AND I HAVEN'T CHANGED?
MEG SAVED ME.
OKAY. THEN HOW DO YOU EXPLAIN ME?
COCKROACH.
MY FATHER WAS MEANT TO BE A TREE. HE NEVER MADE IT THAT FAR. AND THE FEW OTHERS I'VE FOUND THAT CAN LIVE OUT THERE, THEY ALL HAVE STRANGE STORIES IN THEIR FAMILY HISTORIES. THEY ALL HAD TREES.

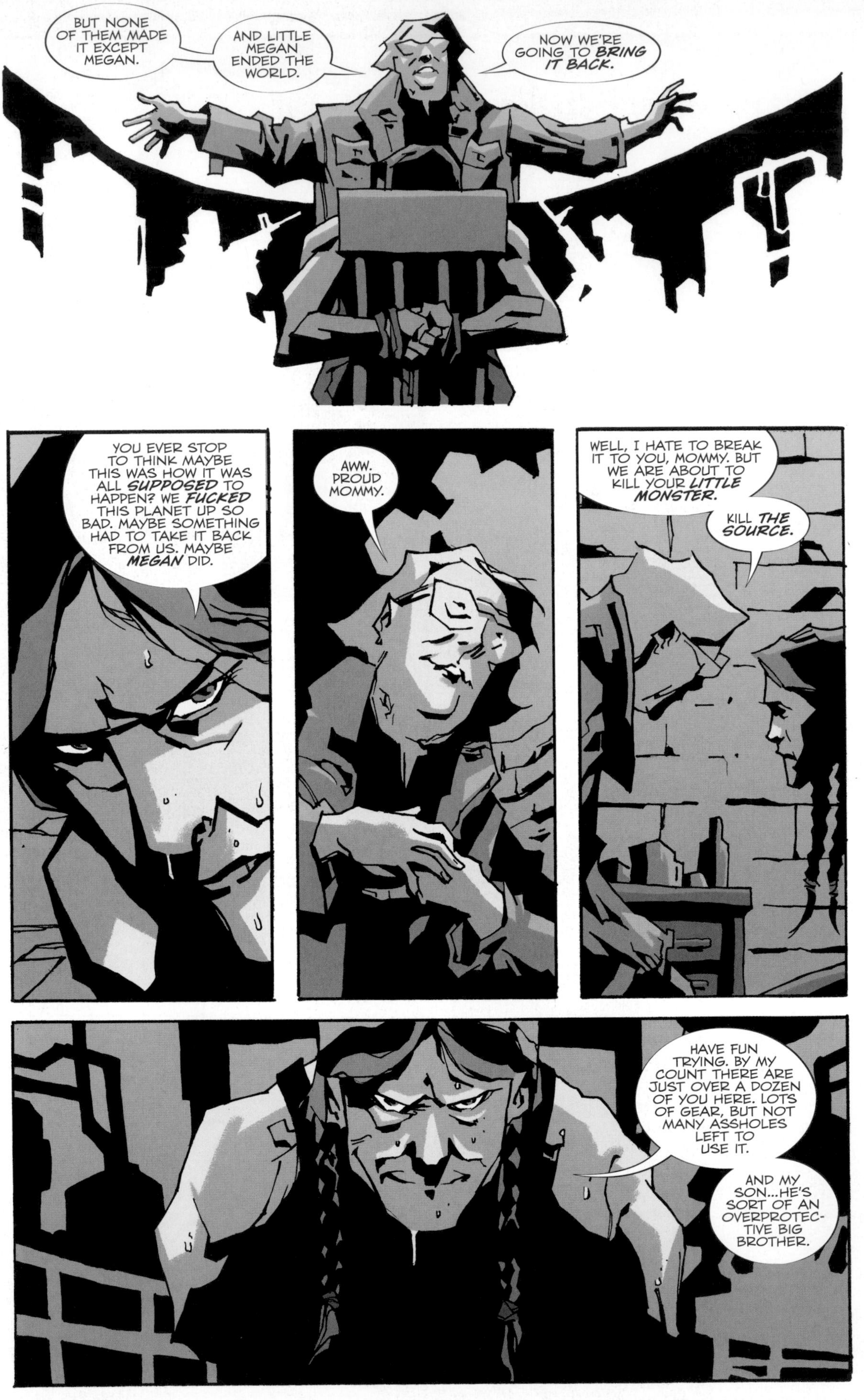
BUT NONE OF THEM MADE IT EXCEPT MEGAN.
AND LITTLE MEGAN ENDED THE WORLD.
NOW WE'RE GOING TO *BRING IT BACK.*
YOU EVER STOP TO THINK MAYBE THIS WAS HOW IT WAS ALL *SUPPOSED* TO HAPPEN? WE *FUCKED* THIS PLANET UP SO BAD. MAYBE SOMETHING HAD TO TAKE IT BACK FROM US. MAYBE *MEGAN* DID.
AWW. PROUD MOMMY.
WELL, I HATE TO BREAK IT TO YOU, MOMMY. BUT WE ARE ABOUT TO KILL YOUR *LITTLE MONSTER.*
KILL *THE SOURCE.*
HAVE FUN TRYING. BY MY COUNT THERE ARE JUST OVER A DOZEN OF YOU HERE. LOTS OF GEAR, BUT NOT MANY ASSHOLES LEFT TO USE IT.
AND MY SON...HE'S SORT OF AN OVERPROTEC-TIVE BIG BROTHER.

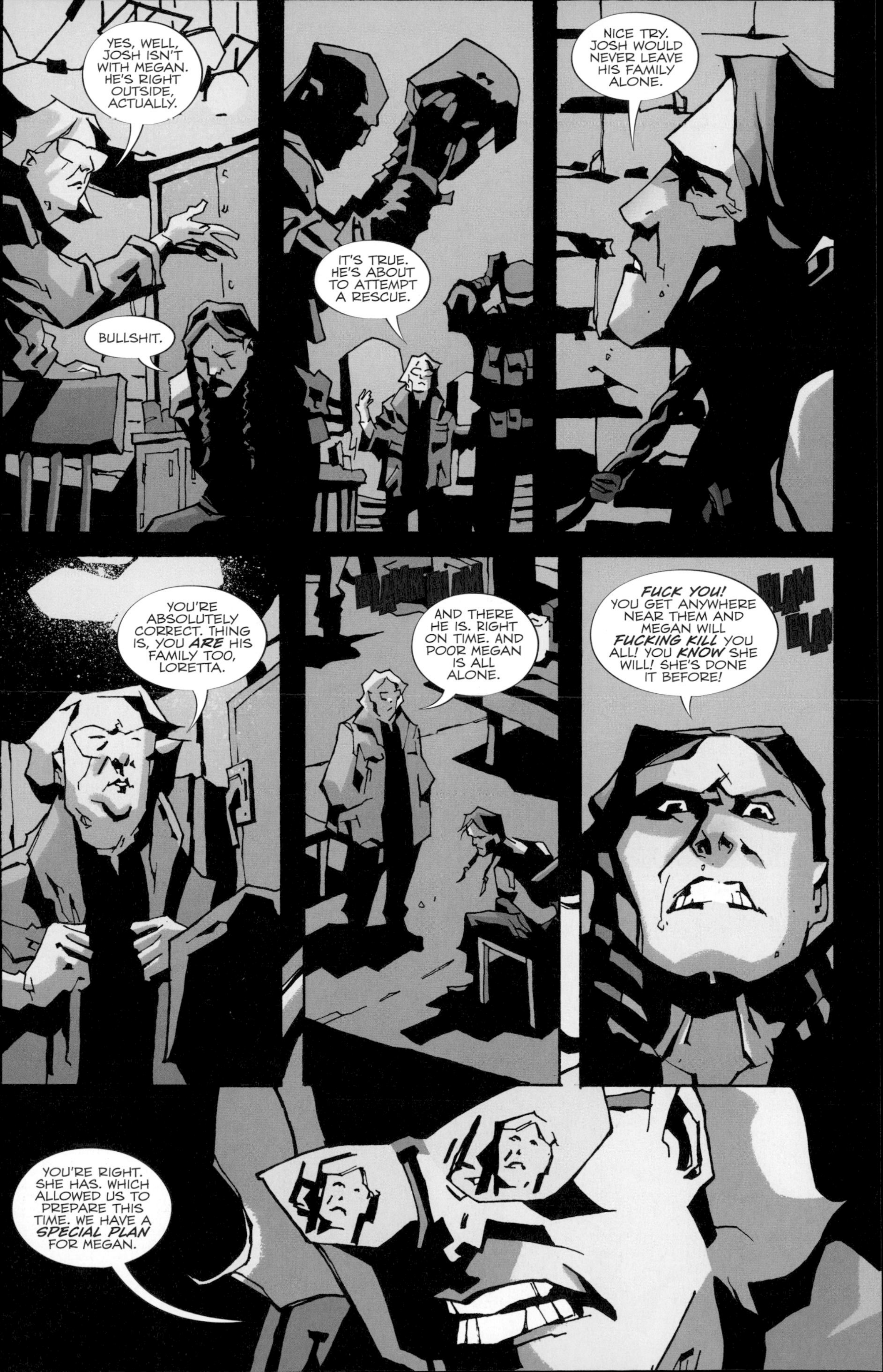
YES, WELL, JOSH ISN'T WITH MEGAN. HE'S RIGHT OUTSIDE, ACTUALLY.
BULLSHIT.
IT'S TRUE. HE'S ABOUT TO ATTEMPT A RESCUE.
NICE TRY. JOSH WOULD NEVER LEAVE HIS FAMILY ALONE.
YOU'RE ABSOLUTELY CORRECT. THING IS, YOU ***ARE*** HIS FAMILY TOO, LORETTA.
AND THERE HE IS. RIGHT ON TIME. AND POOR MEGAN IS ALL ALONE.
FUCK YOU! YOU GET ANYWHERE NEAR THEM AND MEGAN WILL ***FUCKING KILL*** YOU ALL! YOU ***KNOW*** SHE WILL! SHE'S DONE IT BEFORE!
YOU'RE RIGHT. SHE HAS. WHICH ALLOWED US TO PREPARE THIS TIME. WE HAVE A ***SPECIAL PLAN*** FOR MEGAN.

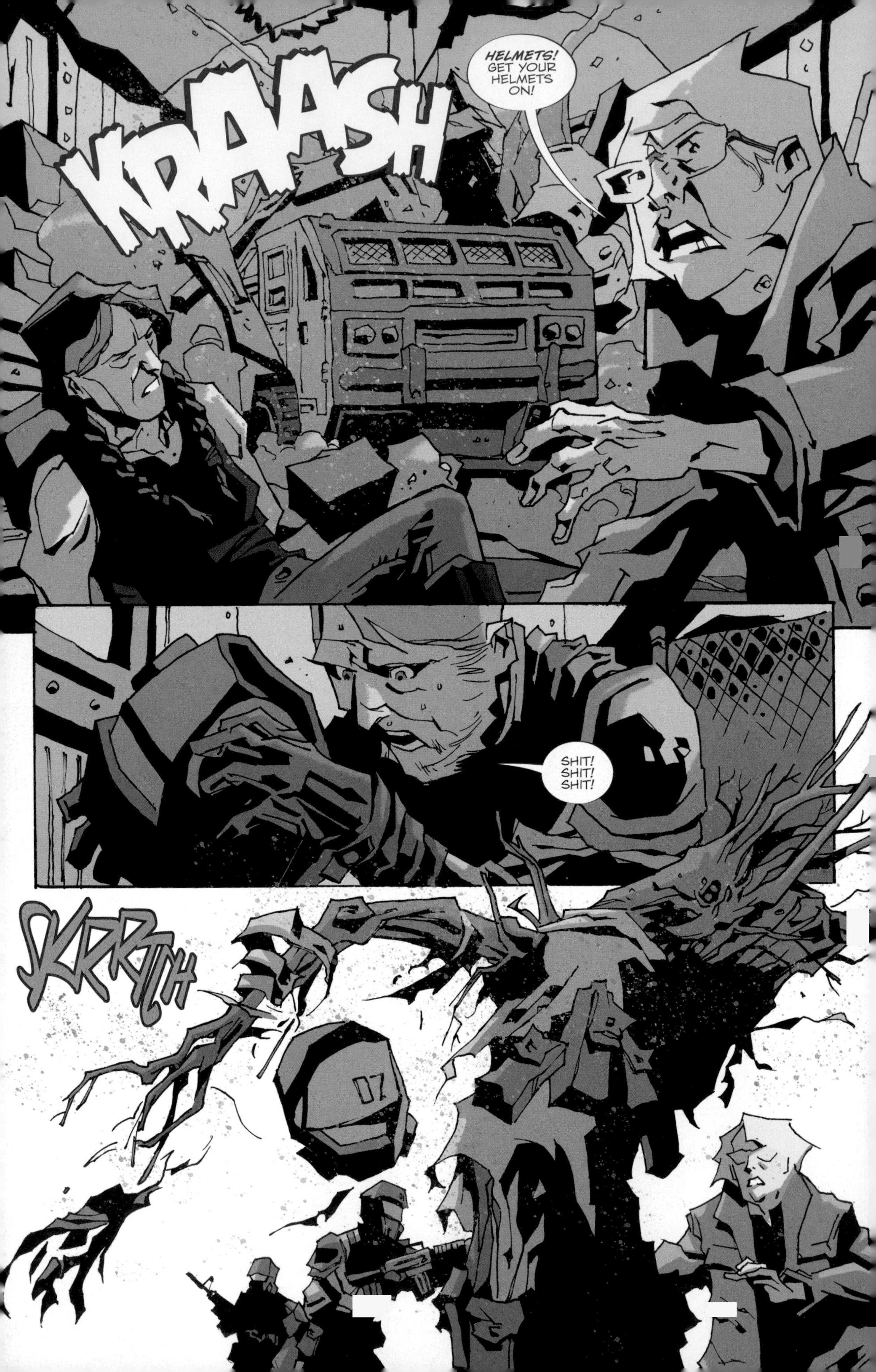
KRAASH
HELMETS! GET YOUR HELMETS ON!
SHIT! SHIT! SHIT!
SKRRTCH
07

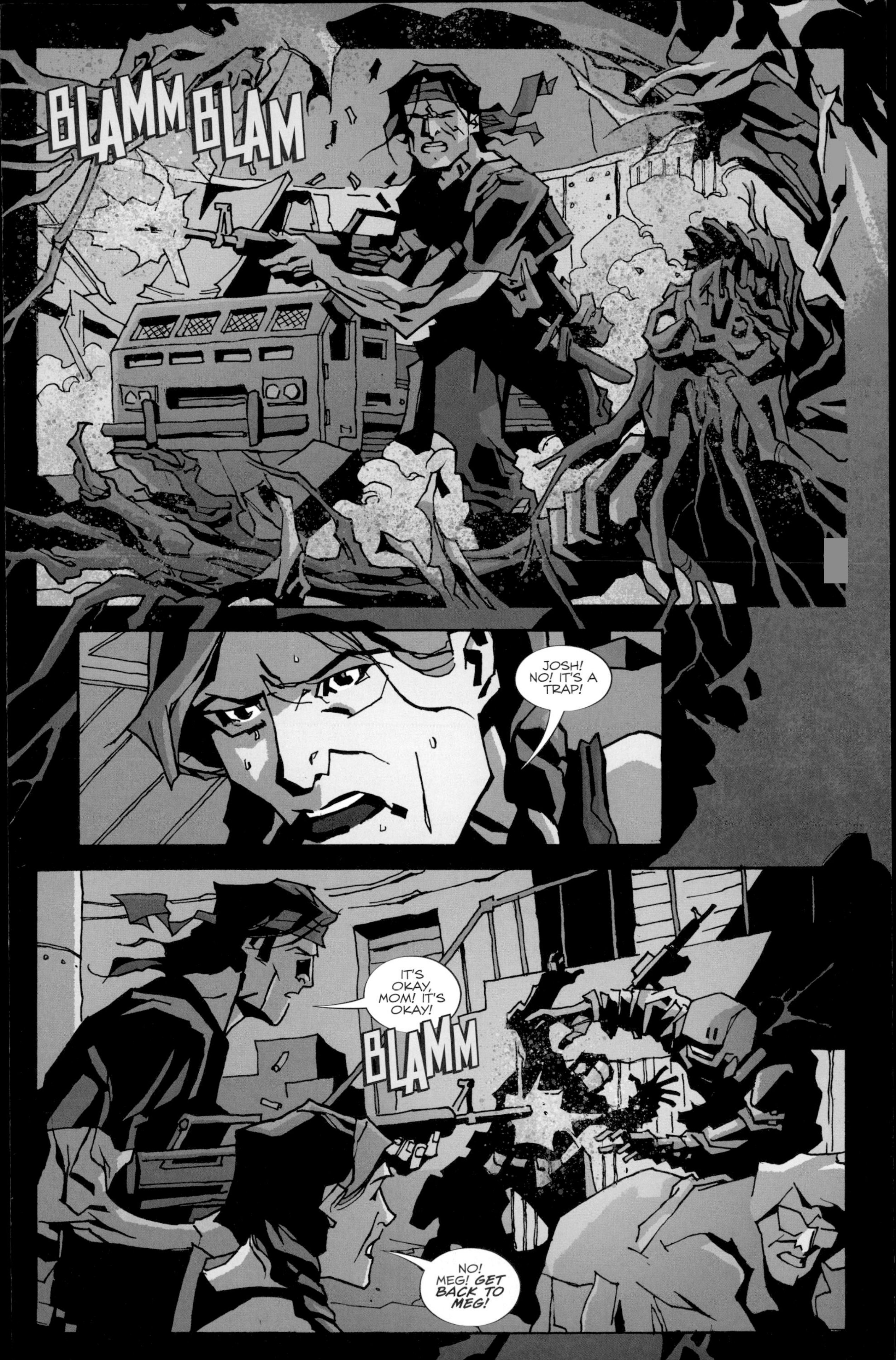
BLAMM BLAM
JOSH! NO! IT'S A TRAP!
IT'S OKAY, MOM! IT'S OKAY!
BLAMM
NO! MEG! GET BACK TO MEG!

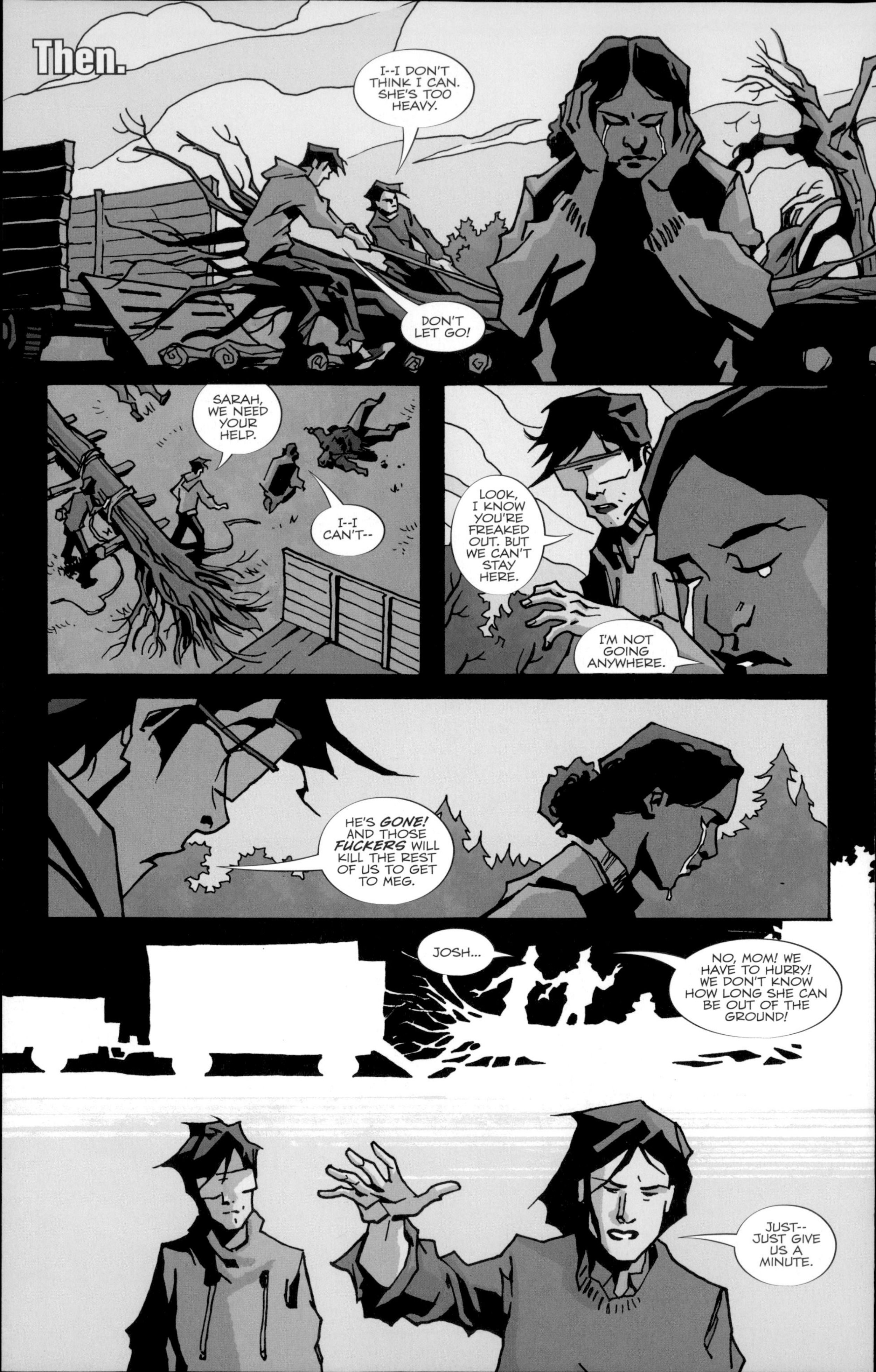
Then.
I--I DON'T THINK I CAN. SHE'S TOO HEAVY.
DON'T LET GO!
SARAH, WE NEED YOUR HELP.
I--I CAN'T--
LOOK, I KNOW YOU'RE FREAKED OUT. BUT WE CAN'T STAY HERE.
I'M NOT GOING ANYWHERE.
HE'S GONE! AND THOSE FUCKERS WILL KILL THE REST OF US TO GET TO MEG.
JOSH...
NO, MOM! WE HAVE TO HURRY! WE DON'T KNOW HOW LONG SHE CAN BE OUT OF THE GROUND!
JUST-- JUST GIVE US A MINUTE.

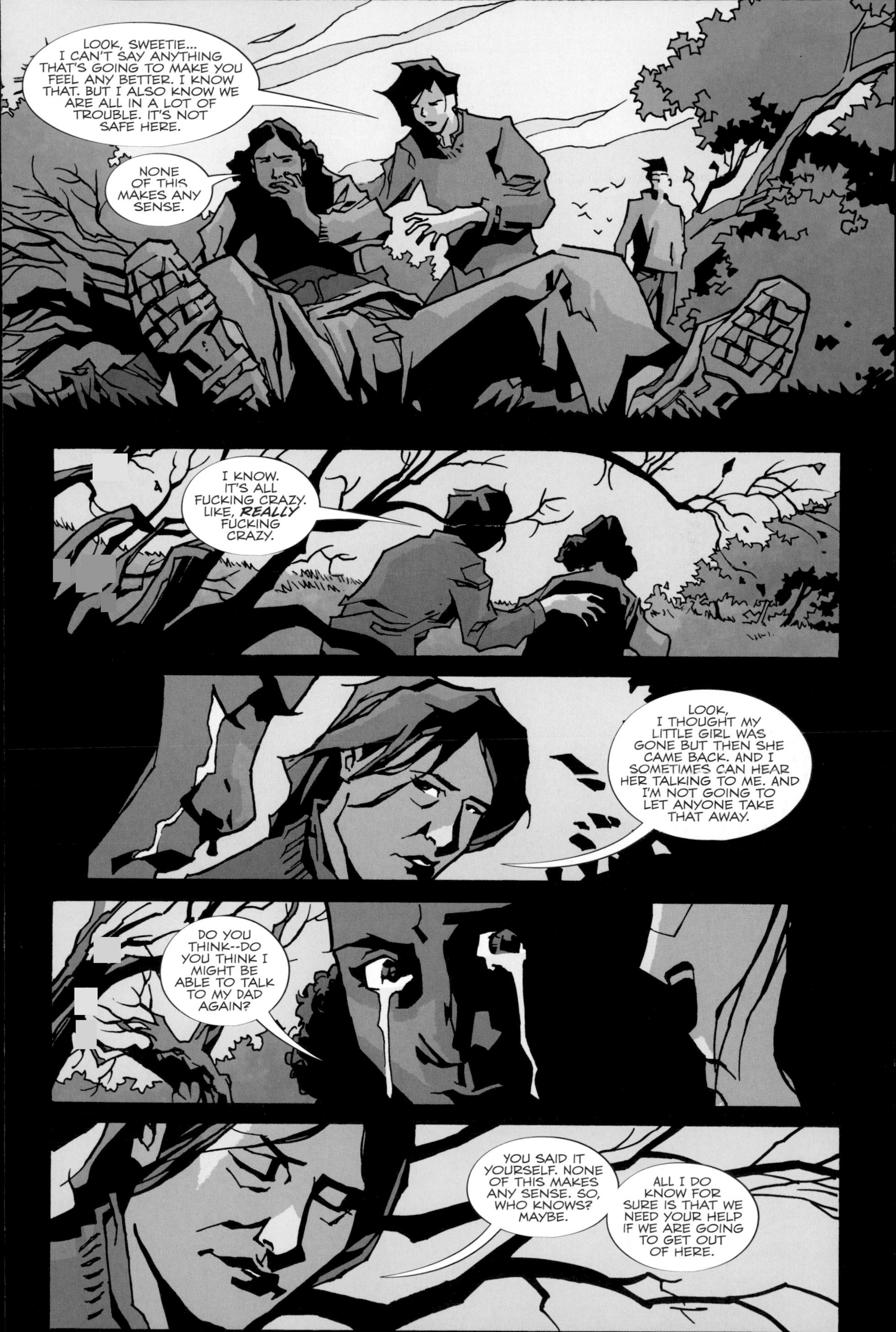
LOOK, SWEETIE... I CAN'T SAY ANYTHING THAT'S GOING TO MAKE YOU FEEL ANY BETTER. I KNOW THAT. BUT I ALSO KNOW WE ARE ALL IN A LOT OF TROUBLE. IT'S NOT SAFE HERE.
NONE OF THIS MAKES ANY SENSE.
I KNOW. IT'S ALL FUCKING CRAZY. LIKE, *REALLY* FUCKING CRAZY.
LOOK, I THOUGHT MY LITTLE GIRL WAS GONE BUT THEN SHE CAME BACK. AND I SOMETIMES CAN HEAR HER TALKING TO ME. AND I'M NOT GOING TO LET ANYONE TAKE THAT AWAY.
DO YOU THINK--DO YOU THINK I MIGHT BE ABLE TO TALK TO MY DAD AGAIN?
YOU SAID IT YOURSELF. NONE OF THIS MAKES ANY SENSE. SO, WHO KNOWS? MAYBE.
ALL I DO KNOW FOR SURE IS THAT WE NEED YOUR HELP IF WE ARE GOING TO GET OUT OF HERE.

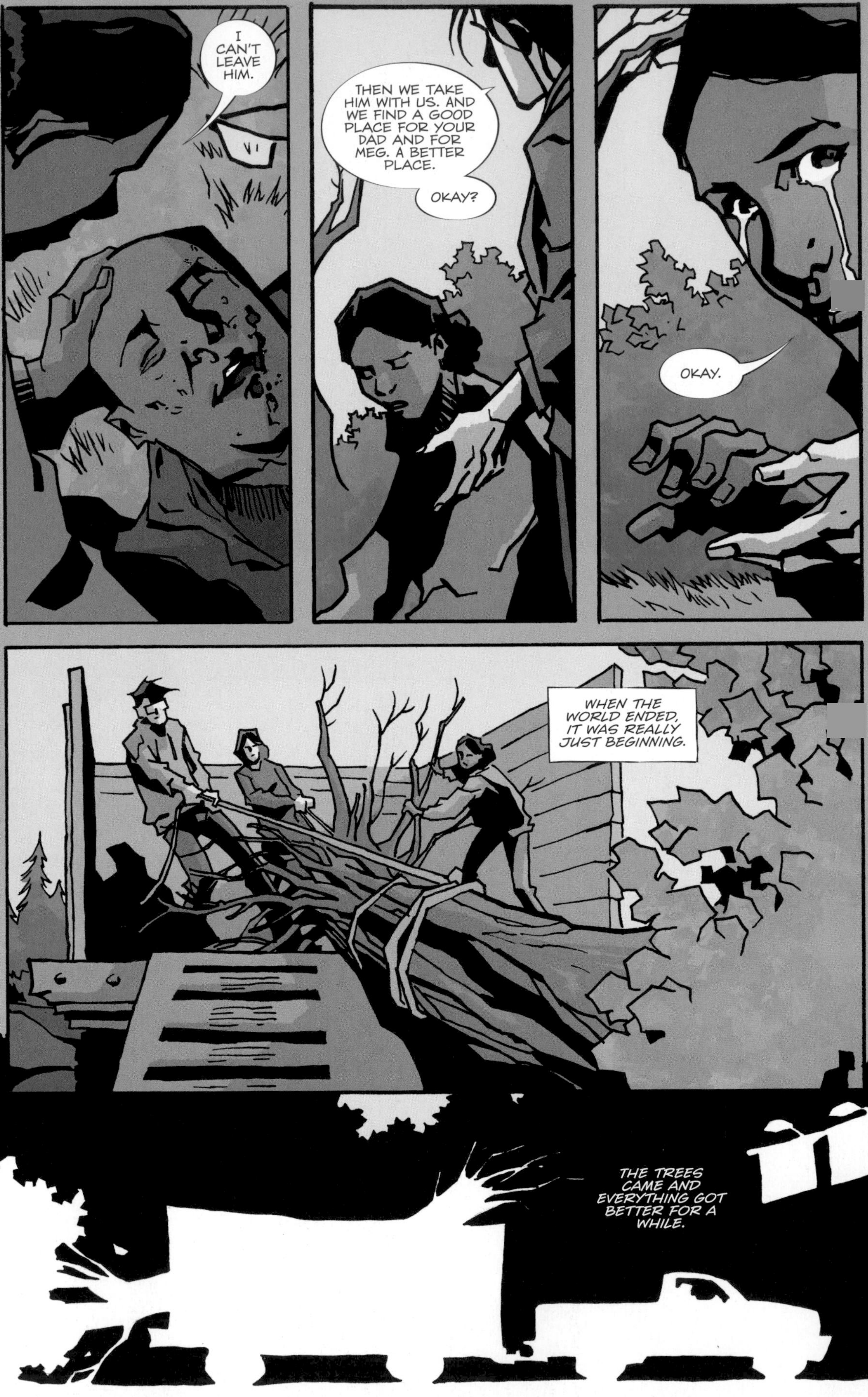
I CAN'T LEAVE HIM.
THEN WE TAKE HIM WITH US. AND WE FIND A GOOD PLACE FOR YOUR DAD AND FOR MEG. A BETTER PLACE.
OKAY?
OKAY.
WHEN THE WORLD ENDED, IT WAS REALLY JUST BEGINNING.
THE TREES CAME AND EVERYTHING GOT BETTER FOR A WHILE.

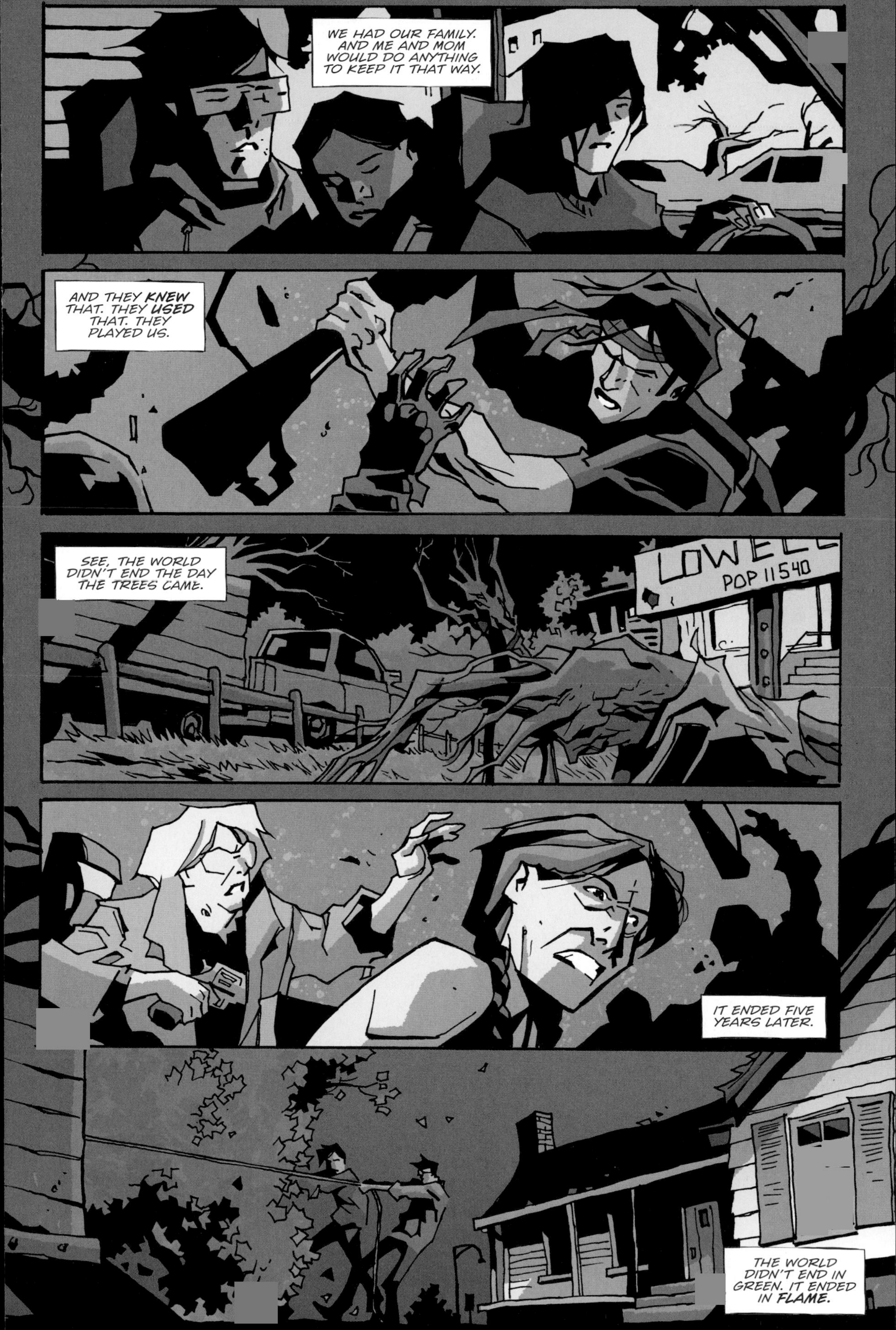

WE HAD OUR FAMILY. AND ME AND MOM WOULD DO ANYTHING TO KEEP IT THAT WAY.
AND THEY **KNEW** THAT. THEY **USED** THAT. THEY PLAYED US.
SEE, THE WORLD DIDN'T END THE DAY THE TREES CAME.
POP 11540
IT ENDED FIVE YEARS LATER.
THE WORLD DIDN'T END IN GREEN. IT ENDED IN **FLAME.**

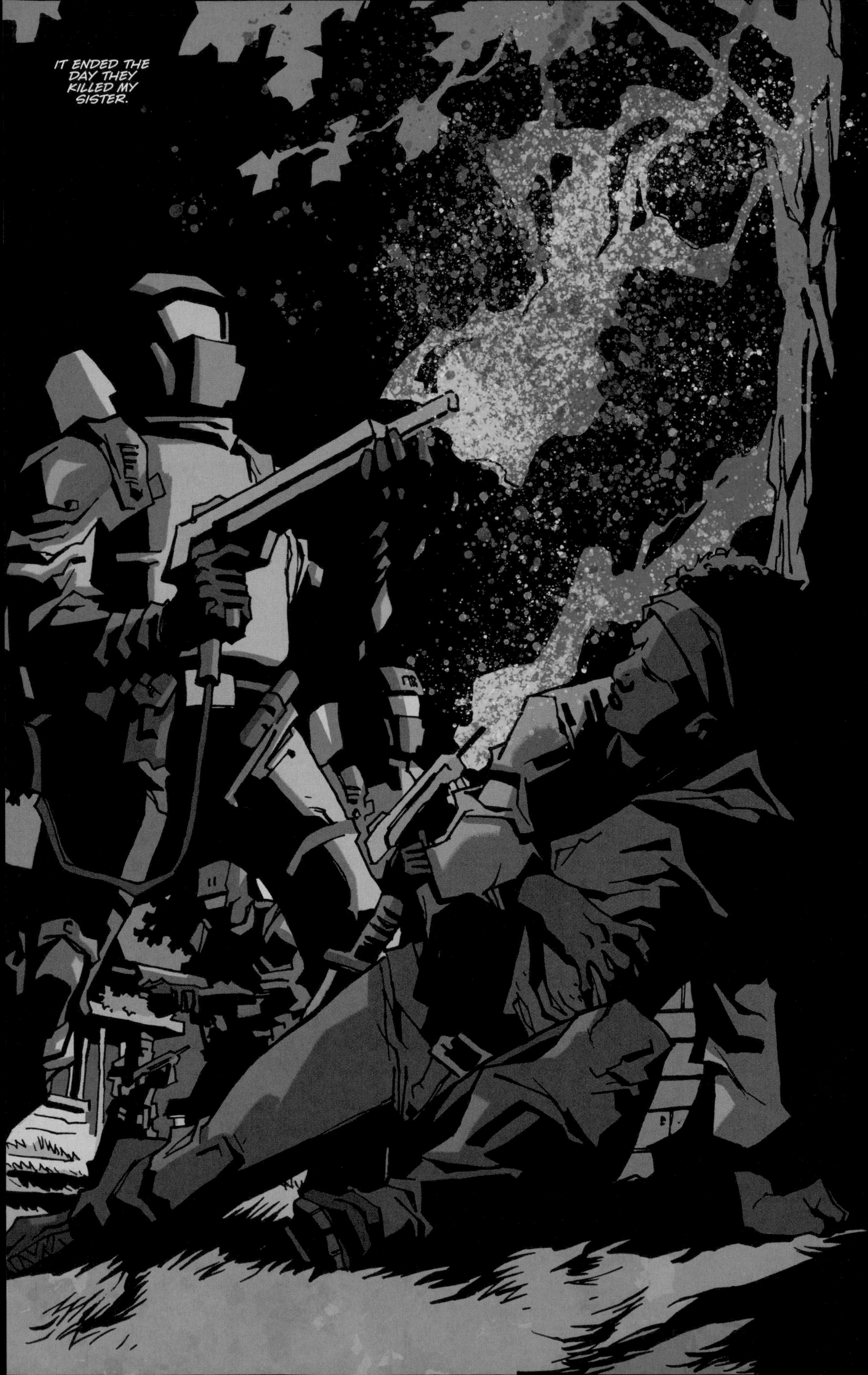
IT ENDED THE DAY THEY KILLED MY SISTER.

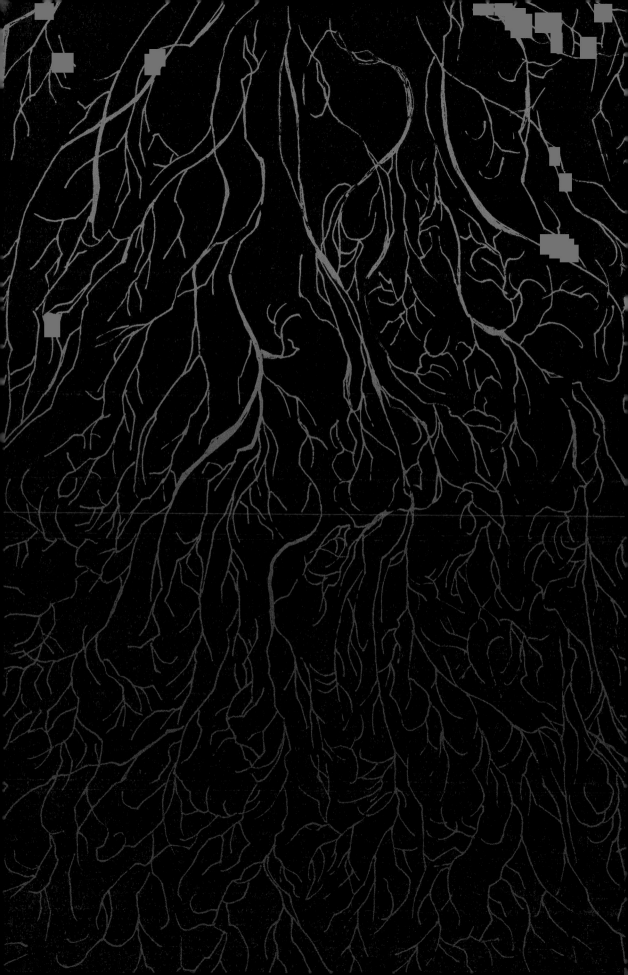

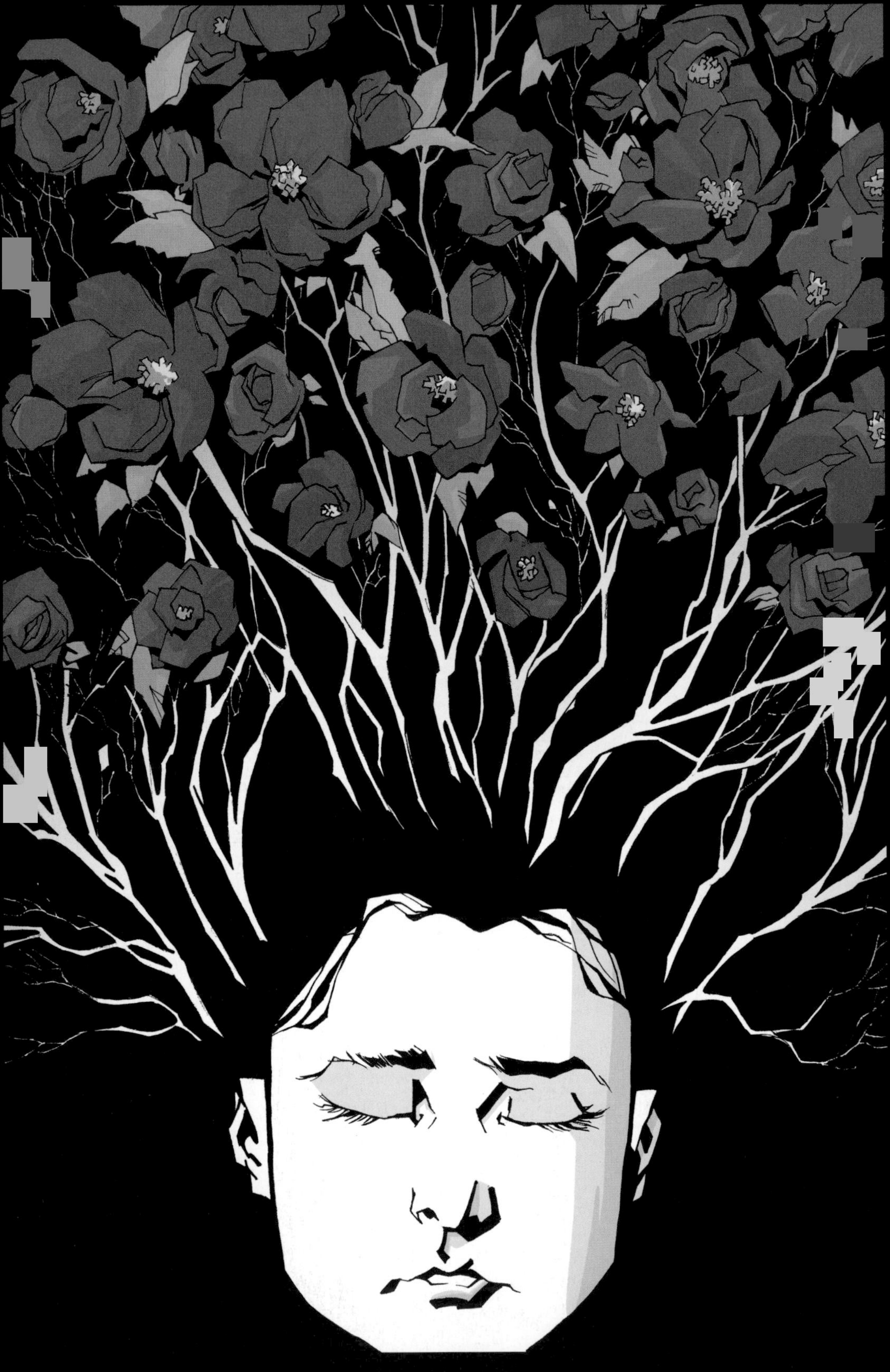

CHAPTER
TWELVE

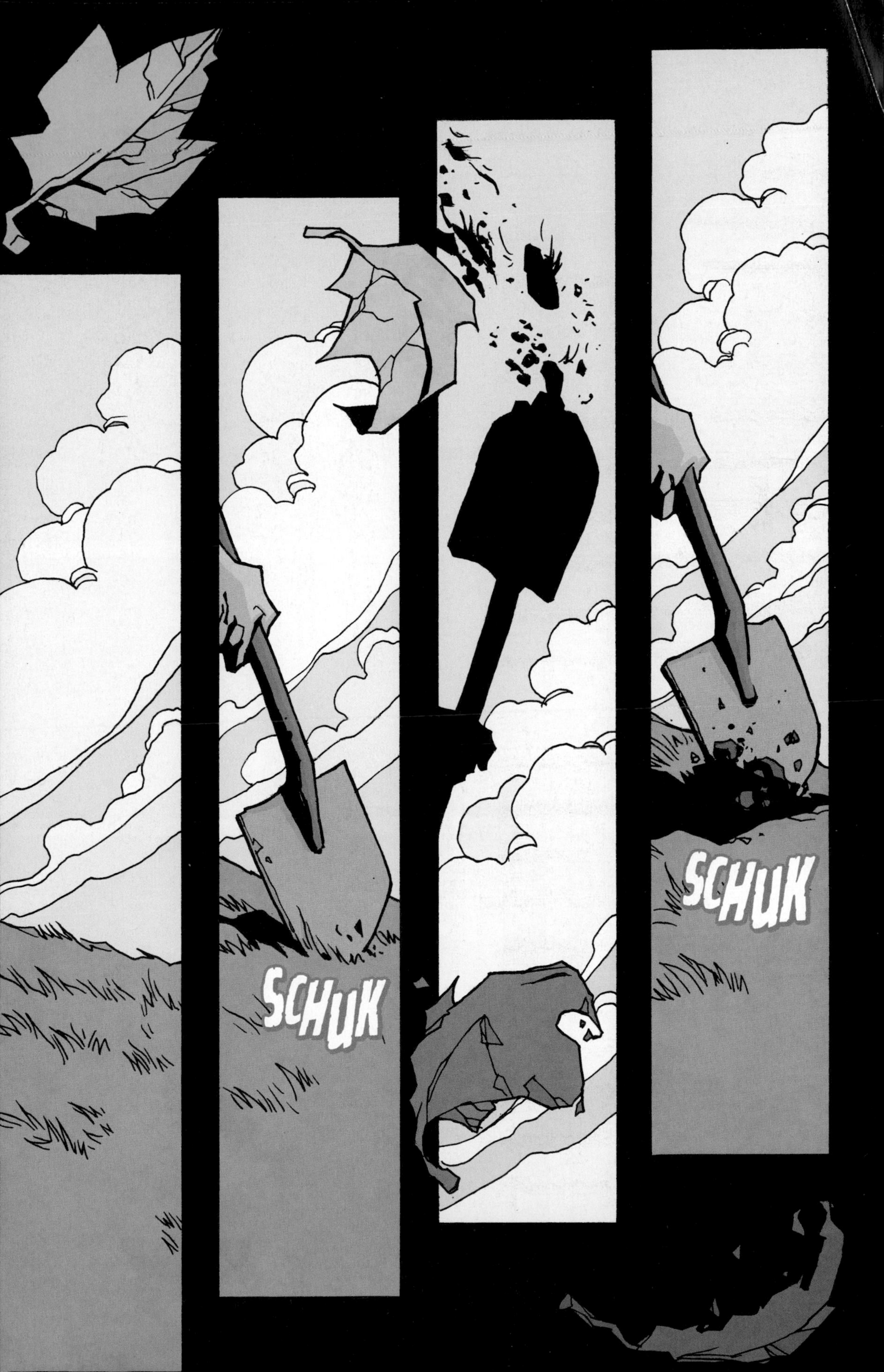
SCHUK
SCHUK

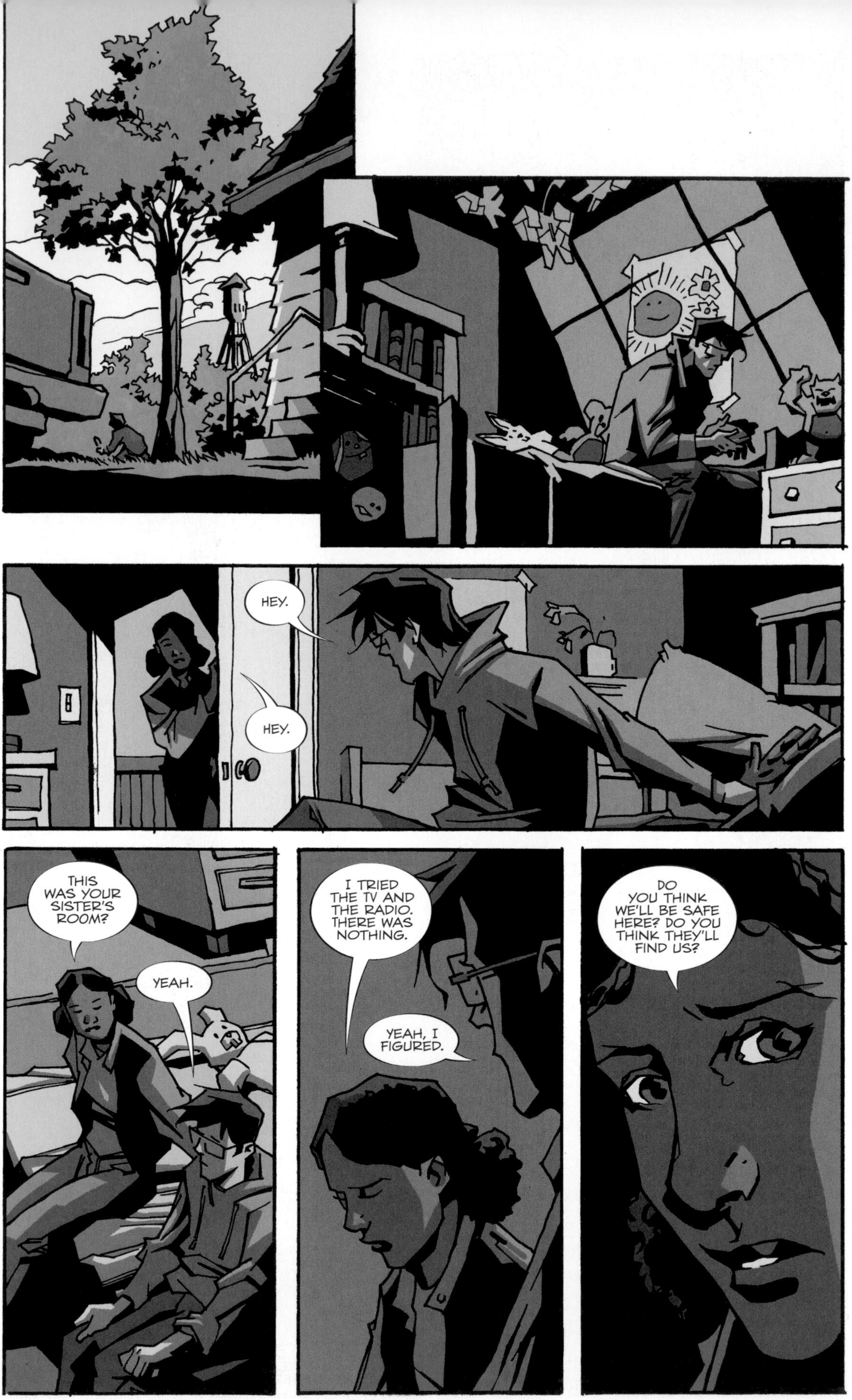
HEY.
HEY.
THIS WAS YOUR SISTER'S ROOM?
YEAH.
I TRIED THE TV AND THE RADIO. THERE WAS NOTHING.
YEAH, I FIGURED.
DO YOU THINK WE'LL BE SAFE HERE? DO YOU THINK THEY'LL FIND US?

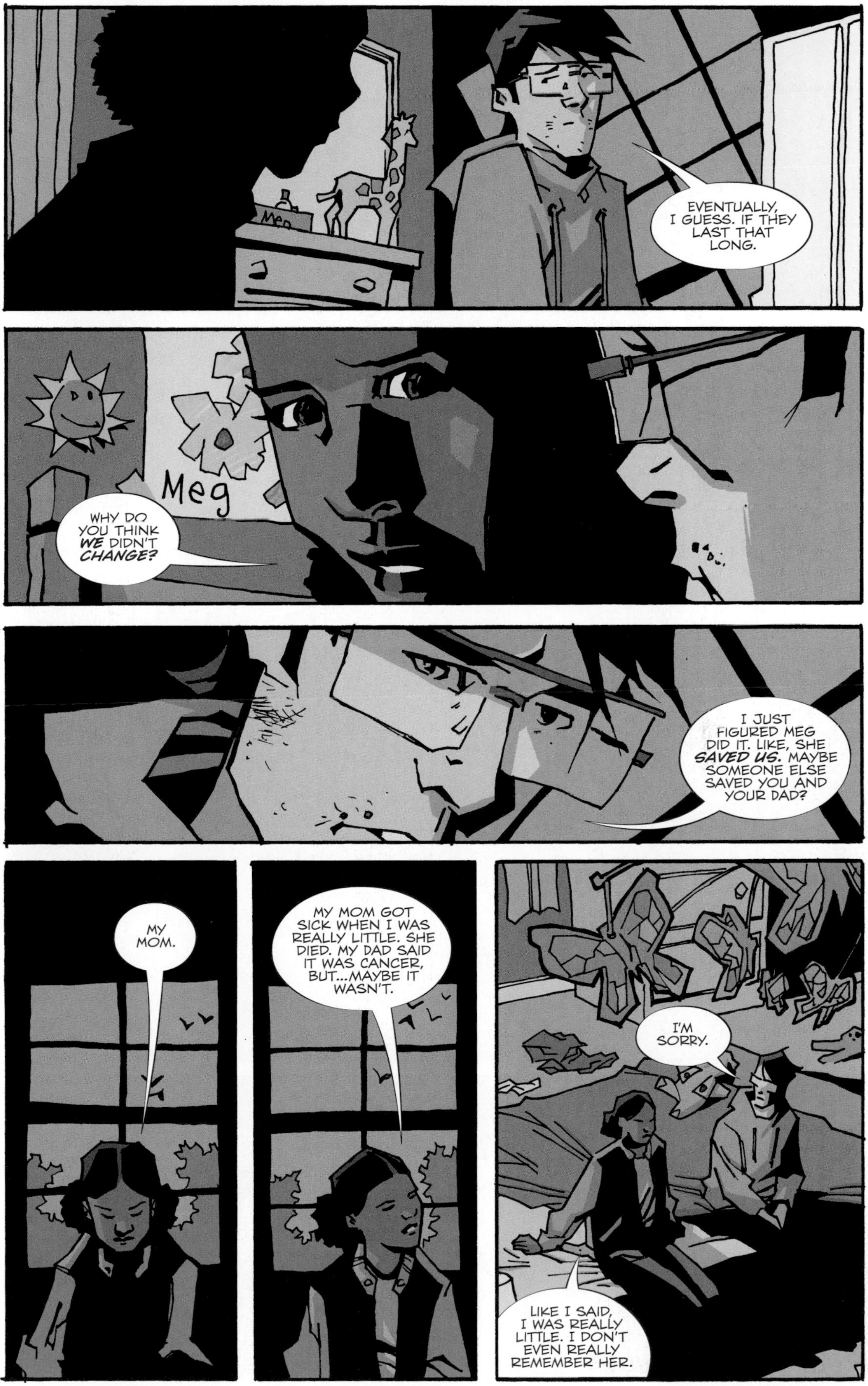

Meg
EVENTUALLY, I GUESS. IF THEY LAST THAT LONG.
Meg
WHY DO YOU THINK *WE* DIDN'T *CHANGE?*
I JUST FIGURED MEG DID IT. LIKE, SHE *SAVED US.* MAYBE SOMEONE ELSE SAVED YOU AND YOUR DAD?
MY MOM.
MY MOM GOT SICK WHEN I WAS REALLY LITTLE. SHE DIED. MY DAD SAID IT WAS CANCER, BUT...MAYBE IT WASN'T.
I'M SORRY.
LIKE I SAID, I WAS REALLY LITTLE. I DON'T EVEN REALLY REMEMBER HER.

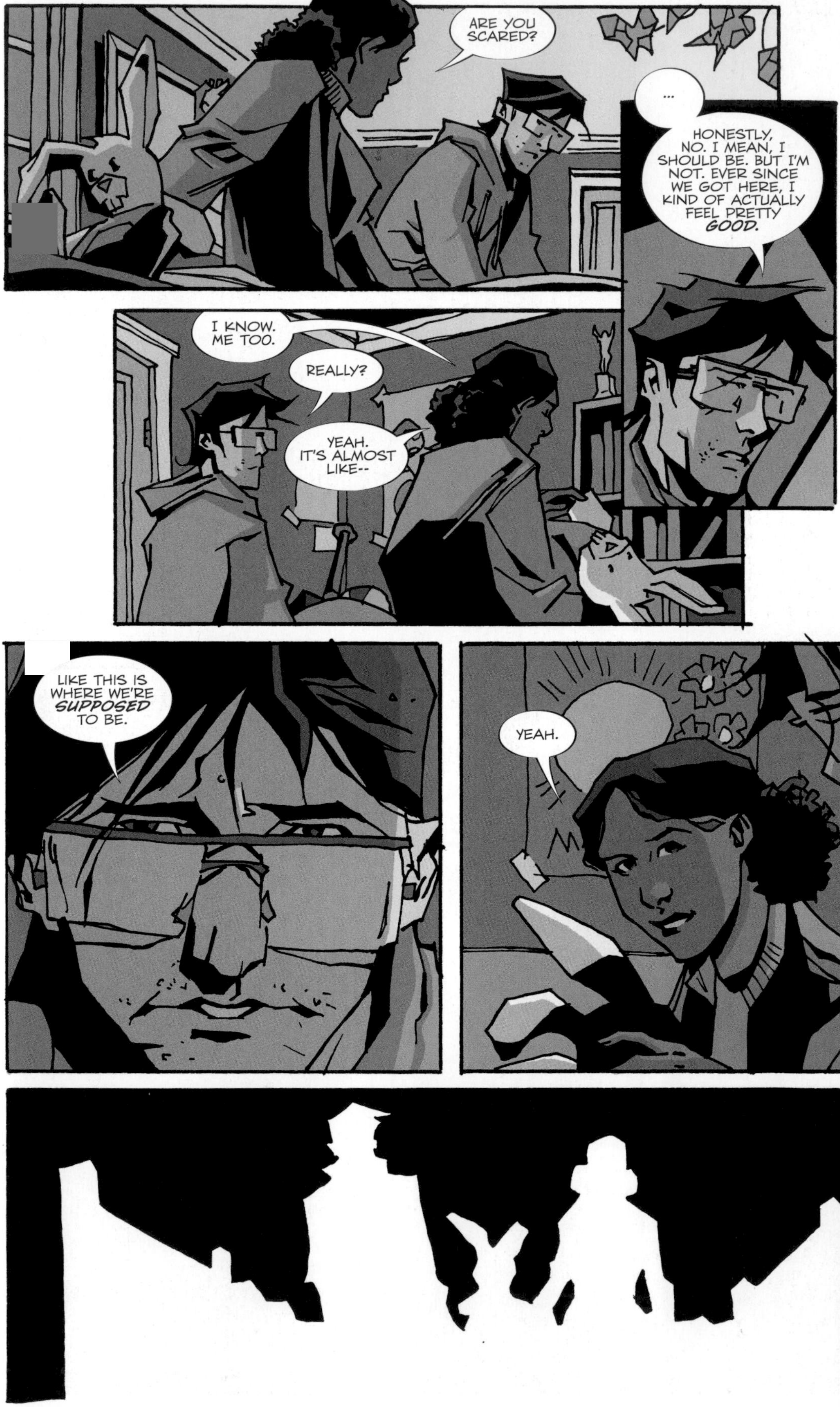
ARE YOU SCARED?
...
HONESTLY, NO. I MEAN, I SHOULD BE. BUT I'M NOT. EVER SINCE WE GOT HERE, I KIND OF ACTUALLY FEEL PRETTY GOOD.
I KNOW. ME TOO.
REALLY?
YEAH. IT'S ALMOST LIKE--
LIKE THIS IS WHERE WE'RE SUPPOSED TO BE.
YEAH.

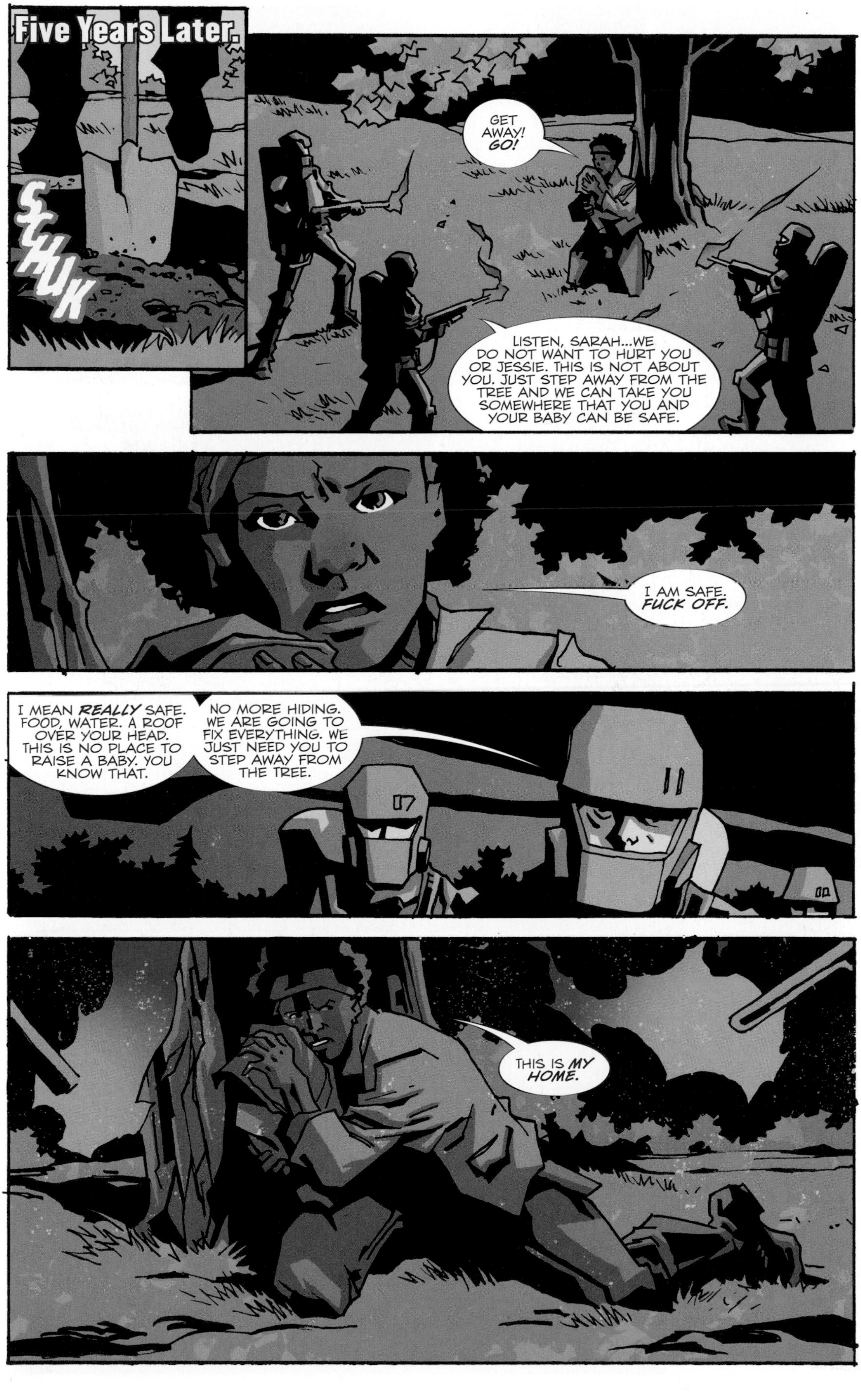

Five Years Later.
SCHUK
GET AWAY! GO!
LISTEN, SARAH...WE DO NOT WANT TO HURT YOU OR JESSIE. THIS IS NOT ABOUT YOU. JUST STEP AWAY FROM THE TREE AND WE CAN TAKE YOU SOMEWHERE THAT YOU AND YOUR BABY CAN BE SAFE.
I AM SAFE. FUCK OFF.
I MEAN REALLY SAFE. FOOD, WATER. A ROOF OVER YOUR HEAD. THIS IS NO PLACE TO RAISE A BABY. YOU KNOW THAT.
NO MORE HIDING. WE ARE GOING TO FIX EVERYTHING. WE JUST NEED YOU TO STEP AWAY FROM THE TREE.
THIS IS MY HOME.

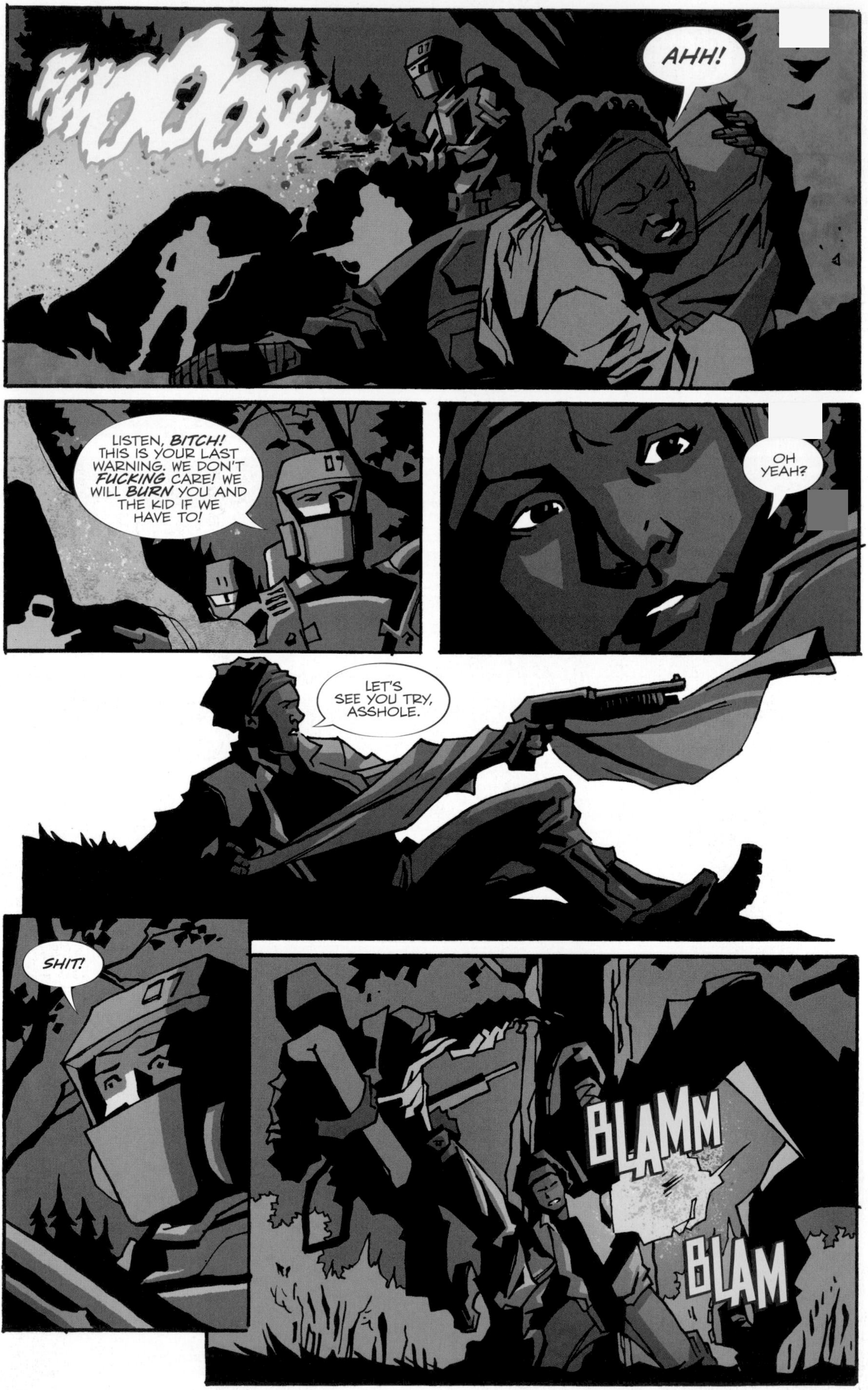
FWOOSH
AHH!
LISTEN, BITCH! THIS IS YOUR LAST WARNING. WE DON'T FUCKING CARE! WE WILL BURN YOU AND THE KID IF WE HAVE TO!
OH YEAH?
LET'S SEE YOU TRY, ASSHOLE.
SHIT!
BLAMM
BLAM

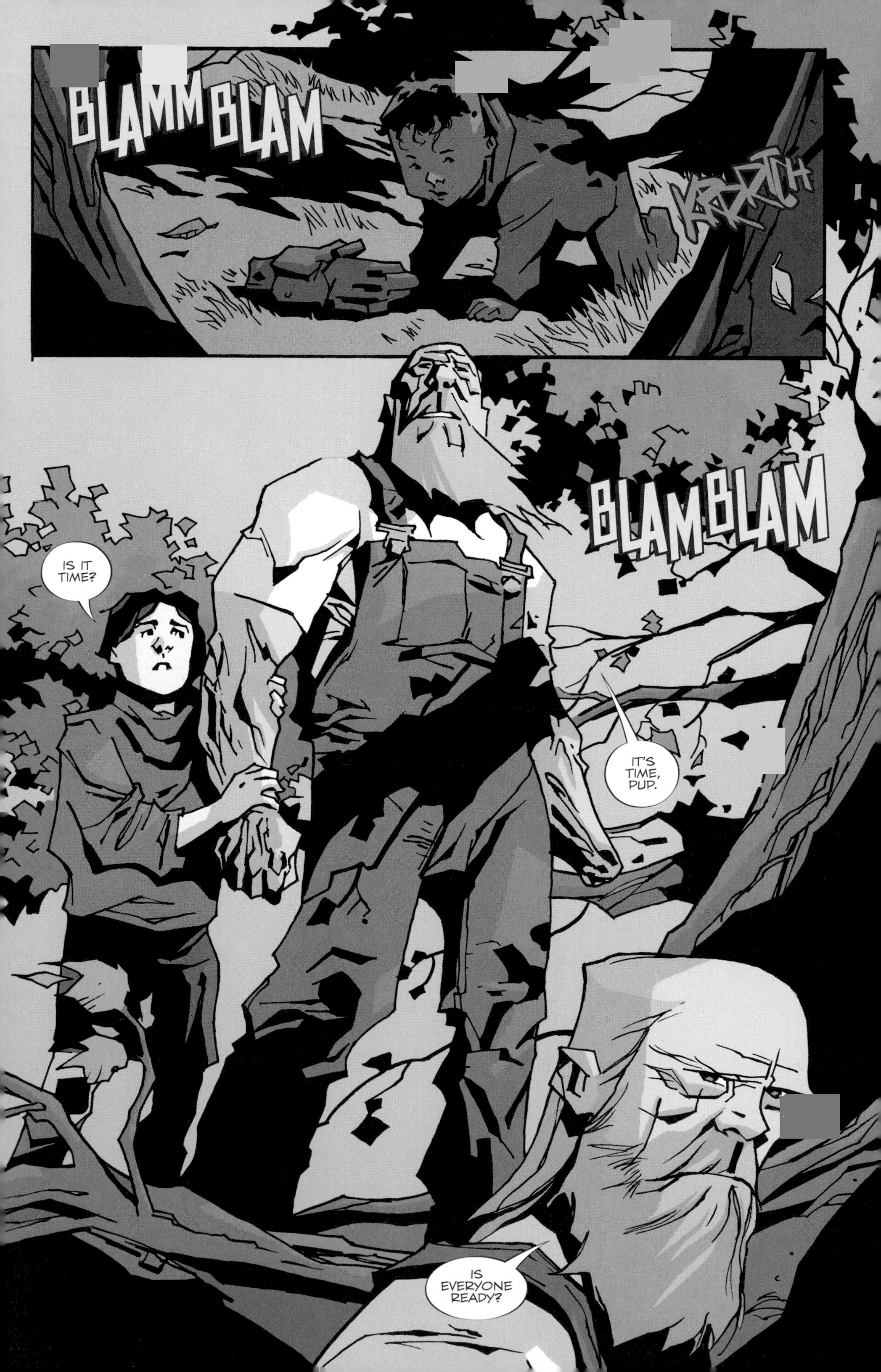
BLAMM BLAM
BLAM BLAM
IS IT TIME?
IT'S TIME, PUP.
IS EVERYONE READY?

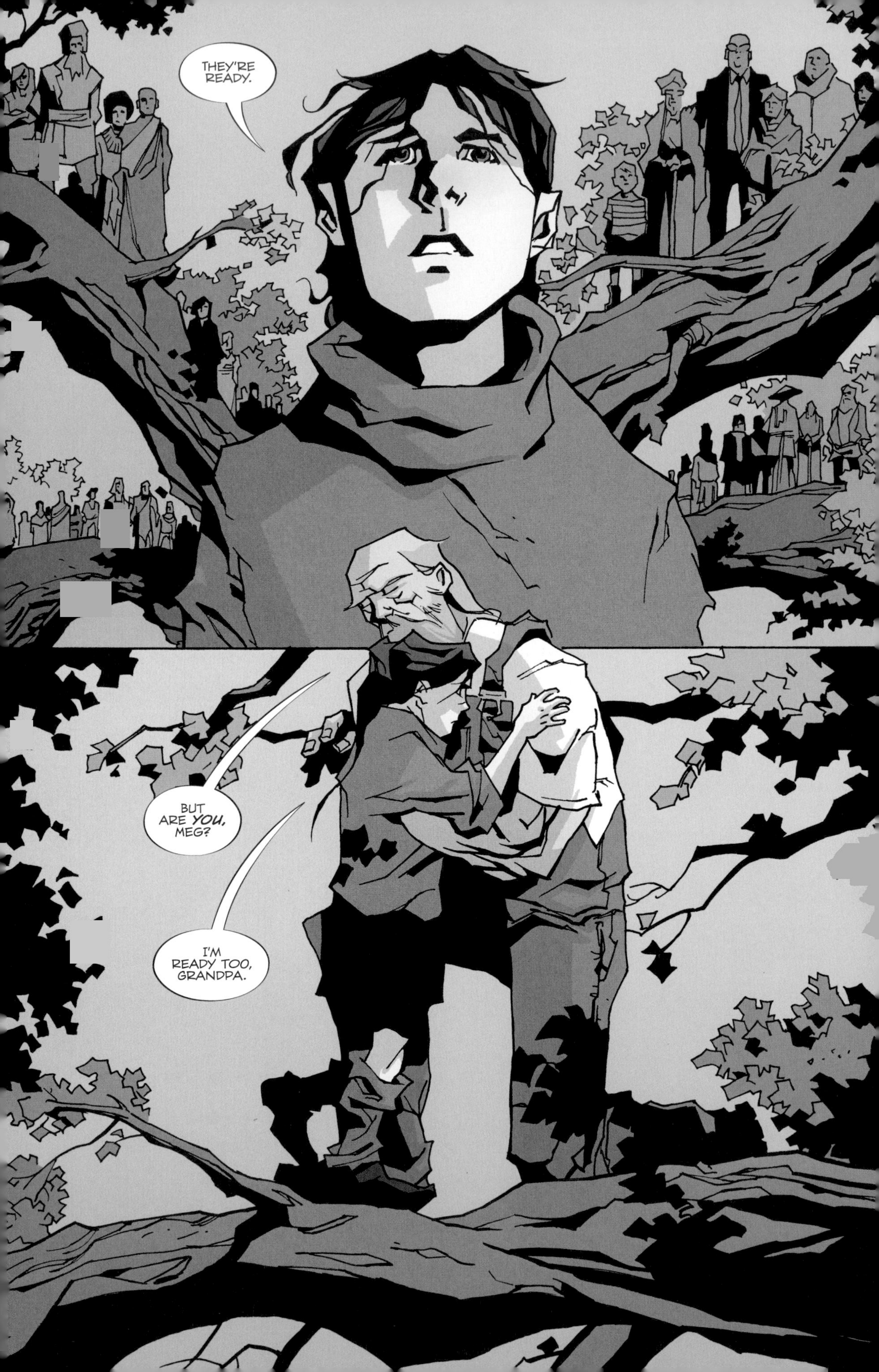
THEY'RE READY.
BUT ARE YOU, MEG?
I'M READY TOO, GRANDPA.

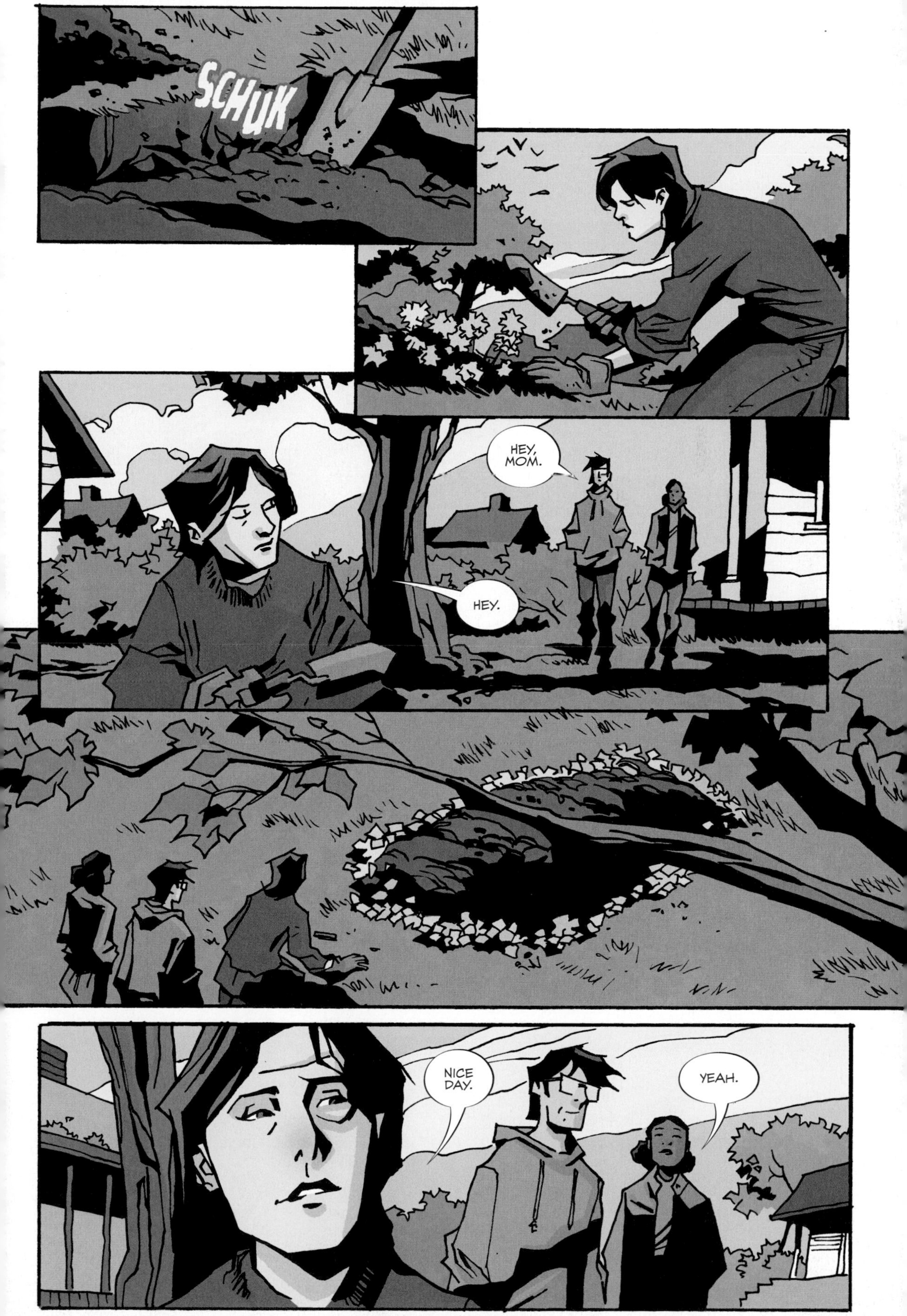
SCHUK
HEY, MOM.
HEY.
NICE DAY.
YEAH.

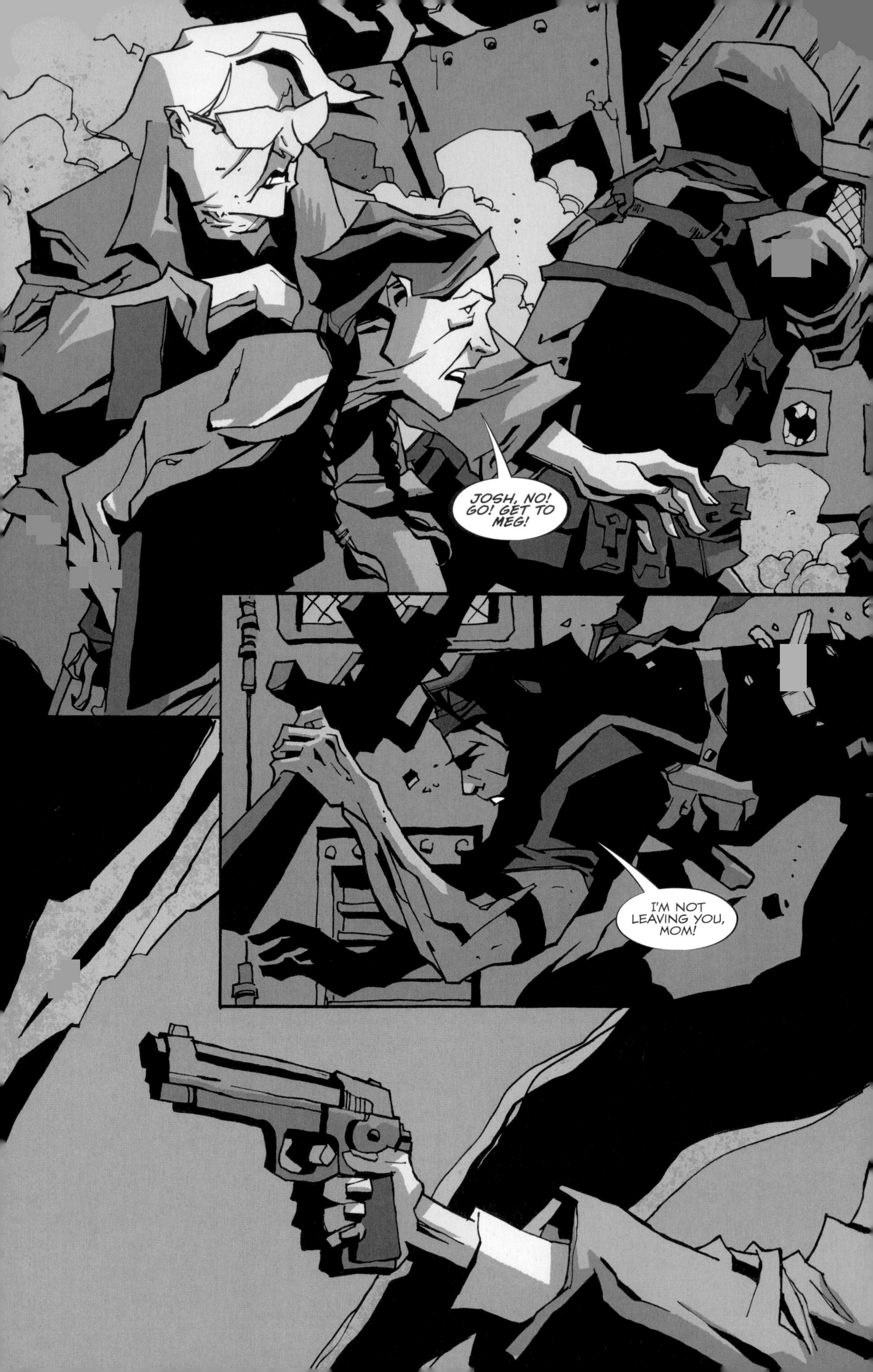
JOSH, NO! GO! GET TO MEG!
I'M NOT LEAVING YOU, MOM!

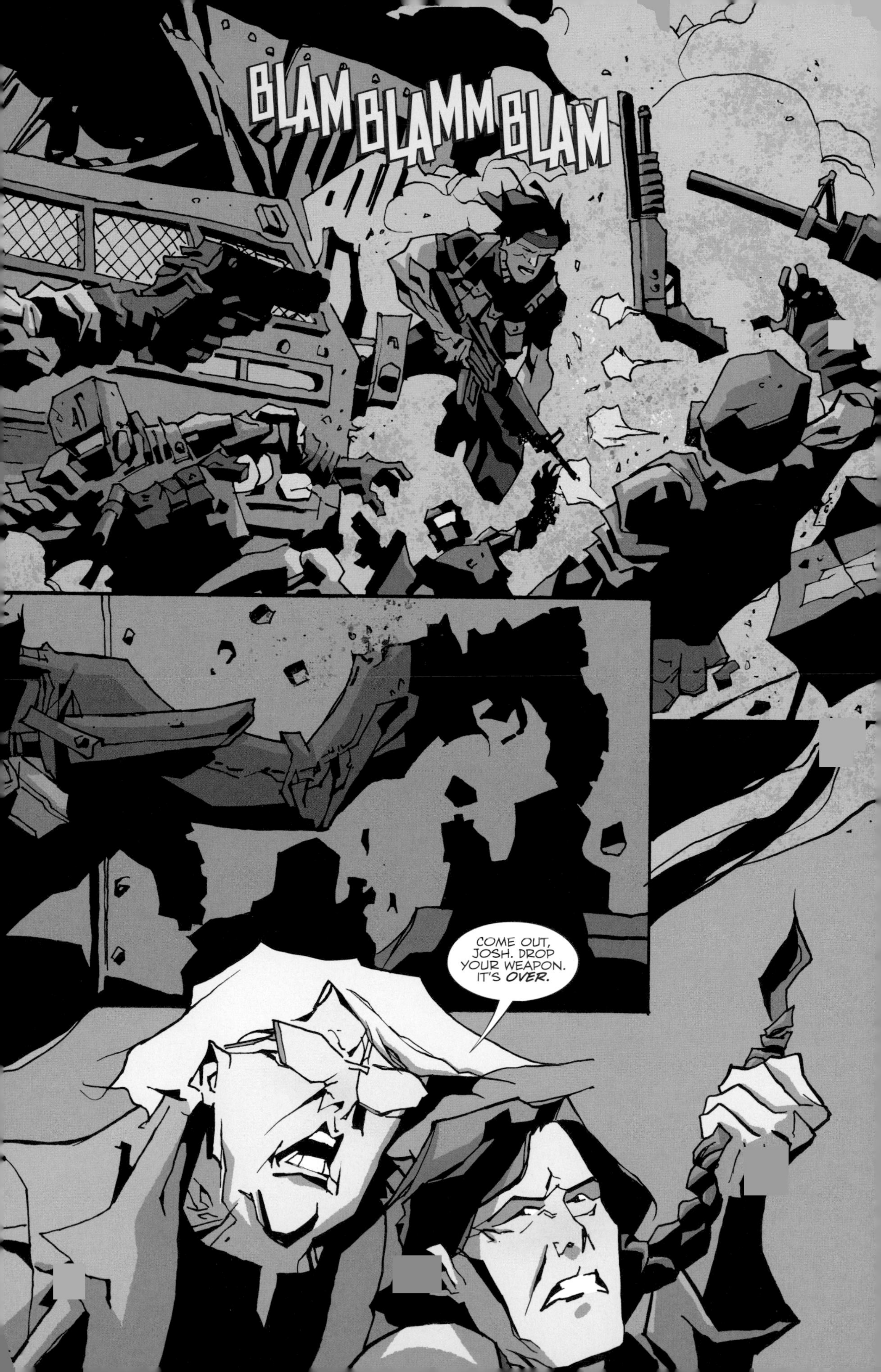
BLAM BLAMM BLAM
COME OUT, JOSH. DROP YOUR WEAPON. IT'S *OVER.*

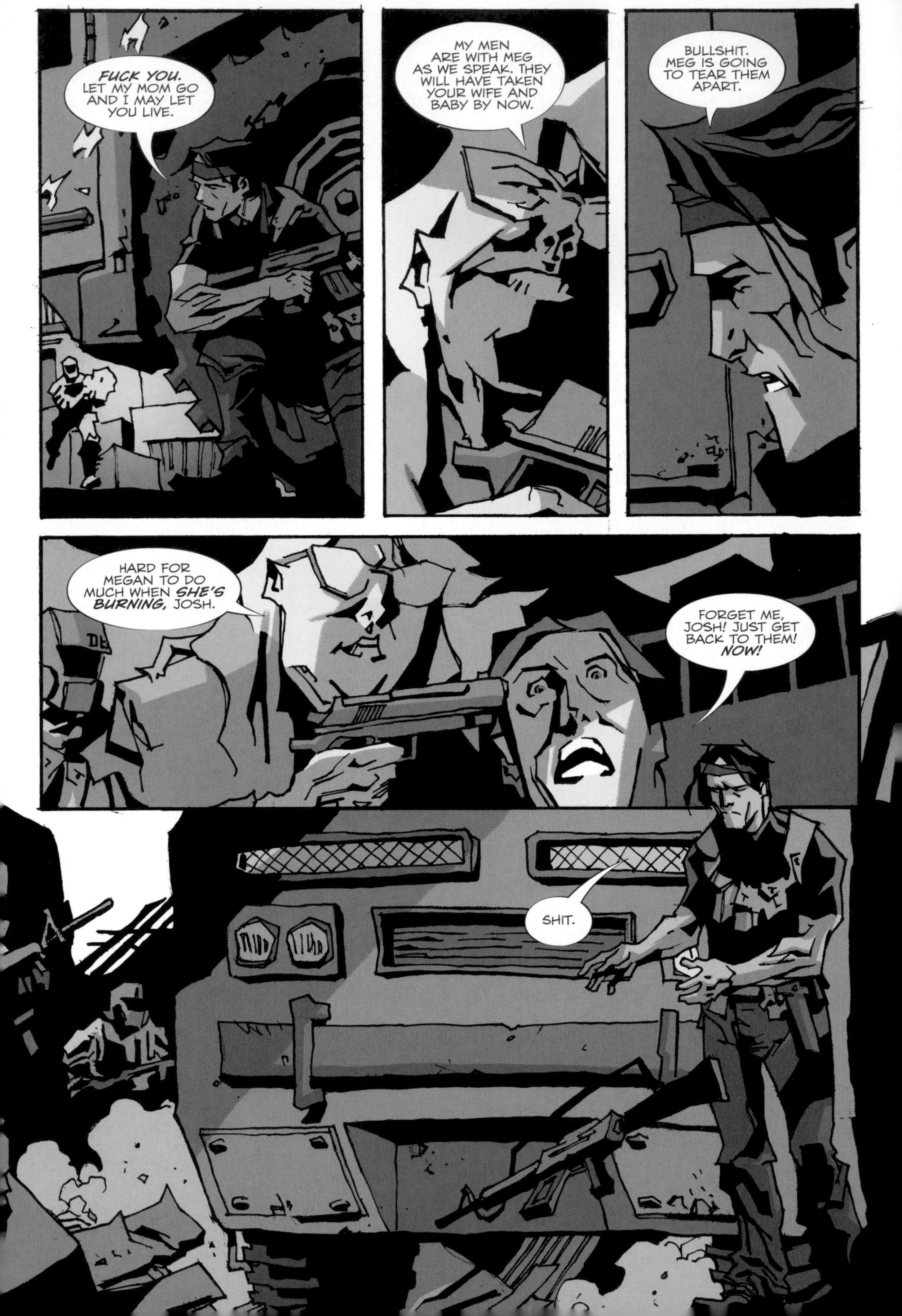

FUCK YOU. LET MY MOM GO AND I MAY LET YOU LIVE.
MY MEN ARE WITH MEG AS WE SPEAK. THEY WILL HAVE TAKEN YOUR WIFE AND BABY BY NOW.
BULLSHIT. MEG IS GOING TO TEAR THEM APART.
HARD FOR MEGAN TO DO MUCH WHEN SHE'S BURNING, JOSH.
FORGET ME, JOSH! JUST GET BACK TO THEM! NOW!
SHIT.

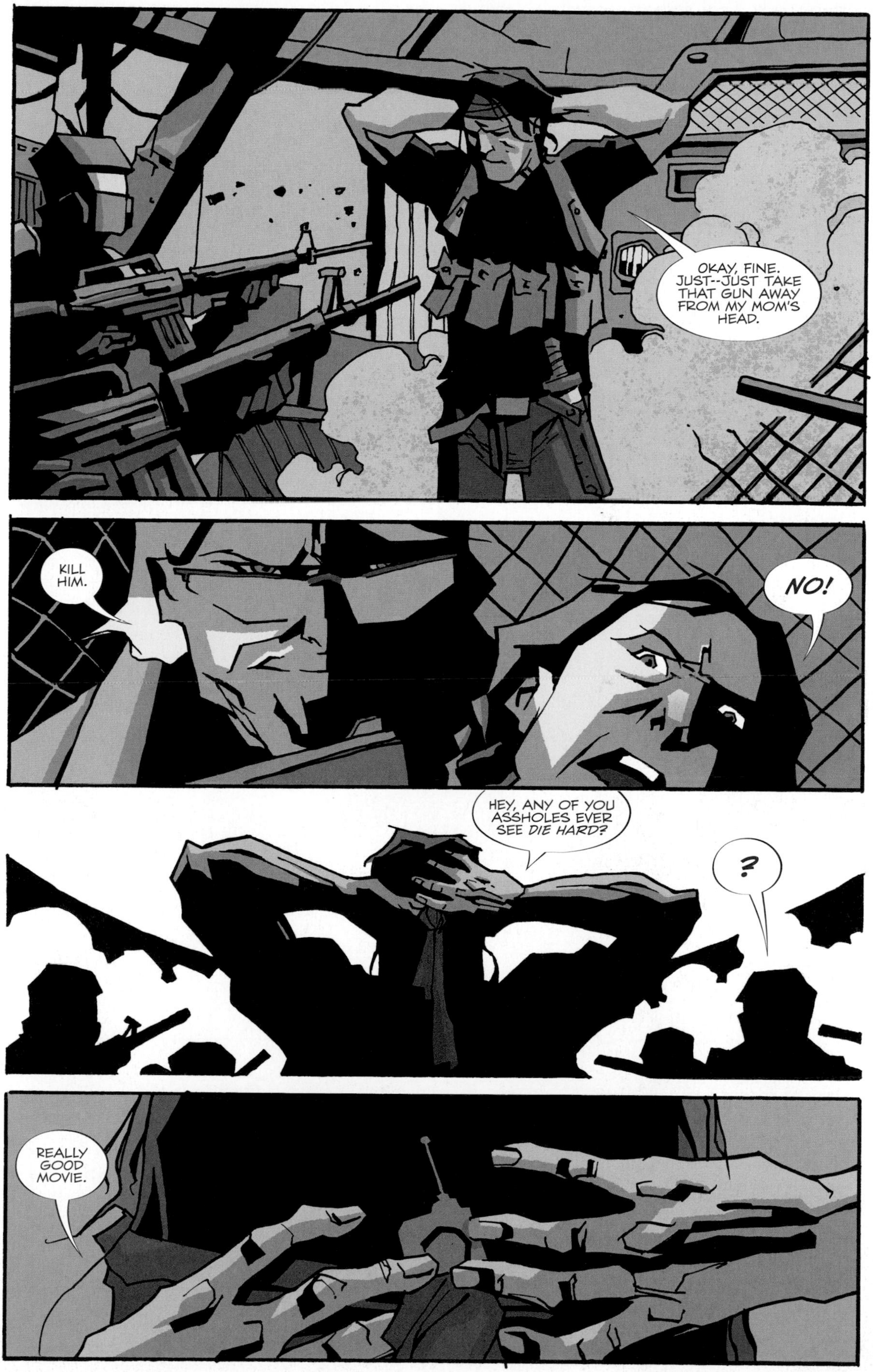
OKAY, FINE. JUST--JUST TAKE THAT GUN AWAY FROM MY MOM'S HEAD.
KILL HIM.
NO!
HEY, ANY OF YOU ASSHOLES EVER SEE *DIE HARD*?
?
REALLY GOOD MOVIE.

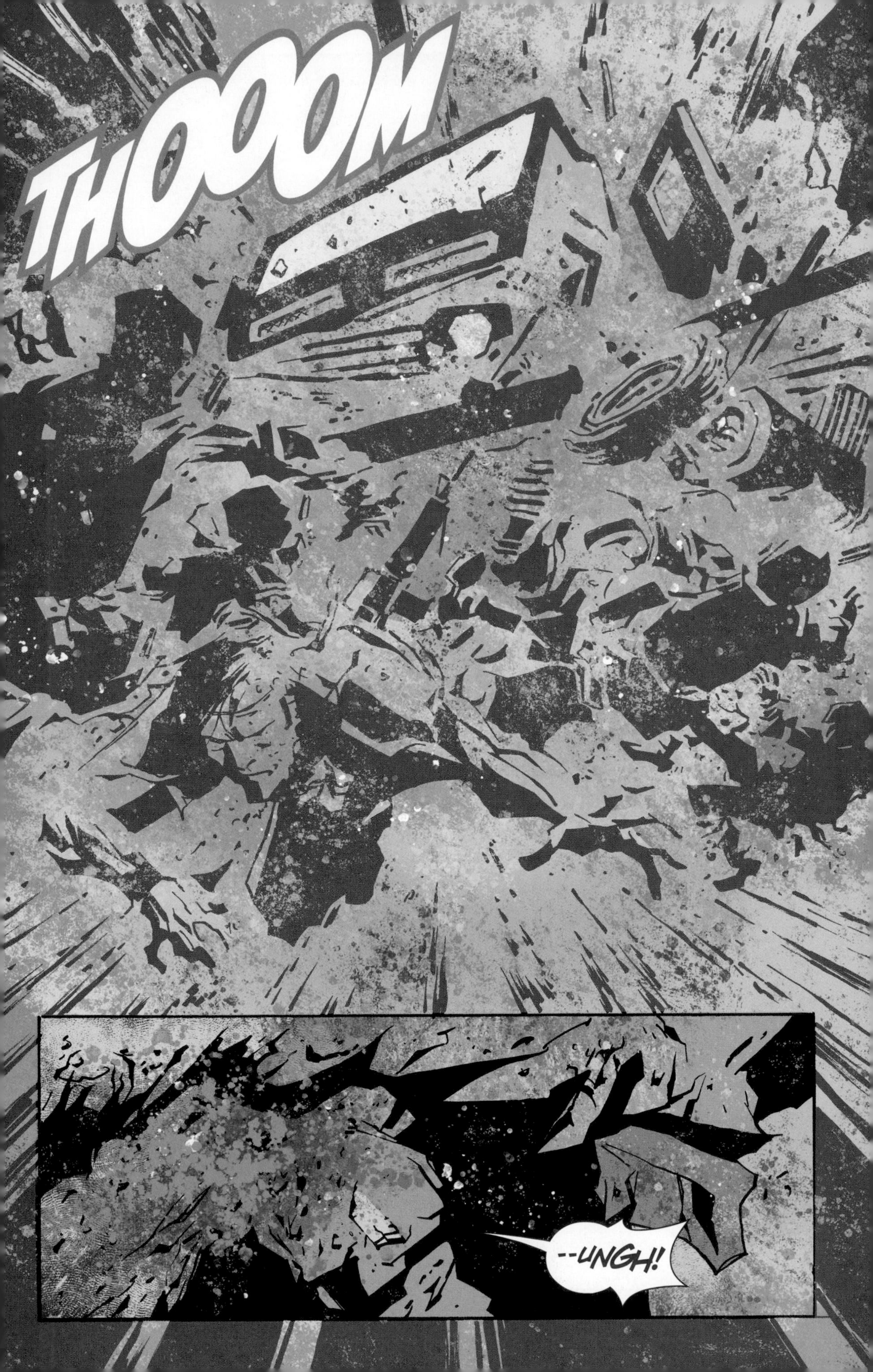
THOOOM
--UNGH!

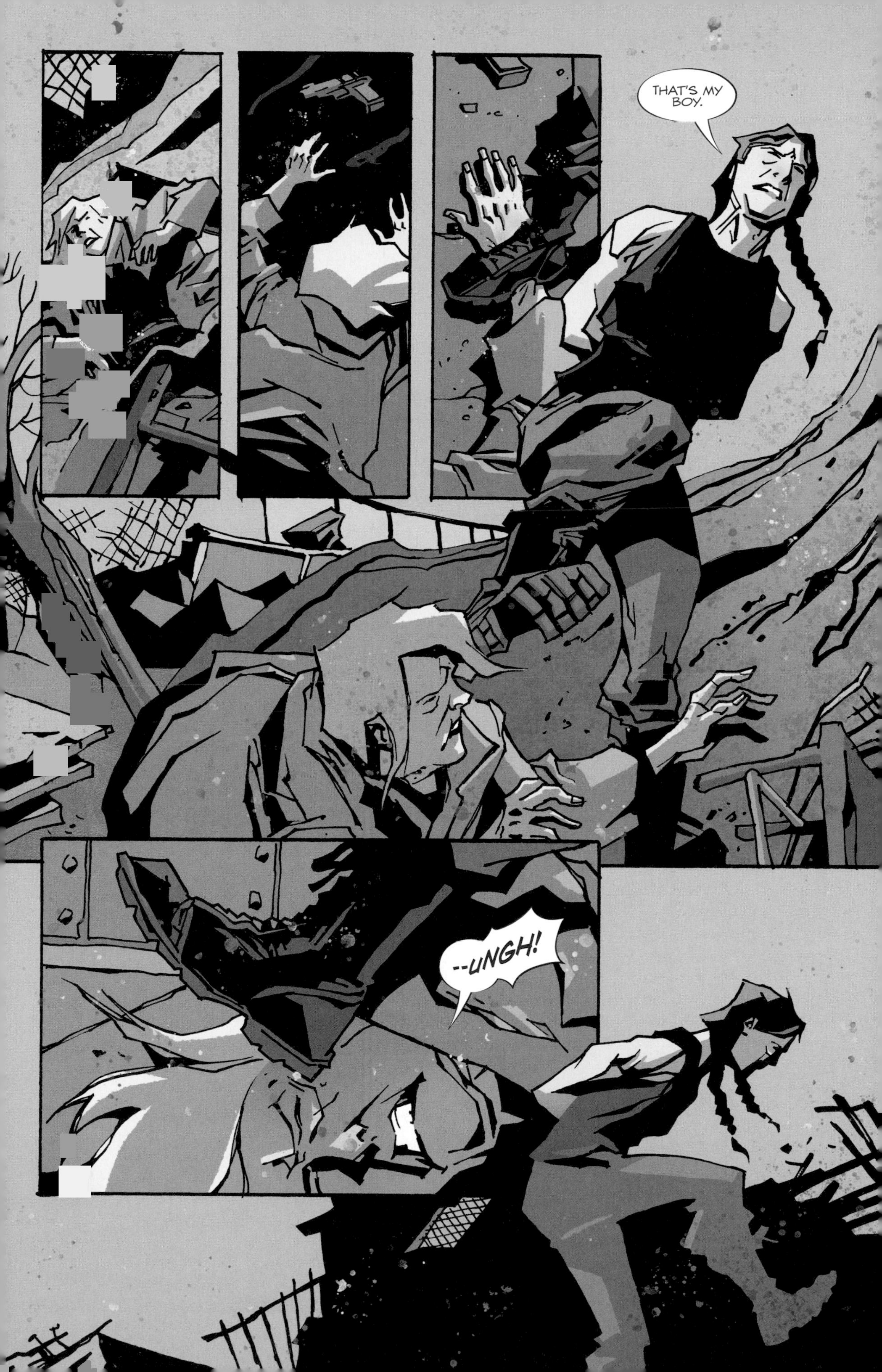
THAT'S MY BOY.
--UNGH!

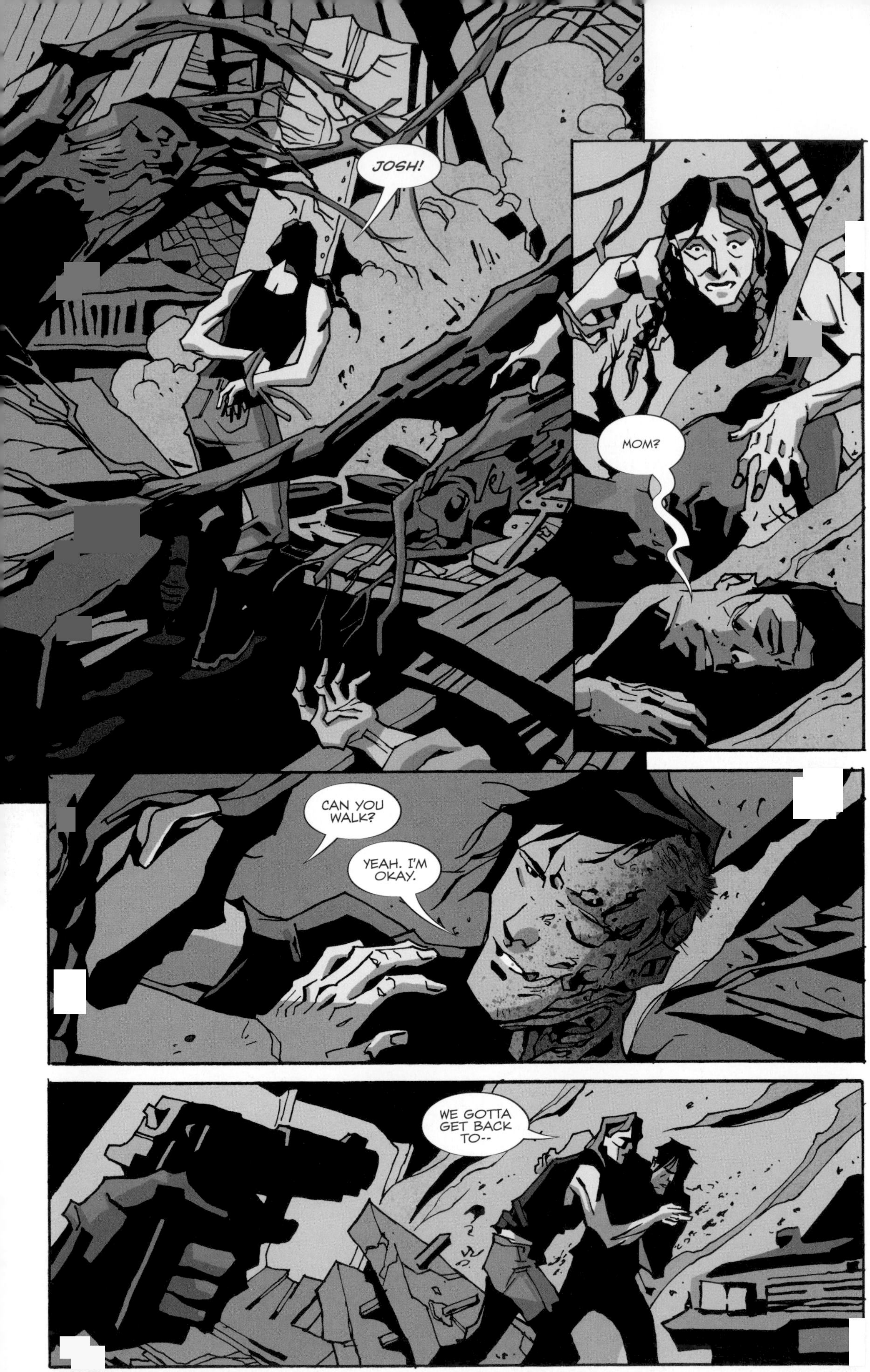
JOSH!
MOM?
CAN YOU WALK?
YEAH. I'M OKAY.
WE GOTTA GET BACK TO--

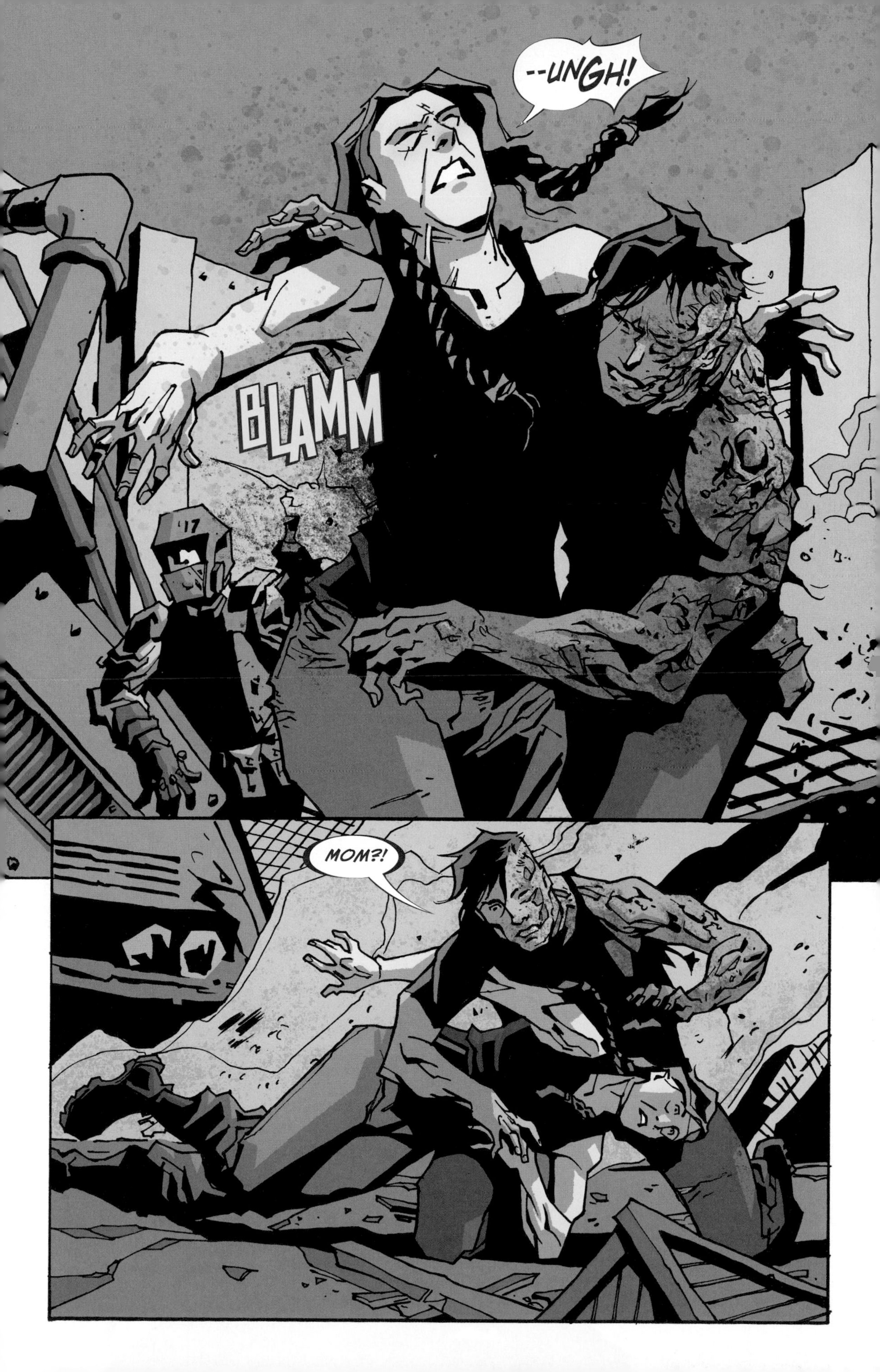
--UNGH!
BLAMM
MOM?!

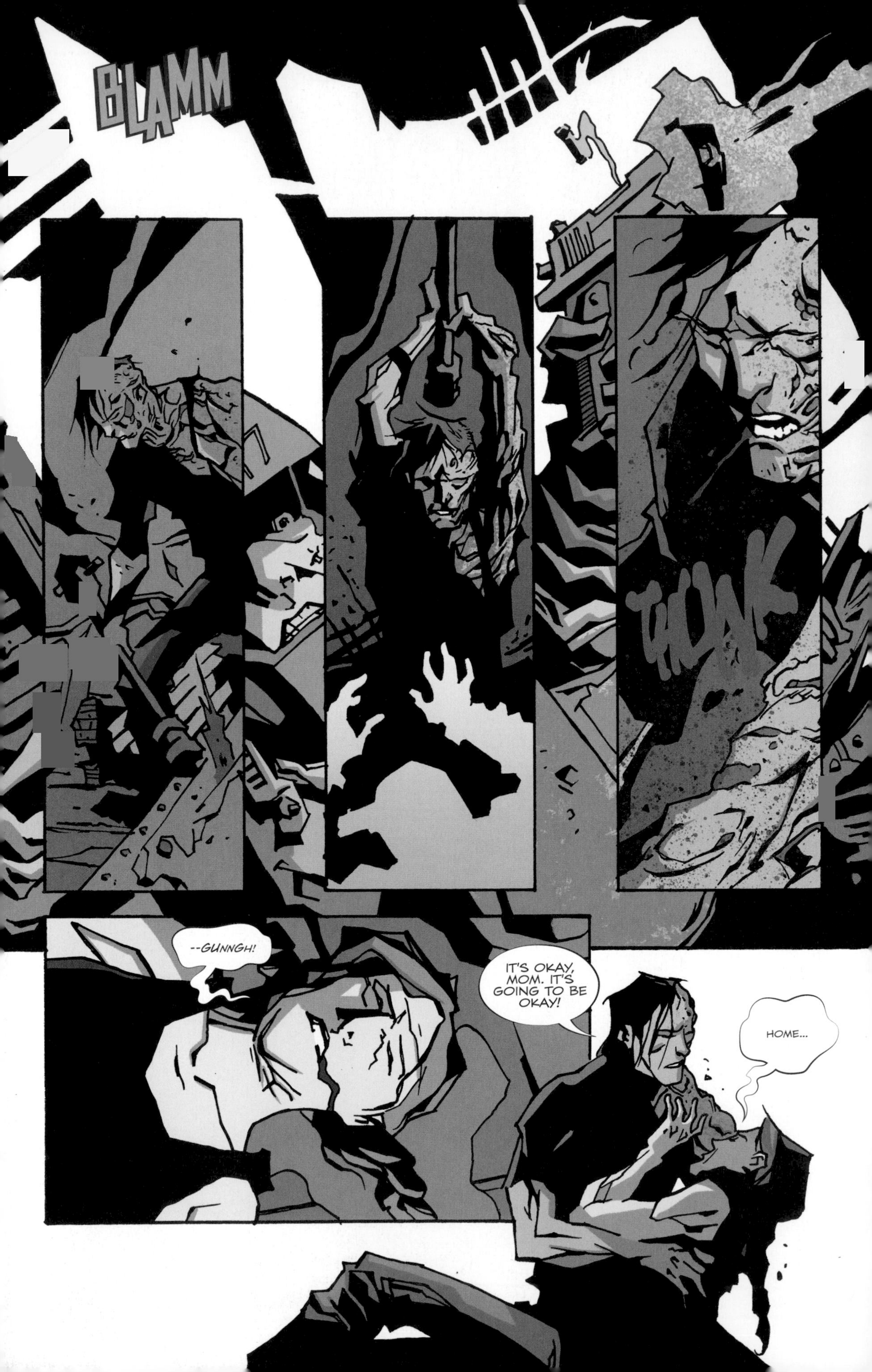
BLAMM
THUNK
--GUNNGH!
IT'S OKAY, MOM. IT'S GOING TO BE OKAY!
HOME...

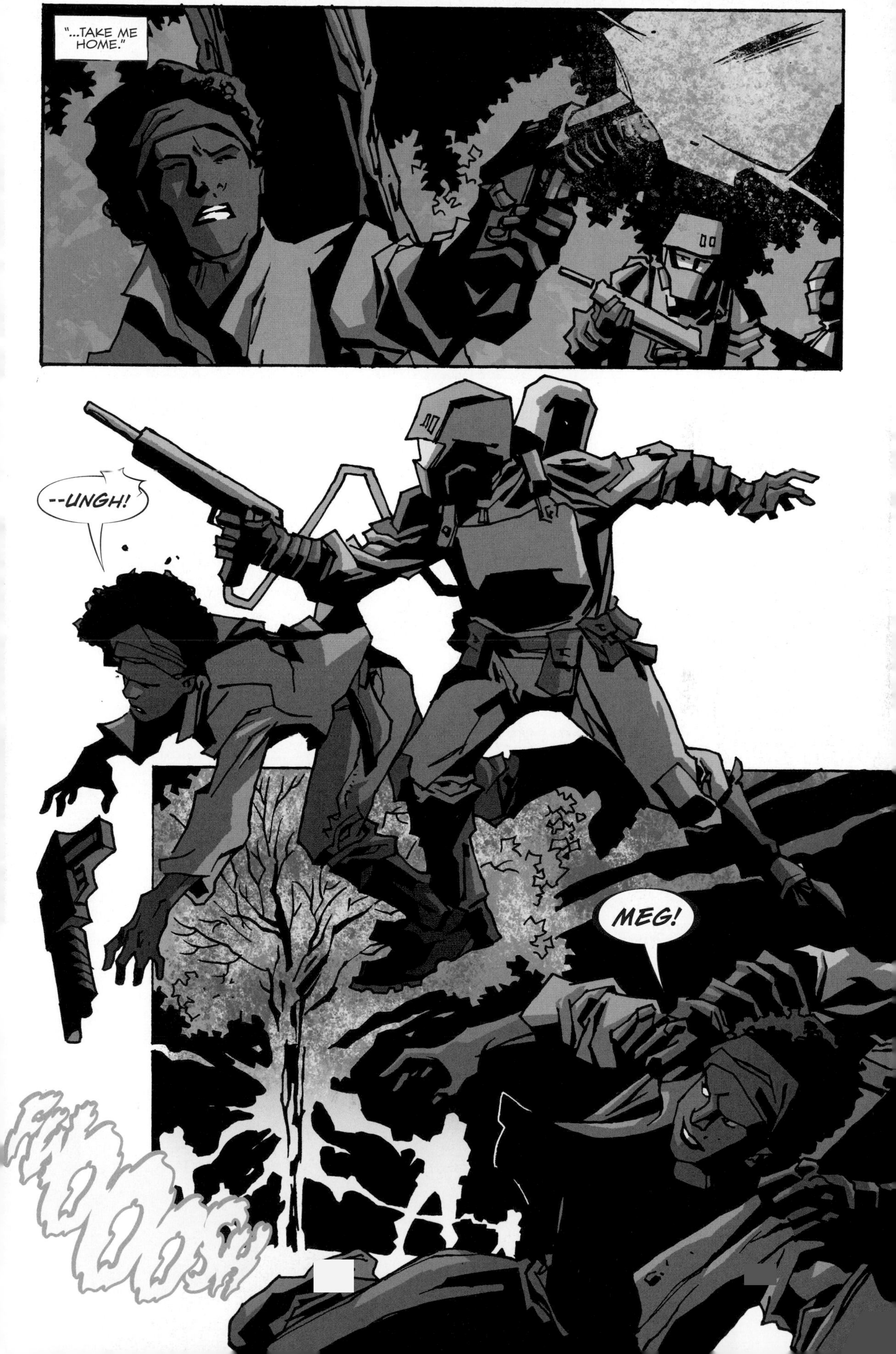
"...TAKE ME HOME."
--UNGH!
MEG!

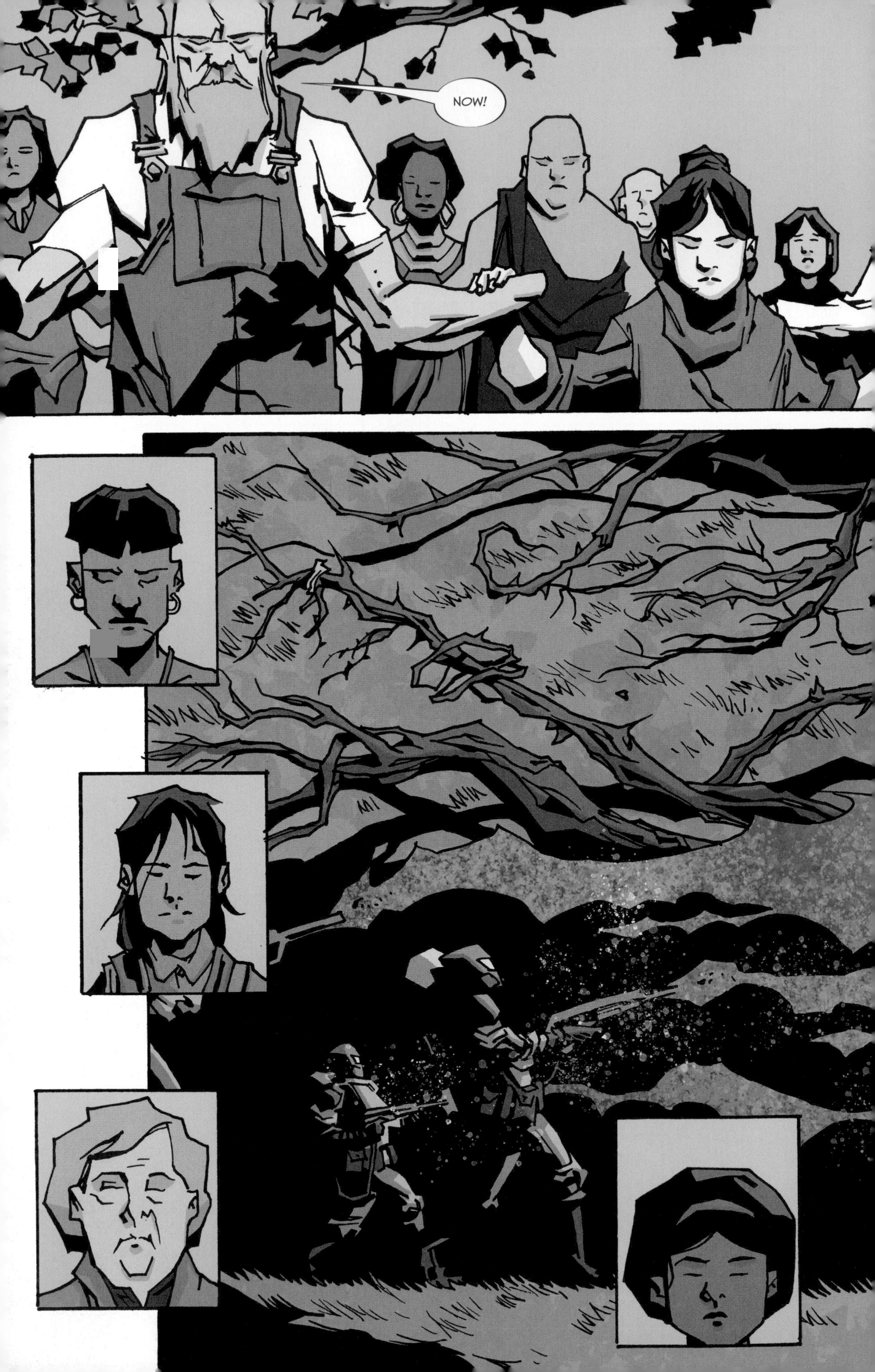
NOW!

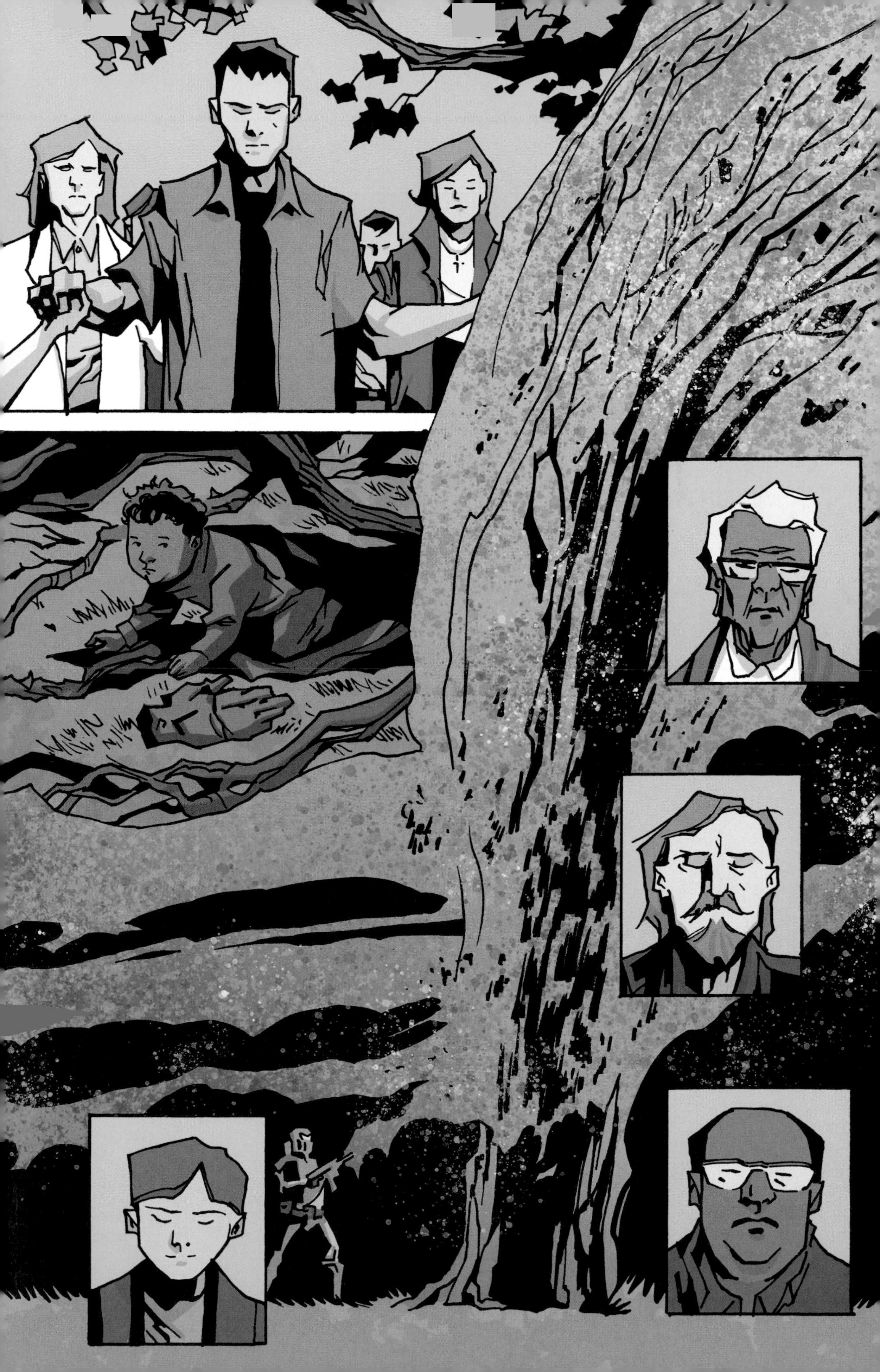

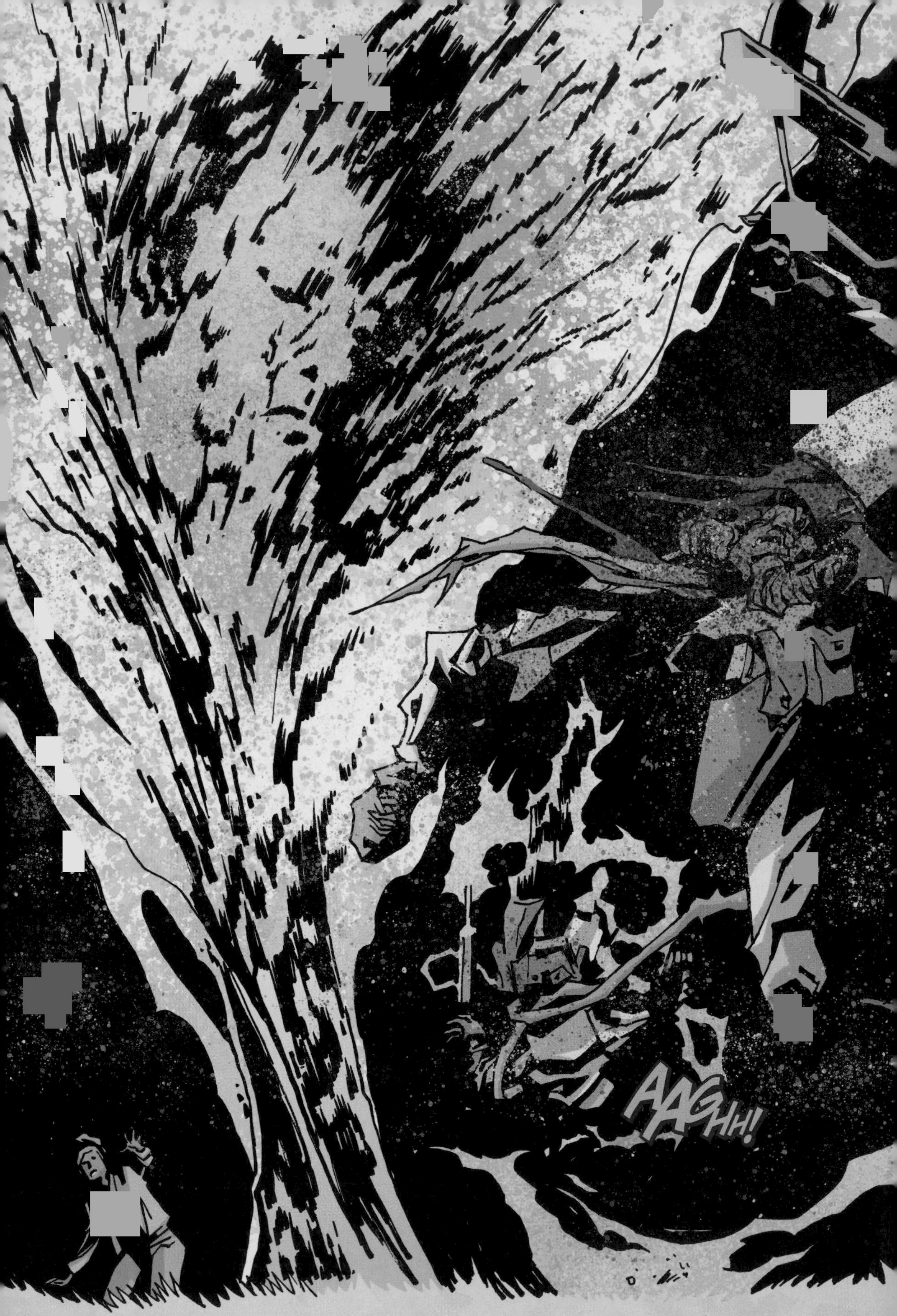
AAGHH!

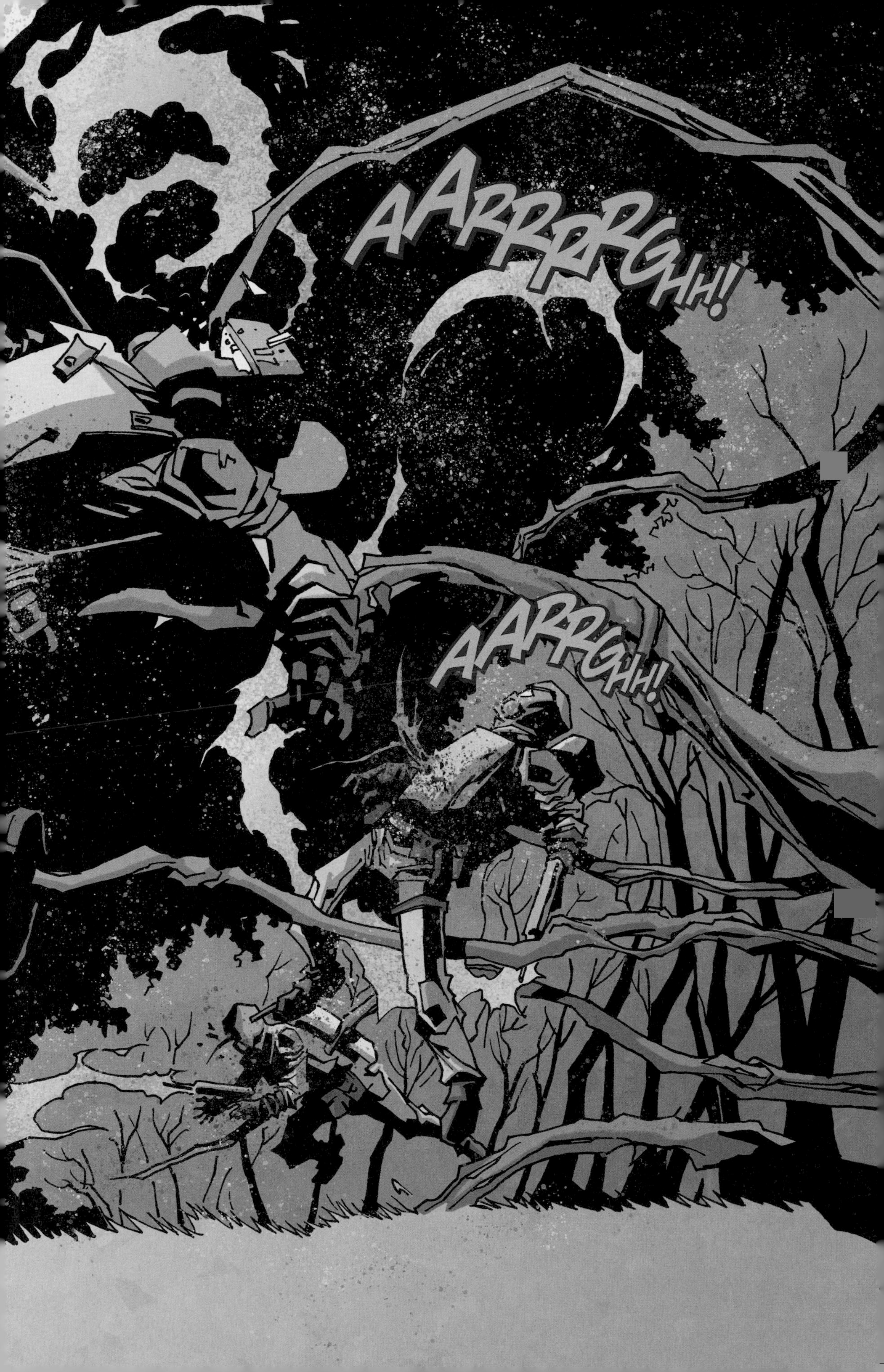
AARRRRGHH!
AARRRGHH!

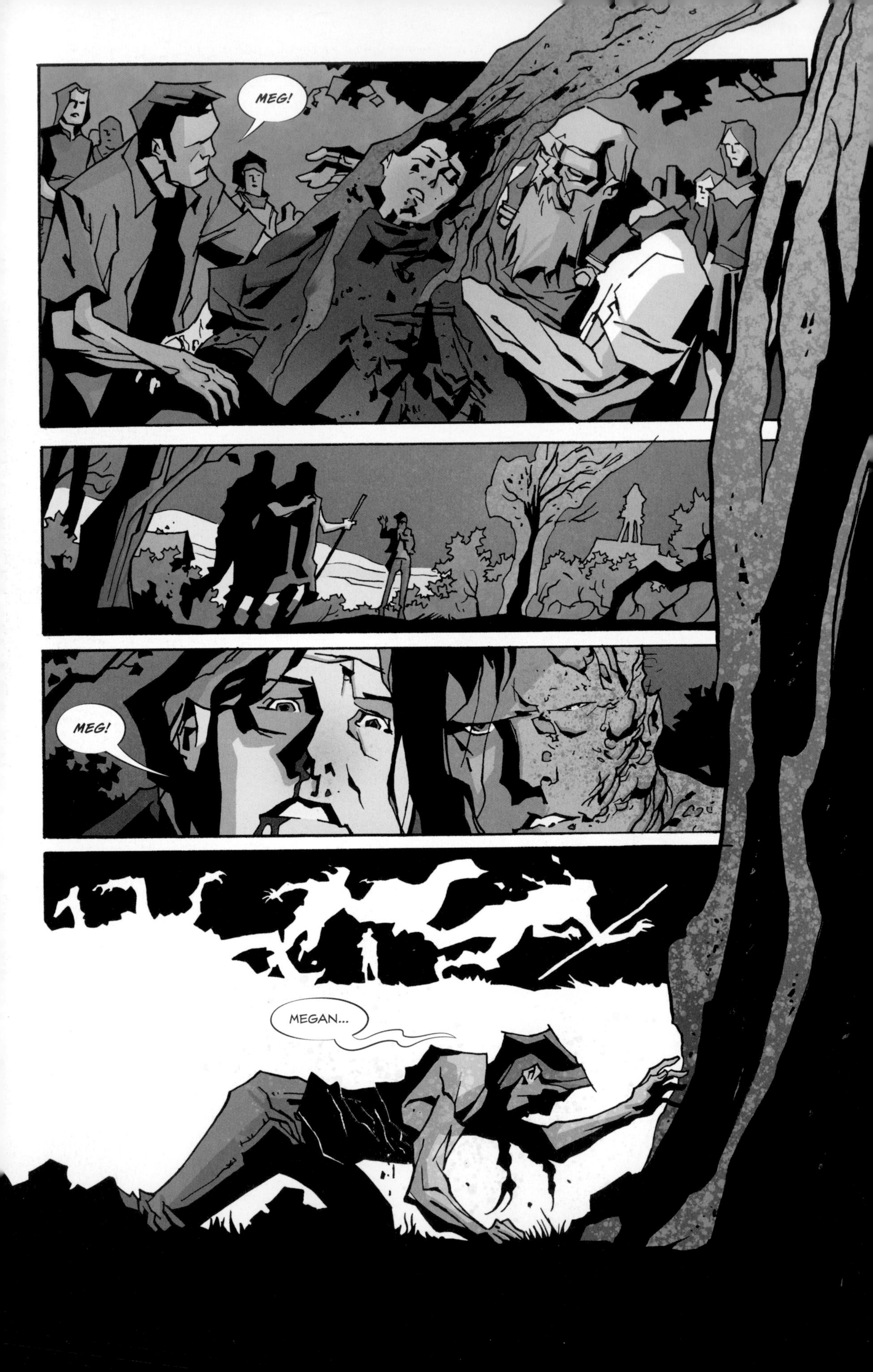
MEG!
MEG!
MEGAN...

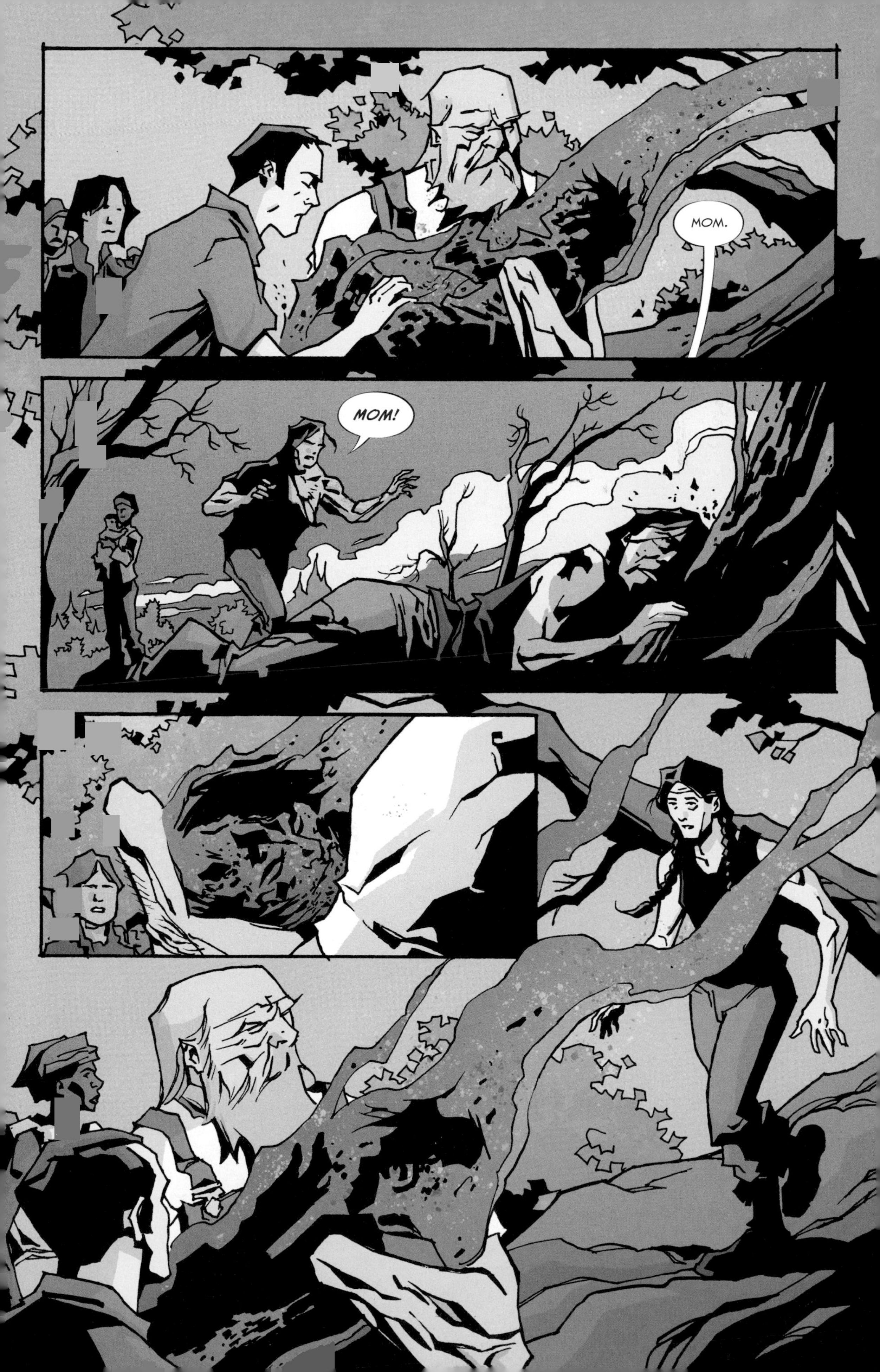
MOM.
MOM!

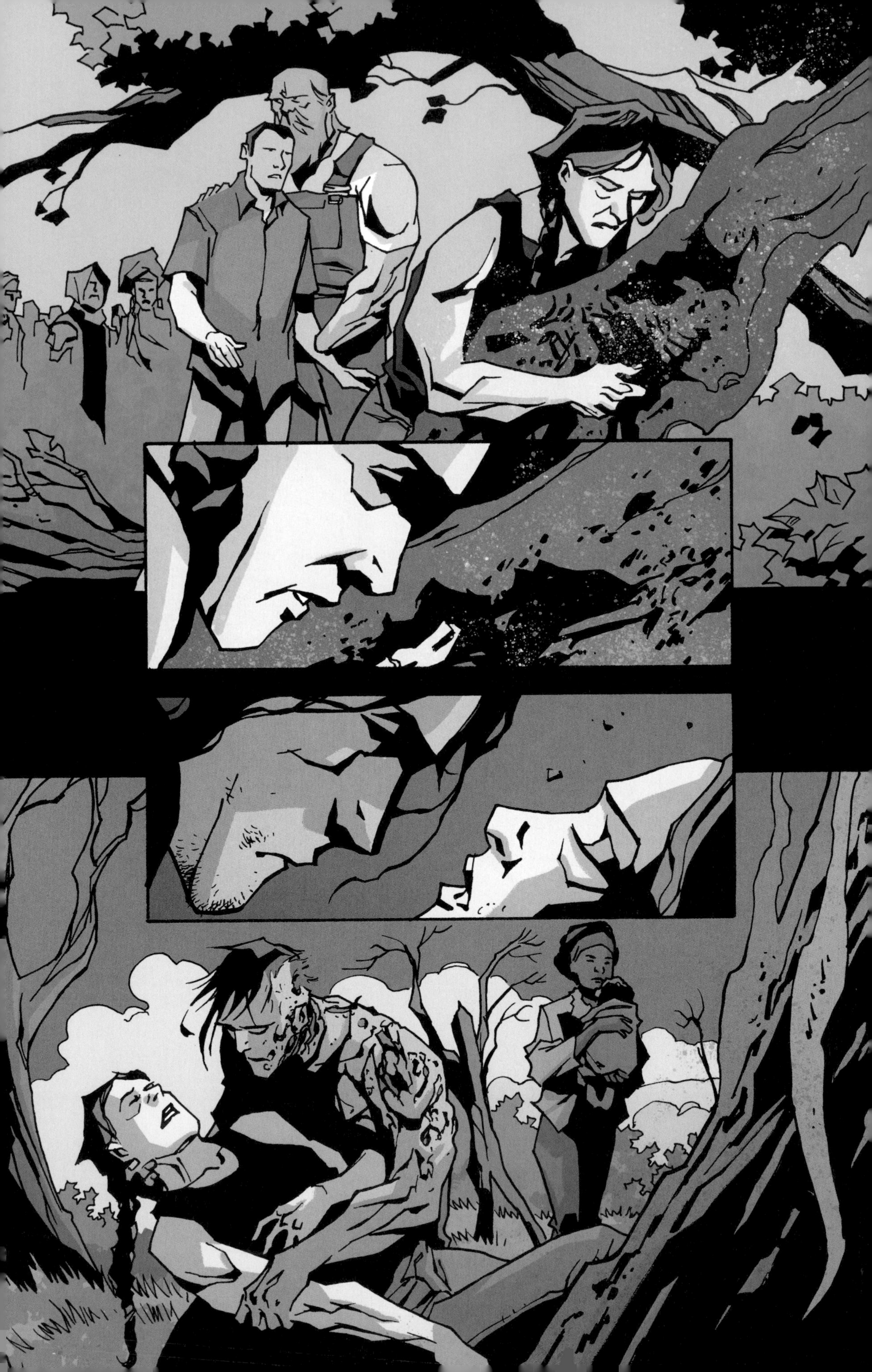

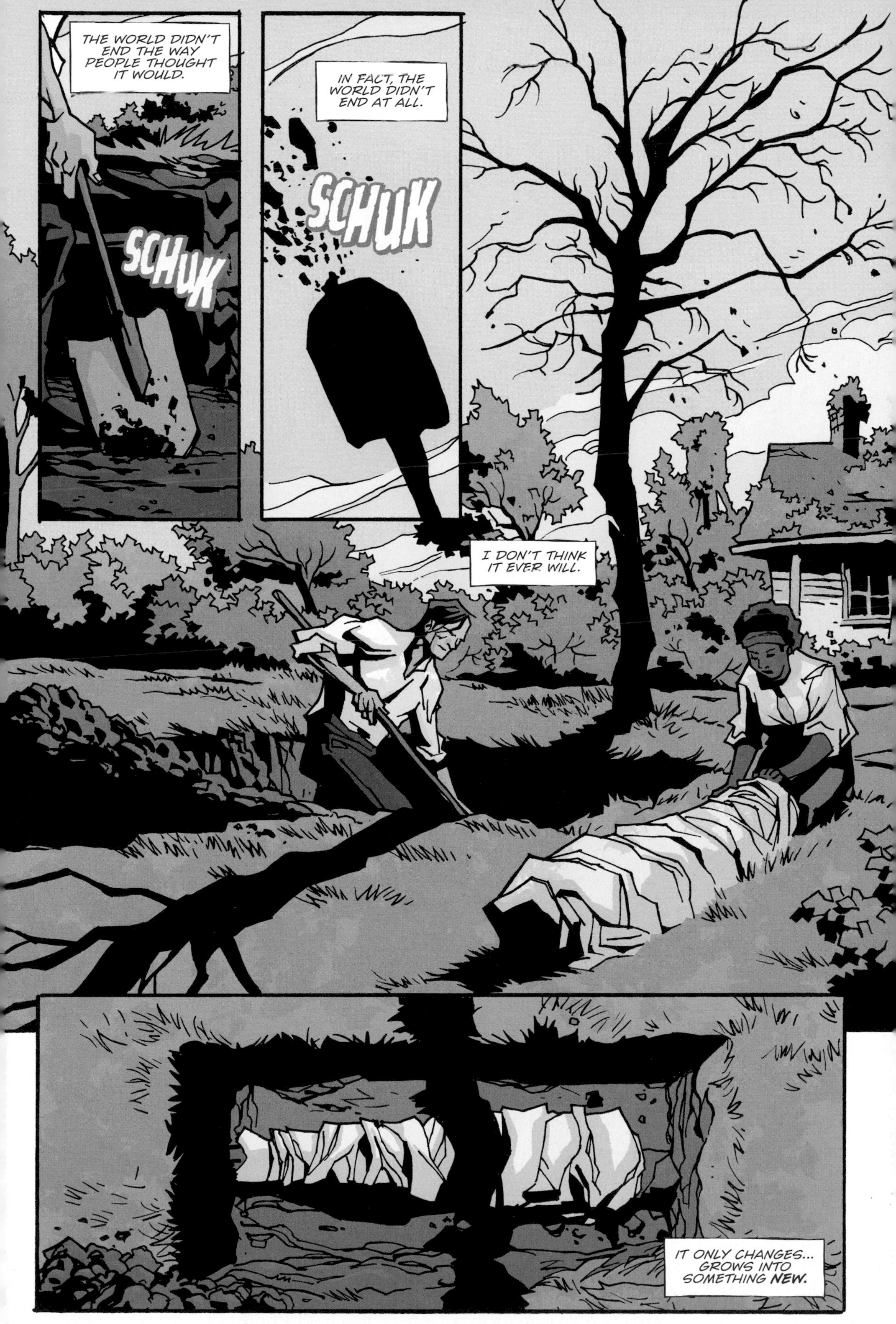
THE WORLD DIDN'T END THE WAY PEOPLE THOUGHT IT WOULD.
SCHUK
IN FACT, THE WORLD DIDN'T END AT ALL.
SCHUK
I DON'T THINK IT EVER WILL.
IT ONLY CHANGES... GROWS INTO SOMETHING NEW.

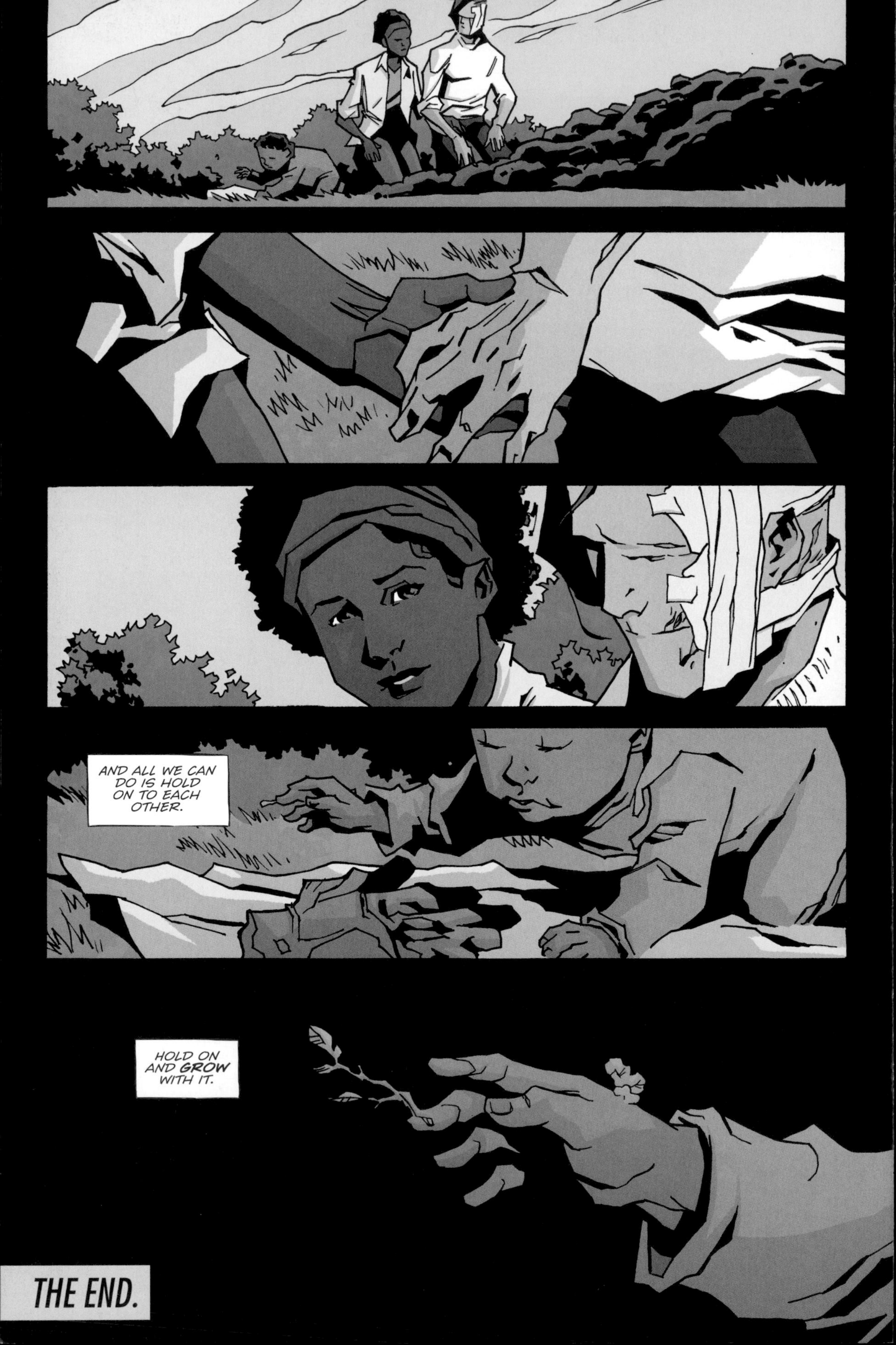
AND ALL WE CAN DO IS HOLD ON TO EACH OTHER.
HOLD ON AND GROW WITH IT.
THE END.

Notes:

A MIGNOLA CLUSTER OF EERIE FIGURES IN HAZMAT SUITS TURNS TO THE READER.. UPON CLOSER EXAMINATION WE SEE THEIR FACE-PLATE VISORS ARE FULL OF NEW GREEN LEAVES & SMALL BLOOMS. BEHIND THEM, THE RUINS OF A FREEWAY.

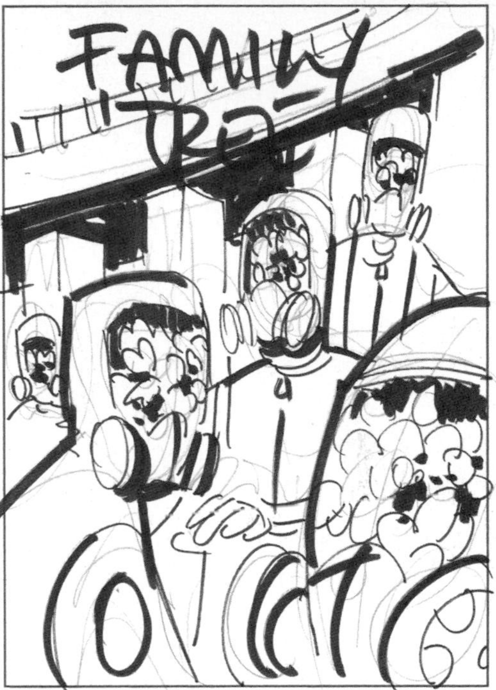
FAMILY

FAMILY TREE ISSUE 9 PAGE CVR A

Notes:

JUDD'S UBIQUITOUS WOODEN HAND SITTING IN A STREAM OF BLOOD, SMALL GREEN LEAVES AFLOAT ON THE CURRENT THAT BREAKS AROUND THE PROSTHETIC. THE HAND FORMS A FRAME SHOWING THE RESTING FACES OF THOSE WHO HAVE PASSED ON TO THE WORLD TREE, NAMELY: MEG, DARCY, JUDD, & UNNAMED OTHERS.

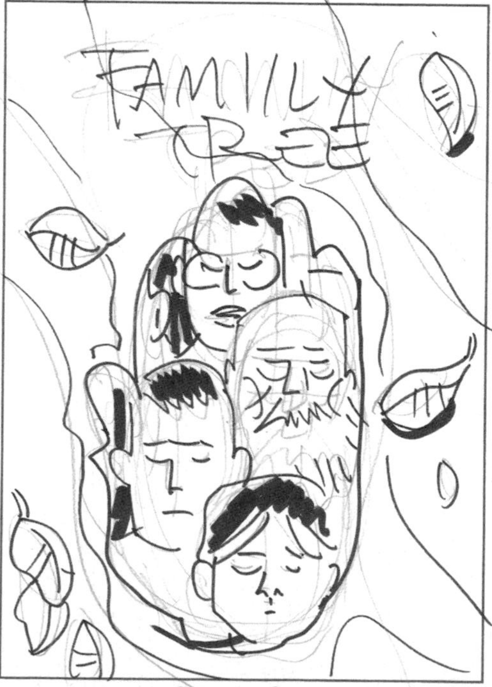
FAMILY TREE

FAMILY TREE ISSUE 9 PAGE CVR B

COVER PROCESS BY PHIL **HESTER**

Notes:

BAD-ASS JOSH HOLDING AN AXE. THE JUNGLE CLOSES IN AROUND HIM, DARCY'S/ JUDD'S WOODEN HAND HANGING FROM HIS NECK.

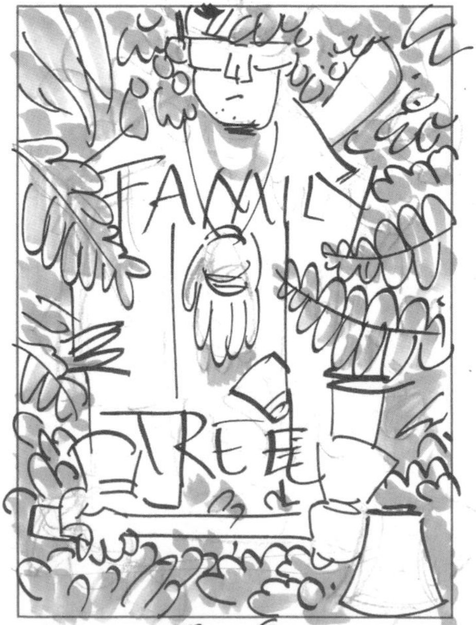
FAMILY
TREE

FAMILY TREE ISSUE CVR PAGE C
#9

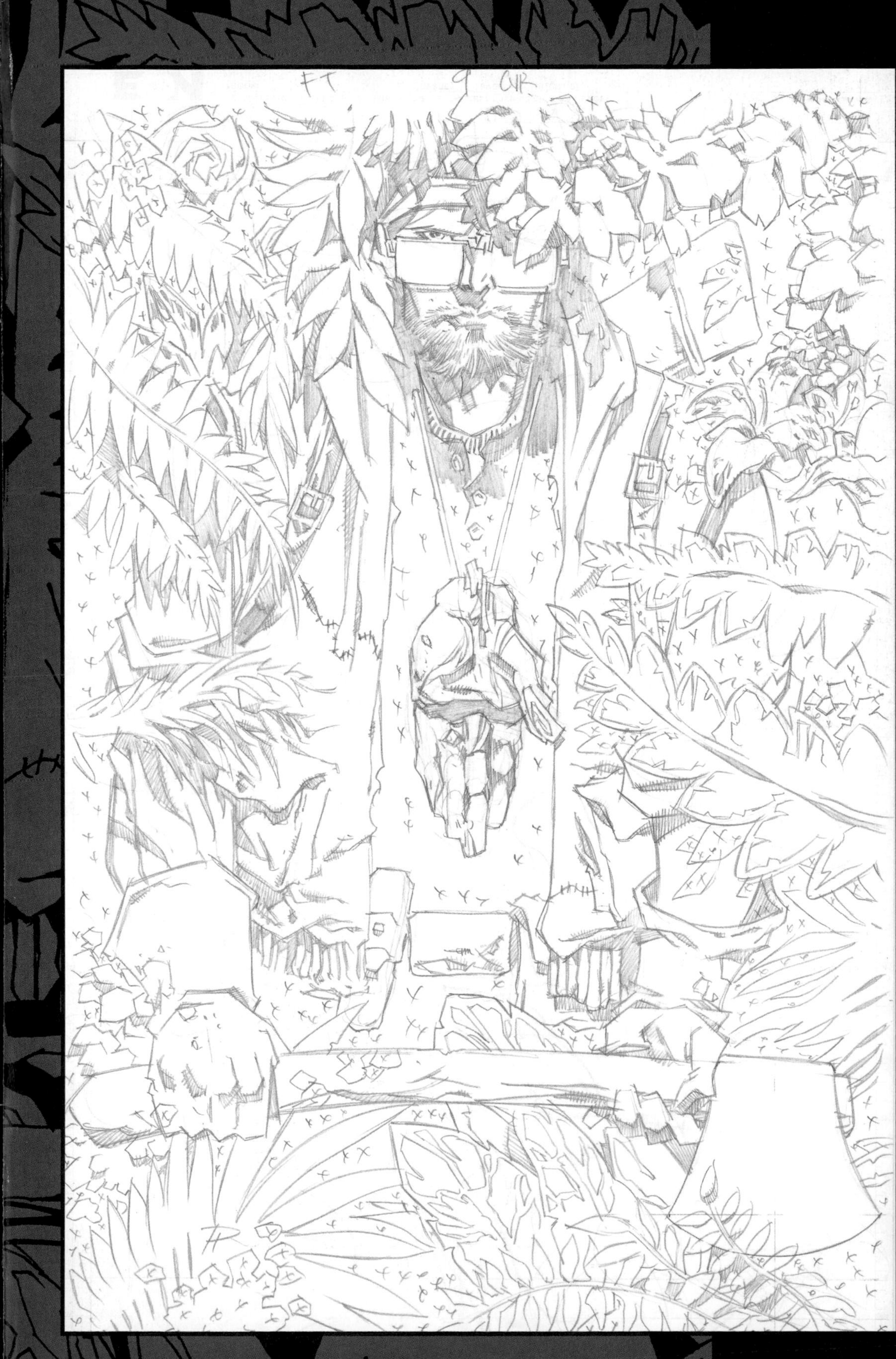

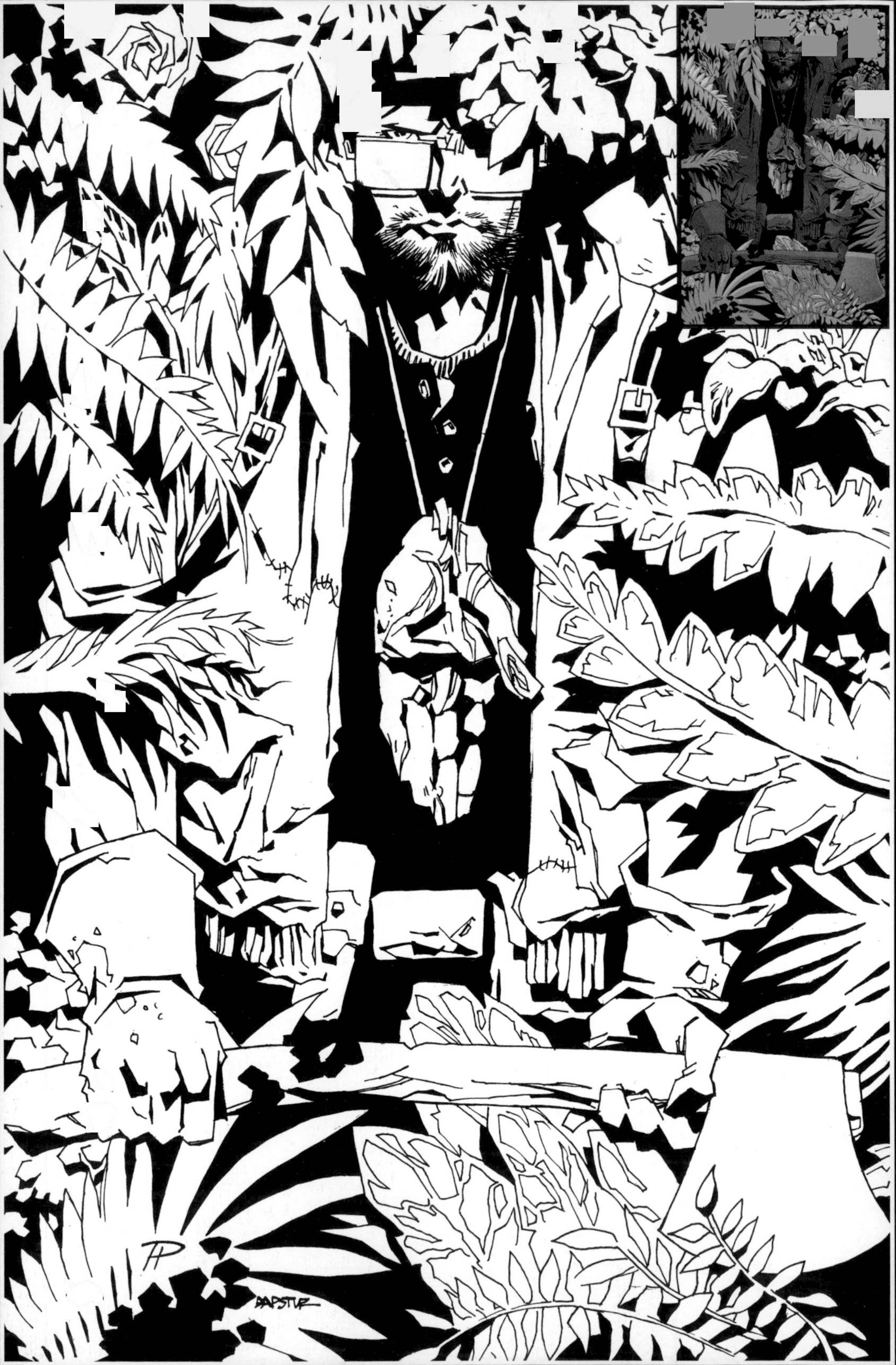
GAPSTUR

INKS BY ERIC **GAPSTUR**